DMessenger

EVA'S THREEPENNY THEATRE

EVA'S THREEPENNY THEATRE BY ANDREW STEINMETZ

GASPEREAU PRESS   PRINTERS & PUBLISHERS   2008

Something new is needed. My business is too hard, for my business is arousing human sympathy.

In memory of Eva Mathilde Steinmetz

CONTENTS

SPEAK LOW

Eva likes to talk. My recorder is running. I ask her if she needs anything, a glass of water, an ashtray.

'Are you sure?'

She sits up straight and slaps her pack of cigarettes on the table. The time to rehearse has passed. Eva knows the material, knows more than her character. She glares at me through her thick glasses. Her role today is straightforward: I would like Eva to talk to me about her connection to *The Threepenny Opera*: *Die Dreigroschenoper*, by Bertolt Brecht. This chapter in her life intrigues me. Since the last visit, I have gone on a six-week fact-finding safari through the savannah of secondary materials, following as closely as I could in her footprints. Now I want *her* to describe those times and put everything back how she left it.

What an amateurish undertaking this seems. She is eighty-two. And here I am, scavenger of a kind, aspirant family historian with literary ambitions. I shift in my seat on the pink brick patio. What poor tools my portable recorder and tin microphone are—a flimsy design, like flypaper—for capturing a life. Eva's known me since my first doughy baby photos. She saw this coming: the telephone call from Montreal, the rented car, the long weekend away. And as we preamble, in this backyard in London, Ontario, Eva grins mischievously, pleased for the spectacle.

'Please, speak low, so that the sound will not distort.'

She rubs the notch set within her sternum and as I reposition the microphone between us one last time, fleetingly I imagine performing an emergency tracheotomy with a ballpoint pen.

1

MONKEY LIFE

O my monkey time! Now we start. For years and years when I was asked for my birthday wish, or if there was anything special I wanted for Christmas, I always said: the best thing for me would be a monkey. A monkey? What would you feed him? Where would you keep your ape? Everyone laughed. I was a joke. What did I know? It was impossible. They treated me like a special, stupid girl. Even if I hadn't seen a real monkey before, I wanted a monkey.

Then the day came and I saw my monkey in the pet shop. That was marvellous. He was definitely the monkey I was looking for. In a wood box, standing in the corner. There was a small sign. *African Monkey. Tanganyika.* He was alone. This is Germany, I said. Here in Germany we have winter and snow. He was bewildered. Everything was new. He didn't know what he was doing, in a packing crate, with nothing but a bowl of water—poorest thing, he had no clue.

I stayed in the shop one hour and before I left told him, Don't give up! I'll come back to get you!

I told the shopkeeper my birthday was coming. He offered me a candy from his apron.

No, I said. Does the monkey make music? I was thinking of an organ grinder's capuchin.

Not yet, he answered.

Then I went. Straight away I returned home and I cried and

cried, until my brother found me. Hermann Hans was the authority. He was the eldest. Anneliese was next. My younger sister Romy and I were nothing.

Hermann Hans agreed to help. Maybe he could create something—just give him some time, he was on my side.

A day went by, a week. It all depended on Hermann Hans. I waited. There was nothing I could do but blow on my fingers.

Finally Hermann Hans went to Father and told him these three things. Eva has her birthday. Eva found a monkey. And, third, he thinks, *Eva should get that monkey*.

I got that monkey.

Bimbo. I was seven. I have no clue where I learned how to take care of a monkey but I was totally alone and held responsible for his upbringing—from eating to shitting to combing his hair. From the start Bimbo was my monkey, nobody else was up to the challenge.

He came home in a cage, a fantastic thing that Father set up in the front hall. Bimbo played the butler, ready to take your coat at the door. A smallish man with a wrinkled stomach and stiff hair on his nipples. That was Bimbo. In the winter one of the maids, the red-haired one, made him a sweater, a green thing like Austrians wear in the Alps. My sister Anneliese thought that was crazy. He has his hair! But she didn't know. Bimbo liked clothes. Romy and I dressed him up. We sat him on the floor in an old shirt and read him stories. We showed him picture books. He enjoyed himself. Only Anneliese didn't like monkeys. Bimbo was dirty. He was impure. She predicted he would get sick. In fact, she never accepted him.

Half the time he was out of his cage. Sometimes I took him to school with me. I went with Bimbo sitting on my shoulder, thinking he was a bird up there. When company came to the house, he jumped into their arms, grabbed their hair, scratched them on the neck. Everyone experienced Bimbo. Even Pastor Kohler.

Bimbo liked to explore. I spanked him when he made a mess and stole things from us. When he made trouble, Anneliese or one of the maids put him back in the cage. I had to fight for his freedom. I taught him good and bad, black and white. He learned the price of peace. He learned to fear. There came a point when I had only to tell him, *Die bose Schwester kommt*—she's coming, the bad sister is coming—and he stepped in line. When Anneliese was home he went to the toilet nicely. He read books on the floor. He would drink from a cup. Entering his cage, he closed the door with his tail. He obeyed every rule and followed the line of command. He was civilized. But when I was alone … he showed me. The full monkey! When I cleaned his cage he ambushed me. He climbed straight up and crouched on my head. He peed over my front. Pulled my face to his armpit. I had to put up with his rebellions, his attacks, sabotage, all his wildness. When I went in the cage to sweep the straw and his mess, he would ride on the broom. We waltzed. And when it was over and time for me to leave, he would shit again and paint my legs with it.

It was unbelievable what I went through, really unbelievable. But I learned quickly how to think like a monkey. This saved me. When he yawned, he was ready to pounce. And when Bimbo concentrated in one direction, I knew he planned to attack in the opposite direction. In the end I could catch him in mid-air!

Pastor Kohler was yellow eyed. Too weak, Father declared, to make the sign of the cross without pausing for a wafer.

Evangelisch. Lutheran. Pastor Kohler carried a miserable face. His eyes were slow. His skin was thick. He didn't go outdoors, or hunting often, that's for sure. In the winter he had his cough. Influenza, his Spanish mistress. She moved into his lungs and hung laundry over his ribs and stayed on until spring.

Anneliese knew him well. Anneliese was involved in the church. She invited her pastor everywhere. She knew every pastor in the book but Kohler was her favourite. He suffered under Anneliese's eyes. Romantic as a worm, he wriggled through the front door. He landed in our house regularly. There was an arrangement. He and Father had some business. Anneliese stood in the corner, served tea, and seemed to know everything before it happened.

Anneliese scolded me each time Pastor Kohler arrived at the house because Bimbo never stopped scratching himself. It was true: lice dropped out of Bimbo like salt. And Bimbo was a great performer. He jumped onto Pastor Kohler's shoulder and waited, and when the pastor coughed, Bimbo stuck his fingers in and stretched his mouth open. My sister went mad. Bimbo grinned. He exposed a harmonica of teeth.

Next, Bimbo started to sing. Nobody could stop him now. When he decided to sing, nobody could change his mind.

Finally Father would call: Quickly, Eva, come. Put Bimbo back in his cage, please lock him away.

But I know Father once let Bimbo loose, out of the cage, just when the pastor arrived at the door. Father also played monkey life.

One day disaster struck. It was some kind of festive dinner and my whole family, my father and sisters and brother, and Pastor Kohler, who was invited to celebrate with us, was at the table, silently waiting to thank the Lord. The proceedings were elaborate and slow, quite slow. Bimbo didn't like it. He was incredibly impatient with us. The table was set in silver and crystal. He could see idiots. The maids delivered our food on long trays. Nonsense. What were we doing?

During dinner Bimbo started to sing. We ignored him. But Bimbo wanted something. He saw it on the table. A fish or cabbage. He wouldn't stop. He wanted it!

He crouched. He moved around the table, low, this way, that way, jealous of what we had.

No, I said. BIMBO, NEIN!

He knew. He knew it was forbidden. He turned away, but you know they have those long arms. They can stretch across trees.

Bimbo, out! Behave. Bimbo. NEIN.

He was furious. Bimbo was a macho. It was unacceptable to him to have me treating him in this way, in front of all the others. So he grabbed the end of the cloth and the table came down, dishes, dinner, everything. That was the beginning, the end was coming.

A year later, when Romy was only pre-school, she stayed with Bimbo when I was out of the house. She played in front of his cage and read him books. She sang songs. They learned the alphabet together. Bimbo advanced and Bimbo played nicely with Romy when there was no one else. But soon as he heard me coming, he ignored her. Ach, go away, he scowled, leave me alone with the older one. And then one day Bimbo was frustrated and he bit Romy. He bit her badly. That's when Father said, It's over, Eva, you have to take Bimbo away.

Of course there was always the rumour that they spread tuberculosis. So there was no mercy. Bimbo was stripped of his rights. He was crushed into a powder, into a nobody. If something was found broken, if something was missing, if somebody lost their ring or hat, it was Bimbo who did it. Everyone blamed the monkey. Bimbo was defenceless, under every circumstance he was found guilty. Like the old joke in Germany. Long before Hitler, when something bad happened, some catastrophe or awful thing, people would say: it is the fault of the bicycle-riders and the Jews. Or the window-washers and the Jews. Always the Jews, the Jews went without saying. In folk tales, in jokes, the poison was deep in the well.

I carried him to the zoo. I had no choice. Bimbo was put in a cage with the other monkeys, a colony of seven or eight. It was a horrible place. They fought over food. Competition was fierce. They didn't get washed. The place was shit. And of course Bimbo never adjusted. The others bit him. They ganged up on the weakest. They rolled Bimbo on the ground, whistling and picking at him. He was teased, hurt, and he never understood. He was bitten and pinched, no mercy at all.

Who can watch that happen and do nothing? Everyone knew, and everyone did nothing.

Day after day, we said goodbye. I came after school and stood in front of the cage, and he grabbed me from inside and we hugged. Our eyes closed together. I cried for weeks. Until I said, Stop it, Eva. You have to stop! It's over now. This is Germany. We have winter and snow.

Even later, when I started in theatre, the other actors told me I had to get rid of my monkey movements. I still had my monkey stamp on me.

CABARET

"I don't know how far it's progressed, but I don't expect her to live more than five or six months. Five months is generous. I imagine she's already jaundiced, that's what happens with these cases." Roland, making humane music of logistics. Only a retired physician like my father can so conscientiously devise an action plan from the natural history of a terminal diagnosis. "They may put in a shunt. Otherwise we'll see, maybe Eva can come stay in Montreal, the last couple of weeks, where I can take care of her …"

Cancer of the pancreas. I hang up the phone and go back to bed. Almost at once I wave off the covers and return to the front room. I feel obscurely hurt and annoyed. Thwarted, I look out the window. There is no traffic on the streets. No pedestrians, no progress, an unconscious morning. I lift the telephone and start dialing but replace the receiver before striking the last digit.

Two weeks later, she opens the front door and immediately places her hands on the top of her head, while taking a step back, as if being taken prisoner. Marvellous, she purrs. Taking her second step, she stumbles and trips over Ningal, her borzoi.

Hello Eva, I manage to blurt out—but I am interrupting. She shoos the neurotic Ningal away. Then holds me straight, at arm's length, gripping my wrists. Looking deep into my eyes, her pupils dilated, she sings: "The world is poor and man's a shit. That's all there is to it."

She's my grand-aunt. My grandfather's sister. But I'm as good as a grandson to her.

So good you could come, she says at last. I have cancer of the panzer tank.

Eva instructs me to put my bags upstairs, in Pavel's half of the house. Pavel is away in Cleveland for a dog show. He's taken the whippets. Klee, Davenport, Rachel and Gould.

She calls the upstairs East Berlin. Here we are in the West, she says, in her kitchen during lunch, and we have everything. Wine. Garlic. Goose fat. Blue cheese. Rye bread. Poor Pavel must make do with what he can find on the black market.

Poor Pavel, as Eva calls him, is Polish. An ex-electrician, in his middle fifties. Ultimately he's a bridge player and a borzoi expert. All of Eva's live-in male companions since her arrival in Canada have been this way. European card-playing dog people. Gay contract bridge whippet and borzoi breeders from the former Eastern Bloc.

Where does she find them? Or, do *they* find *her*?

During lunch, Eva discreetly brings my attention around to Ningal, who is recuperating, within eyesight, in the living room.

She's been depressed, Eva whispers. She's unhappy that we didn't send her to Cleveland—don't look! Eva admonishes me but too late. Ningal, muzzle on her forepaws, eyes aimed down her snout, is watching us from the sofa. Listening to our every word, I bet.

She's an old bitch, Eva continues. Do you remember her mother? Yes, I remember, but I'm unsure if I should risk naming the mother—who is surely deceased—thereby causing further upset to the child. No matter. Eva is on the case. She mouths the letters, managing full caps: N-A-T-A-S-H-A.

I answer with a slight nod. (Eva had Natasha when she lived in the Eastern Townships outside Montreal, our neighbour for the summers.)

Eva winks at me. What's this now—Morse code? Ridiculous. No. Eva is adamant. She winks again and this time draws my eyes over to Ningal, who is up and standing on the sofa cushions, ears perked.

Ningal holds our gaze for only a second before she points her muzzle at the heavens and howls.

After lunch we clear the kitchen table and take our coffee outside on the patio. Eva takes me by the hand on a quick tour of her gardening, to show me the chives and greenish tomatoes—pausing, first, to acknowledge the sunshine (she raises her face to the sky and shuts her eyes), then, in a few paces, to administer formal introductions to some Latinate shrubs and bushes in flower.

One moment. Eva excuses herself and goes into the house just as the sun moves behind the clouds. I follow the murmur of her voice, a Doppler effect as she passes down the hall, from kitchen to bedroom. When she comes back out, she's carrying a stack of photo albums and a Bata shoebox.

Help me get rid of these, she says. Take the ones you want. Then she lays out her albums on the plastic patio table. Six or seven, and the box full of large black and white prints. Sepia tones and then, brash arcs of colour. There are hundreds of photographs to sift through and countless Evas to examine. This is a retrospective. Eva in Breslau, Eva in Baden-Baden, in Vienna, Zurich, post-war Berlin. So many incarnations, embodiments, spirits of the age. I am invited to select the ones I want, buffet-style: seven-year-old Eva posing with Bimbo inside the house on Briskestrasse; Eva at twenty-eight in Zurich, seated by the dormer window of her top floor apartment, posture perfect, adjacent her music stand and with an accordion strapped like a cartridge belt across her front; Eva in the Eastern Townships of Quebec, playing a game of Scrabble indoors with her old friend (and sister-in-law) Pinguin; and Eva photographed in this very backyard in southwestern Ontario, where this minute I sit across the table from the dying Eva.

This one was taken the day I was *certified doomed by that doctor*. She slides it across the table. In her eighties, Eva projects her lines for every house on the block.

I take a look at the Polaroid. It must have been taken by Pavel. Eva stands by her rose bushes; pink explosions offset the marble-toned whippet formed like soft ice cream at her ankles. She holds in one hand a glass of sparkling white wine. Relaxed, her free hand guesses at her hip. A casual arrangement, this, an amateur's shot. I study her eyes. Is there anything there, any sign of capitulation? There is none. Nothing in the picture tells you this woman is doomed. Late in the day her eyes have adjusted to the light. They penetrate the eye behind the camera with defiant and mocking composure.

When I return to my apartment in Montreal, three days later, I take with me some of Eva's records. Django Reinhardt and Stephane Grapelli. Paul Desmond. Louis Armstrong. Lotte Lenya. In the big front room on rue Esplanade I play them. Over the next several weeks, I am indoctrinated. Eva's music becomes my music. Armstrong's gay and swinging version of "The Ballad of Mack the Knife" is a surprise. It's a free interpretation, jocular, all-American. But Lenya is the authority on Kurt Weill.

Lenya *is* the cabaret. Eva swears by it.

A teenage Eva was just starting out as a stage actress in Breslau in the late 1920s when Brecht and Weill arrived from

Berlin, via Le Lavandou in the south of France, to work-shop a new play. *Die Dreigroschenoper*: their adaptation of John Gay's 1728 *The Beggar's Opera*. Like the original, *Die Dreigroschenoper* was set in London's Old Soho. The script was based on a German translation made by Elisabeth Hauptmann, one of Brecht's many female collaborators.

As Eva tells it, Eva appeared in a workshop version of the play—presumably in the summer of 1928, June or July, since *Die Dreigroschenoper* opened in Berlin at the Theater am Schiffbauerdamm on 31 August of that year.

My role, she confesses, was quite small. It was not a speaking part.

Eva played one of "die Huren," the whores.

WORKSHOP

Kurt Weill at the piano. Slight and balding, wearing the round black-rimmed glasses described in the newspapers. The conductor is Theo Mackeben. White-gloved but without baton, Mackeben leads the eight-piece street orchestra through a ballad. The theme continually repeats, with the single instrument variations sporadically added then subtracted: the accordion re-announcing itself, then the banjo, then mandolin, rousing the others along the passage of a lazy striptease that, looking at the singer, does seem past imminent. 'The singer': for heaven's sake, what else to call her?

From his seat near the back of the auditorium, sheltered by the mezzanine, the visiting actor Karl Paryla is set to enjoy the afternoon rehearsal. "Peachum's Morning Hymn." "The 'No They Can't' Song." "Wedding Song For The Less Well-Off." "Pirate Jenny." He uses his spyglasses to read. "Song Of The Insufficiency Of Human Endeavour." "The Cannon Song." The list is tacked to the wall opposite Weill. Weill is pumping away at the foot pedals, inching the piano across the stage. "The Ballad of Sexual Obsession." Wonderful, *Schön*. This is Weill's *Gebrauchsmusik*. Cabaret-style ballads sung by petty criminals, beggars, whores. Class disharmony given musical form. The orchestra a ragged street gang.

When Paryla heard from his old teacher Max Ophüls

about the work Brecht was doing at the Lobetheater, he decided to come right away. Just last night he had dinner with Ophüls at Hotel Monopol. Ophüls—artistic director of the Lobetheater—was much taken by the young genius from Augsburg. Brecht is an innovator! He's making montage! Brecht is from a new class! Brecht, yes, *is* a shit disturber. Having only partially digested Ophüls' summary of Brecht's aesthetics, Paryla waits to see how all this theory will translate onto the stage.

The singer is a pretty barmaid. Lotte Lenya, surely. The composer's young wife. She confronts her imaginary audience with a city coldness that makes Paryla cringe. Low-Dive Jenny, the proverbial tart. Is she not positively worn out from supporting the opposite sex? Indeed she is weary. Lenya presumably has been chosen to sing Jenny's part because she can't read a note of music. Touching the hem of her dress, she sips from her cigarette and snatches at the lyrics, recounting how lust is transformed into cash … how business is business. Hoarse, slight, gaunt, she spits "Pirate Jenny" over the barricade of her front teeth.

Meanwhile a group of actresses is being positioned on the set by Brecht's assistant, Elisabeth Hauptmann. This, Paryla can see, is being done painstakingly, according to protocol, as Ophüls explained it to him the night before. Hauptmann carries a black portfolio of sketches. She cradles the portfolio in her arm, referring to the drawings whenever an enquiry arises from one of the actresses. Caspar Neher, the set designer, has imagined the Soho brothel. But Hauptmann is responsible for bringing the whores of Turnbridge to life.

Paryla remembers one or two of these girls, now kowtowing to Hauptmann, from his own time at the Lobetheater.

Eva, the new girl, is late. Paryla anticipates her arrival. No one else seems aware of her absence. They are preoccupied, surely, taking short-orders from Hauptmann. *You, stand here, and you, over there. Don't move. No one move. Wait until Jenny is done singing.* These instructions turn a minor role on its head and make the actor feel part of the production's metaphysics. Without instruction, the actors are apt to betray an air of uncertainty. The theatre is a complex organism. Paryla knows this. It can easily suffer. It is not the hardiest illusion. No. But today, something was on the actors' minds, something is bothering them, besides Hauptmann's minimalist directives. Of course: today Brecht is scheduled to introduce his concept of Epic Theatre and a new technique of acting to the company.

This has been attempted once before, with disastrous results. Epic Theatre requires, first of all, Epic Actors. Last week, the cast was instructed to forget everything they had learned about acting. Brecht wanted catharsis. Purification. The purging of pity and fear. But all this, Brecht wants, before the actors set foot on stage! His method, as it happened, was *anti-illusory*. Imagine that. No easy sell to the insecure amateur—and most of them, on stage now, are amateurs. The supporting cast is composed of a group of local actors, as it always is. Parochial Parrots. Insecure ... well, weren't all actors insecure?

Not this one—Eva strolls across the stage in costume: red stockings and a black corset. She is striking. She joins the others, who have stopped the exercise and are seated on chairs in a semi-circle. Her serene humility is accentuated when she comes to sit *on the stage floor*.

It is time. Finally, Brecht makes the grand entrance. Blue poplin jacket. Cap and cigar. Workman's trousers, and socks rolled down around his ankles. He nods to Hauptmann and she claps her hands. Her attitude smacks of righteousness. The music stops. The orchestra members put down their instruments. Kurt Weill lights a cigarette. Lenya exits. Jenny's girls, then a good half of Peachum's army of beggars, wandering in from the canteen, join the assembly, body language resigned to today's sermon.

Eva, Paryla surmises, is the least convincing. Nothing about her technique, no. During the morning exercises in which they practised mime Eva showed good control, fine technique. Watching her and the others move through their vignettes in a shroud of silence, Paryla had the odd sensation that he was being mocked. He guessed she was one of the more experienced of the lot, though this wasn't the case. She is new to the theatre. What is it about her, then? Beauty. Beauty like hers is not credible. It is too much for any technique of acting.

Yet Eva's attention to Brecht is total. She is stolen by the moment. Paryla can see that very well. She has discovered something special—has she?—the kind of thing you can search for an entire lifetime and perhaps never find.

Is it Brecht himself, this young heathen from Augsburg? Not according to Ophüls.

It is not Brecht. Then what? The life of the theatre? The art of acting? Never mind alienation, estrangement … detachment. What about acting and becoming? Or simple improvisation? Paryla himself believes in the latter. The dialectic of acting and becoming, the synthesis is—

There is no other method in the theatre's vast repertoire to overturn a heavy glacier like the self.

BRISKESTRASSE, GOOD NIGHT

Our mother died slowly for us. She gradually went extinct under the roof of that magnificent house on Briskestrasse. Those attacks she had went on for years. But we had no name for it, no Latin, no diagnosis. It was too complicated. My brother Hermann Hans always had a different explanation, which I never understood. Nobody really knew. Was it this part, or that system? Her blood, her soul—was it sour? TB, the kidneys. There was no cure. Only curiosities. We lived in the dark ages. We were guided by the candlelit figures of the detached and the devout who came and went, the doctor and the pastor, who escorted the family through week after week in the lost cause. They led us in circles, up the stairs to the second floor and around the side of Mutti's bed and then back down the stairs and again up the stairs, around we went until Mutti was discovered—dead. Oh yes, dead as the field mouse in winter.

For the children there was certainly nothing more fantastic and strange than to have the kind of mother we could imagine. She was our captive, tangled under the sheets, chained to the bedpost, she stirred her blankets in bed. Mutti was stuck. On her pillow the head lay, browned, like the top of a wooden spoon, a face, features burnt, black on the sides. She was stuck with a poisonous sack, a full belly. And there was an odour. Her dying spread through the house, room to room. She leaked into the walls. Terrific, we whispered to each other, Just amazing. The children never walked by the door to her room alone. We went two by two.

We dreaded her, in fact. We were raised by Father to respect authority, but we grew up in fear of the mother we imagined. She died, aching and turning, a dark bruise that turned my stomach. We all knew, right from the beginning, that the end was near: in the beginning was the word, and the word was *hopeless*. But what a performance. She died when my sister Romy was three, and Romy went mute. Romy absorbed the whole show, without blinking, without intermission. Then at Mutti's funeral: Romy froze at eye-level.

Pastor Kohler stuck us on the wagon and we went. We arrived, pulled by horses, holding flowers. Romy was plunked in Anneliese's lap and Hermann Hans was sent on ahead with Papa: father and son led the charge in the front carriage.

The box lay on the flat-back wagon. We clopped over the stones dressed in perfect black. Three carriages followed behind. At the cemetery, Pastor Kohler raised his hand and drew us out of our seats, one by one. We jumped to the ground and stood by the gravesite, this black hole, necks stiffening, shivering in a line like prisoners about to be shot.

Time had stopped. I stood with my back to Breslau, ready to be pushed, tumbled into the gaping hole. Our row of faces held one expression. Child to child, dust to dust. Our hearts bled. Mutti was lowered by rope and the box was covered with earth. Through prayers, we waited for the sign to drop our flowers. Then we *threw* them at the ground.

Afterwards the pastor brought us back home to our life.

My father was left standing holding the shit bucket. He stood behind the horse, and pushed the family forward. He was left with three children, and Romy full of sand. Romy frozen. Romy packed up to her eyeballs. He married again, once, for peace and quiet, and for Romy's sake. But that was another catastrophe. The Second Mother arrived too late to save us. She stepped out of her carriage under a veil, wearing her black hat, with a lone feather sticking up like a shark's fin. Fabulous. The house, our villa, the garden, were magnificent. She inspected the children who were lined up along the inside hallway, and understood right away that the mistake was all hers. She stayed for the opening night, and left the next morning or the morning after that.

At home I knew only my little corner. On Briskestrasse we lived in this tremendous house with high windows and oval ceilings. A villa surrounded by trees and gardens, and at the end of the carriageway, there stood the front gate. Beyond the gate, Breslau, Silesia and the rest of Germany.

Our father was a limb-maker. A leather tradesman. From Poland to Pomerania he was known as an expert in limb-making. He kept his shop during the day, he worked hard, hour by hour, and then at night he arrived home to his wife dying in the roof over his children.

We knew nothing. We, the children were not supposed to do or know anything. That was called 'privilege.' I wasn't allowed into the kitchen. We were not to play in the garden. The only thing I knew for sure was we were supposed to be rich, the rich people of the neighbourhood.

That was early on. The villa, horses, Mutti upstairs—and we had those two spinster maids. We kept horses in the stables and in the house we kept two maids, through thick and thin, like old house pets. The spinsters with black whiskers. Father relied on our governess and housekeeper to keep order. Both had come from the Grimm fairy tales. They had wandered out of the forest sometime in the last century. And my father depended on them to maintain the house, and to cook. They were his marionettes. They hung from strings and moved according to Father's commands, room to room, washing and cooking and cleaning. Dusting with their giant feathers on poles. They floated over the furniture, flying together in starched aprons until Mutti, awake at noon, fading at dinner, pulled them in, upstairs to her room, by ringing her bell.

Early on, that's how it was. Then it went kaput. Inflation. Unemployment. In Breslau the war veterans, young men, passed the time counting cobblestones. No one could afford a joke. Kaput. My mother died in 1919. Then came riots. The Freikorps and trade unions. Spartacus. Disasters. Zoo.

Eventually the house went, everything was sold. Father was ruined. When he sold the amazing property on Briskestrasse, the next day he could buy a loaf of bread. There was no size in life. No proportion. The villa for a loaf of bread. Wagon for horseshoe. All those catastrophe years: from Briskestrasse to Lehrbeutelstrasse, and next we lived on Garberstrasse.

Kaput. Always we went down: down in house size, down in money, and down with our dead.

Father arrived at the gate by horse and carriage. Like clockwork: through the gate and around the house to the stables. One circle, around the villa: horse, wagon, man. It was impressive. The routine, the precision. Each day we waited for him, early evening, for our father and the sound of carriage wheels, for our father and the horses, the crunch of the wheels on gravel, these things that tied us together, yesterday and tomorrow.

He spent evenings reading. He took his chair in the salon. It had four bowed legs, and lion paws carved into the wooden feet. There he made himself comfortable, up on his pedestal. For hours he followed his newspaper. We lay on the carpet beside the tile oven at the base of his chair—watching him.

To begin, he examined the newspaper, page by page. He

skimmed through it, nose in the air, superficially, choosing from the menu. Inflation. Freikorps. Unemployment.

'Bitte, Papa. Ich ...' *Today it's my turn! Please.* We competed for his attention. Whose turn was it to clean his glasses? Which of his helpers? Each of us wanted to be noticed, except Romy who played her game, deaf and dumb, floating in a fable.

Then he snapped the newspaper, full broadsheets—Achtung! It came alive—he snapped the paper, waving his elbows.

Then, be still. An oblong moment, we waited.

He lowered his eyes. Elbows at rest. He held the newspaper by its top corners, his proper way. High up, out in front. He was gone now, behind the paper. He escaped into propaganda while on the floor we found a quiet game to play or finished our schoolwork.

Above us the pages of his newspaper flapped. Anneliese called it a butterfly. Papa's butterfly. It was the *Völkischer Beobachter.* Oh yes. The People's Observer. The newspaper of the metamorphosis.

Later on he folded his glasses and placed them on the side table. Then he called for the maids. He was tired, he rubbed his eyes, he asked them to bring the thermometer and vinegar. Mutti's thermometer. It was time.

Stay. He told us to remain where we were, be quiet, and next he climbed the stairs.

Up he went to meet our Maker. Wrapped in layers, hair mashed in sweat on the pillow. Twisting away into the sheets. With her poisonous sack, her striped abdomen, webbing under her arms and between her legs. We listened from the downstairs, from underneath, as he climbed. We swallowed nervous laughter. Time for us: time for us the children to crawl through our heads like mice. Time for us to crawl inside our imaginations. Time for us to spy: we followed his steps on the stairs, then along the hall, then as he knocked before he entered Mutti's room. She stirred in her blankets, inviting him in. Then—voices. Their voices in another world. Our parents' voices, far away, outside the villa. Echoing from another world. Another hemisphere. A world in which we had no influence, no weight. Our parents went away.

We don't exist.

We lay on our backs and stared at the ceiling. In the middle of the room Romy rocked on her feet from side to side. She danced away. The other two let her go. Papa was five minutes. Romy transformed. She was our pantomime. A child lost in the woods. Every mime is trapped, as children are trapped: outside memory, trapped inside their own fables. Romy was acting, feeling her way, wandering alone in the dark woods. Touching us, our noses, our eyes. Touching us, as if we had turned inside out.

Then she stops. Romy's face flat with mine. Eye to eye, nose on nose. But no smile on her lips.

She danced over to my brother, Männe. Next, Anneliese's turn to be deformed.

Romy, the clown. Our alien mirror.

We continued our routine, our schoolwork, elbows dipped in the carpet. Soon he was back, downstairs again. Papa in his chair.

He opened his newspaper, flap. The pages fluttered. Not a word to us, no news from above. *At ease, as you were, continue ...* Don't ask questions! We knew never to observe him too closely. But I did. Before returning to the newspaper he turned. He paused a moment. His head turned a fraction and his eyes looked out. Proud, sad, decayed and disoriented. He stared and he counted, drumming his chest with a finger. Hermann Hans. Anneliese. Eva. Romy. Four beats, four in total. Four remaining, under his care.

Under normal circumstances we couldn't go, we were not allowed—not *permitted*—inside Mutti's room. Under normal circumstances her room was off limits. Her door was closed. Do not enter. Do not destroy the fantasy. Do not disturb the dead.

Inside she coughed to sleep. She peed into a bowl. She was taboo. She rang her bell for the maids when she needed water, food or a wash. But that was it.

Sunday morning after church was the exception. Then we saw our mother. Once a week we were led upstairs to the top floor and we saw where she lay. At bed-level, the Feast of Consumption. Swollen, watery and pale. Eyes under collapsing skin. Her bed at the window, curtains in place.

Lamp, table, a pile of books. The finger bell rolled on its side.

Our nights of routine. The circle game. We repeated ourselves—schoolwork, puzzles, stories—until it was time for the maids to march the animals up to bed. We said good night to Papa and the maids took us away. Straight to bed. No talking or whispering. Silent prayers before sleep.

My brother introduced a game, imported from school. On the way up, nobody was allowed to breathe on the stairs, or in the hall, and never outside the door to Mutti's room. For school children, it was bad luck to breathe between tombstones, when passing a cemetery, and it was bad luck for us to breathe outside Mutti's door.

Under Männe's orders, no one breathed. No one dared. Upstairs, in the hall, we transformed in the dark. We changed into owls and bats. *Eulen und Fledermäuse.* Flying mice. Animals with shining eyes! That magic went on for months. It was sensational to be in the group. But in fact Männe was cooking our soup on a burning house. Eventually one of the maids caught on and our father received the detailed report and the game was finished. From then on, we were watched closely: in line, we marched, hands behind our backs. One maid led the way with another maid behind.

Einatmen, ausatmen! All breathing and march.

Upstairs, three sisters. One room, three beds. We climbed under the blankets. In the winter, one common bed would have been the best solution.

After putting us to bed, the maids retreated and finished their work in the kitchen. They stacked the dishes and closed the cupboards, talking, working, making a little noise.

Meanwhile I lay in my bed listening, awake. I pulled the blanket to my chin. I lay like a toad under the moon, my forehead glistening, I waited. I never slept until she produced her cough, a concussion through the walls. Proof to me that Mutti was alive.

One night without warning, we saw a hand. From in the salon—Papa reading, the four children on the floor—we saw it coming. A hand on the wood, fingers on the banister.

Mutti let herself out. She had come from her room, moving down the stairs, holding the railing, she was feeling her way to the bottom.

All of us—including Papa—all of us froze. The maids popped out of the kitchen, just their heads in the door frame.

We froze for a hand. Then, for the full picture. White, shock. The picture no one could describe.

Mutti stared right through us in a dream. Her eyes were opening and opening.

Then she moved a little further down the stairs. I watched her shadow slide loose over the wallpaper. Step by step, I felt myself slipping underwater.

Stop her! Make her stop!

Father stood up and walked directly to the bottom of the stairs. Stop her! She stared over his shoulder. She looked inside us. *She knew what we thought. She knew everything. Still she wanted to join us. Join the group.*

Papa took her hand. Very gently, and she turned with him. Soft hands together, they went back upstairs. The maids followed like bridesmaids in step, lifting that long shadow off the ground.

After she died the maids hung onto the thermometer. Mutti's thermometer. They never exchanged it, and I was terrorized, totally terrorized under their glass stick. In my mind Mutti was stuck to the glass. Wet-smelling taboo. But you see the maids had no feelings for us. They cleaned the house and respected Emil Steinmetz, but not his children. The spinsters came from a different world, and they never cared for us *children.* When I fell sick, I had to hide. I had to pretend. I couldn't let them know. Or else: they would lay me over their knees and tell me not to move.

Stay still, don't move. That was their advice. Don't move, child.

No. I couldn't escape. I was much too frightened.

Don't move, no, I wouldn't move an inch to the side—over her knees, the old Grimm sister pushed the stick into my backyard.

That was special treatment.

On Sunday Pastor Kohler walked us home from church. At the villa, tea was served. In the summertime we ate biscuits and tea at the white table in the garden. Männe in his blue and white sailor uniform. The girls in dresses, neck scarves and ribbons. Pastor Kohler in black and white.

Mutti's window faced the garden. Gauze was sucked out the open window and blown wild by the wind. Everything in our lives was an omen. We shared tea watching the window, afraid she was watching, getting herself ready, into or out of costume.

Pastor Kohler took us up after tea. He balanced an open Bible in his palms and climbed the stairs, carefully he stepped, as if in his hands he was carrying a plate of crumbs. He was transporting the last morsels of food on earth, which he himself was going to serve to the birds of paradise.

It was a formal visit. Our delegation entered the room, we surrounded her bed. The pastor arranged us, in whispers. Anneliese and Männe on one side, Romy and me on the other. We settled. Usually her head sat on the pillow. But sometimes she spoke to us. She asked ordinary questions.

In a trance, we answered: what we were doing in school, what we had learned in church, what games were new and fun to play.

All the while her neck didn't move. She was corpsing! Awful. Shame on us. Männe put on a serious face. Romy held my hand. And Anneliese, upright Anneliese, attentively followed the pastor on his tour from prophet to parable, and then out the door.

Five minutes maximum. Five minutes, and then the pastor served communion. He touched Mother's forehead and fed her the wafer. He placed it on her tongue. She took the white flower into her mouth and we shut our eyes.

Finally, a black curtain went up, a black sleeve. Pastor Kohler lifted his arm, a sign for the children to leave. Auf

Wiedersehen, we said, turned, and went out again through his words.

Years later whenever my brother or my sisters or my father were telling a story, we always would say *This happened two years before Mutti's death* or *This happened one year after she died* or *At the last Christmas* or *During the final summer*. Her death was our zero. And from that point the record starts: time runs forwards and backwards, ahead and behind, up and down like the fever that was trapped inside Mutti's thermometer.

THE EXHIBIT

Stopping at one photograph then another, Eva and I tour the exhibit. Hours pass. Fatigued, we hurry through years and Eva goes for a nap. She returns a couple of hours later and asks me where I've been, where am I right now—Are you still in Germany? Have you gone to Austria? Have you seen the photograph of my quartet in Zurich?

No, Eva, I'm still in Germany; I'm studying a twelve by sixteen print from 1919. This one is of the salon in the house on Briskestrasse. Natural light bursts through the sepia sludge on the windows at the far end of the room. The tile oven runs up one wall. A chandelier hangs over a small oval table. Three chairs. Which of these was my great-grandfather's favourite? Certainly none of them lives up to Eva's description of having lion paws carved into the wooden feet.

Eva sits across from me, providing anecdotes, more names and dates, while I continue to make my way through her photo boxes and albums. We put on our best face when we greet family, some almost strangers, and most from beyond the grave. The experience has a particular quality, familiar yet curiously theoretical, pre-lapsarian.

I begin to sort the photographs, arranging them by era, making mental notes, matching them up with what I've learned through her oral commentary. Soon I have made about ten separate stacks of the loose photographs, some piled higher than others. She watches me as I work, silently amused. The pile of photographs from 1928 and 1929, boom years for Eva, towers over the rest. In contrast, there is next to nothing here from 1935 and 1936, Eva's time in exile in Austria. 1945, 1946, 1947: these are the years Eva spent in post-war Berlin, surviving on ration cards, bribes and the black market. There is no photograph from 1948. But from 1949 on, the photos come, year upon year, and the last piles reach optimistic heights. In the mix we turn up one (c.1938) of Karl Paryla, her husband, and a passport snap (c.1952) of Michael, her son. By 1954, she has put everything into albums.

Is this you? I refer to a studio portrait of Eva taken at the peak of her theatre years, around 1929. She nods, proudly. Wow. We share a laugh. Eva is arresting. Her eyes a deep caramel. I have to hide my real feelings, the force of which surprises me, behind mock incredulity.

Later I come upon this:

```
TEMPORARY TRAVEL DOCUMENT IN LIEU OF PASSPORT
for Stateless Persons and Persons of Undetermined
Nationality.
TITRE DE VOYAGE PROVISOIRE TENANT LIEU DE PASSEPORT.
VORLÄUFIGER REISEAUSWEIS AN STELLE EINES PASSES.
Military Exit Permit. ZONE D'OCCUPATION FRANÇAISE EN
ALLEMAGNE. Le Chef du Bureau des Passeports. Destination
CANADA.
No. 0021241.
Issued at Baden-Baden, August 1949, valid to the 28th of
July 1950.
```

Stateless Persons and Persons of Undetermined Nationality. This category of persons charms me. But at the table Eva dismisses her military exit permit as something out of its rightful place, a non sequitur. She tosses it back into the box. So we move on. Eva translates scribbled annotations. There are countless portraits, her family in all its permutations, sisters and brothers, parents and grandparents. She prods me. I must take what I want. Never be shy.

I select a series of early photos of Eva and her sisters clowning on a park bench. One of Eva with her father, Emil, at the Baltic Sea, both of them in swimming trunks, running hand in hand on the beach. Eva and my father, Roland, in the driveway of the house in Sault Ste. Marie. This one is from the early fifties. Another of Roland standing beside his cousin Michael, Eva's son. Both are dressed in T-shirts and denim. Leather boots. Elvis pompadours. They have strong, youthful bodies. My father is the immigrant James Dean—but minus the teenage angst. Not a rebel bone in his body. Having been sent at fifteen by his parents from South America to live with his aunt in Canada, he is thousands of miles from home with no promise of return. Meanwhile, cousin Michael's good looks are unmistakably mischievous. His pout is downright insolent, in an *East of Eden*, world-of-experience kind of way. Already in 1952, the world (Germany in fact) is calling out, having lined him up for a part in a major motion picture. But Michael's spin in John Sturge's *The Great Escape* is years off.

In all her collection, Eva has only one photograph of my grandfather, her brother, Hermann Hans. There he stands with his best man, on the church steps in Oppeln on his wedding day, 25 May 1936. Holding the hand railing, no smile, aloof, and betraying nothing. Where, oh where did he send his bride, his Pinguin, Suzanne? Where is my Oma? If not for the inscription on the back there would be no way to discern the occasion.

That's him, Eva points to her brother, that's him for sure. And *that*—pointing to the figure in a military uniform by his side—is Rudolf. Hermann Hans' friend from the *deutsche Jugendbewegung*, the German Youth Movement.

THE SÜSSIGKEITSGANGSTER

From a very early age my brother was declared the authority. Mutti's favourite—the only boy in her litter. He was called Männe, this horrible German nickname. It means 'little man'. Männe was in charge. Before the inflation Männe kept goodies locked away in his desk. Männe was the *Süßigkeitsgangster*, the sweet-stuff gangster. Everything at my level depended on him. He stockpiled chocolate. And I remember when our mother, or, later, when one of the maids said, Yes, Eva, you deserve something sweet, go ask Männe for a piece of chocolate, a square of candy, I would knock at the door, softly: Mutti said I could have ... He would shout back: Nein! No you cannot! Away from there! You disturb me. Go away! Leave. You ruin everything!

It was horrible. Horrible how he behaved. I was not ready for that.

Meanwhile the little man was given a private room, and he was encouraged to find his inner peace. *Sein Erlebnis*. He never found it. It was too dark in there. But in fact he was allowed to do whatever he wanted, whenever he wanted. He was encouraged by the maids to become anything it was possible for him to become. He was free to invent himself, day to day, from his mood. Männe tolerated Anneliese, but not the younger two. Romy and I were fluff. Meaningless girls. Anneliese was his ally. I had to carry Romy in my arms, shielding her, always in the other direction, away from them, because we were no match for the older two. We were treated like refugees. Romy and I were never allowed ... we were forbidden ... we didn't have the right papers ... Don't do that! Get out! Leave us alone.

Most of his time was spent behind the door, pooled in the chair, at his desk, making drawings and reading old books. Days, he would sit in his outfit. His green shirt, brown shorts, belt, knee socks, boots. Uniform of his youth group. They were not little Hitlers, not yet, but they were cut the same. During the winter the authority kept to himself. He sat at his desk by the window, a brown-green bulb waiting in the ground. And then in the spring, he stirred. His buttocks shook. In the summertime he and his friends disappeared. They marched into the land and climbed the mountains. In groups of twenty or thirty boys, together they marched out of Breslau. Singing, set free. They marched to the Sudetenland or far north along the Oder to the Baltic Sea. Out of the city and into nature. Arms linked. *I have a Kamerad!* For weeks they survived on the trail. *I have a Kamerad!* Eating wild berries and mushrooms. They drank from streams and rivers. Boys with one or two group leaders. Hiking in the forest. Orienteering and putting up shelters. Camping and building rafts, navigating on the river. Competing in cross-country running races.

Tough as leather, swift as whippets, and hard as Krupp steel.

An orgy of physical activity.

Between the wars there was a code between our boys. Our youth went back to nature and one, two, three, they became the other, the other one. One and the same. They journeyed into the woodland, up river, over mountains, deep, so deep, not to hunt! Not to hunt bison or elk or black bears. There was no hunt for animals. The woodland was theirs. The deformed oaks, and wild-grass clearings. Their fortress ... hung with moss ... the forest floor of black ponds, all this was for them to explore. *Wandervogel. Tramper in Lederhosen.*

At night, outside under the stars, they gathered around bonfires, singing, watching for the flash of an eye, throwing their old stories on the fire.

Männe and the other boys were led up the dark trail into a myth.

When he came home from his summer adventures, he closed his door again. He locked himself from the inside, closed-and-shut, he stuck himself like a clam to the desk.

After Mutti died, he went through a difficult phase. He was forced out of his shell, cracked open. Then what I saw—he was completely unknown. Completely uncharted and unknown to me. He was raw. My brother was this thing, this thing waiting its turn to explode.

I was given a diary for my birthday. I wrote in my diary every day. I turned the pages and the world opened up to me. Meanwhile no one at home said two words to me. In the villa I had to fight for attention. I shoplifted for Anneliese. Guaranteed what I did was wrong. You know, I was an immigrant. I didn't fit in. All along I was living at the wrong address.

In my diary I made up stories about the person no one ever talked about. The person the maids could not see. The person my brother ignored. It was not a whole person or a big person or a small person. But it was me. I started to write a page in the evening. I wrote notes in my diary every day and I was beginning to feel something, I was beginning to grow. Until I had the most devastating experience of my whole life.

I had made him a painting. A scene from nature. Flowers trees mountains. I imagined a place. Somewhere my brother might have gone with his youth group. A woodland haven. I painted tents under the trees. I painted a stream. Black ponds. Wild grass clearings. Someplace he would recognize. I made this for him. A gift, simple. There was no special reason, no occasion to mark. It was not his birthday, not Christmas. The fact was I had started making my painting and while I was still painting I began thinking of him—and so when I was finished I thought, why not, it's a present for Männe.

I wanted to show him I understood, really understood, how important that youth gang was to him.

Off I went to his room, so happy and proud with my gift, and knocked at his door.

Who is there? Who are you? There, terrific. *Who are you?*

It's me. I have a picture for you. I am a girl with a gift. I am no one. No one at all.

And then, *whoof!*

ICH VERZICHTE AUF DEINE GESCHENKE. RAUS!

He broke my heart. I went back to my room and I cried. I opened my diary, marked the date and I started to write using this horrible German nickname. I wrote in my diary: Männe rejects my present. He doesn't want my painting. *Verzichten,* the harsh word. I felt very sad. Destroyed and betrayed. Männe is a primitive, I wrote. He gives no sign, he drops no clues. He lives by his own system. He is unpredictable. Then I stopped writing. When I looked at the pages in my diary I could only think of him, and not of myself anymore. I was so afraid he would take over the space in my diary! So I put it away.

Meanwhile there is another story. It begins when Hermann Hans meets his boy friend, this 'best man' from the photograph, Rudolf, who was also a member of the German Youth Gang. Rudolf's uncle, Gerhard, was a pilot, and famous among the children. Gerhard was shot down at the end of the first war and sent to a French camp. Rudolf had many fascinating stories to tell about his war-uncle.

We played Prisoner of War Hospital in Männe's room with a bucket and a blanket and some bandages. Water and cups and the thermometer. Männe and Rudolf and Anneliese did all the talking: the speaking parts were theirs. That was great, because they knew exactly what to say, and when to say it.

Whenever I opened my mouth, I was attacked.

Not so! Keep quiet, don't spoil our game.

Romy and I stayed out of the way, behind the wires. When it was required by our commanding officer, then we were two more: two more prisoners of war.

When they came for us, Romy and I promised to do exactly as we were told, though it was never much. Männe was in charge. Colonel or captain. The rest transformed into doctors or nurses or soldiers, depending on who or what was needed.

One day I was asked to play, but they sent Romy out. *Ach,* they discarded her. Romy and her head of sand. Go away. Leave us alone.

Why me? I wondered. What's special about me today?

The hospital again was set up inside Männe's room. I knocked on the door, entered. They were ready to start. Männe, colonel, sitting at his desk. Anneliese, doctor, standing beside the bed. Rudolf, the injured, lying in bed. Rudolf was suffering. A wounded enemy soldier. Our own French prisoner of war. Bandaged head. Full of pain. A pink stocking tied to one leg. They told me he was bleeding. But from where? Where was the hole?

You are the nurse.

It was the usual game. Cup of water and rag cloth. Bucket and bandages. Childhood repeats itself. I wet his cheeks and neck. I cleaned Rudolf's face. I pressed my hand to his forehead. *Open your mouth.* Rudolf looked into my eyes. I instantly disliked him.

Find his wound.

Männe and Anneliese stood together on the other side of the bed. I ignored them for now. Instead I reached for the comb on the table. I combed Rudolf's hair. His head felt loose and heavy. It moved like a doll's head in my hands. Next I started to sing. What should I have done? They let me go on singing to the prisoner. Nobody stopped me.

There was no blood. I could see no wound. I was following along.

Find out ... is he a spy?

I looked down at him, bending over from above, moving sideways, swaying, as if he was far, far below. Then I reached and pulled up the left eyelid. I looked under and I saw where the trouble rolled back into his head. He was ugly. He didn't like me. Rudolf didn't approve. He didn't like that I was the nurse.

Männe was seated again. He turned around on his chair, he couldn't be bothered to stand. He said, This one is a spy.

Anneliese stepped in closer. She pointed at the prisoner. Make a full exam. A deep examination.

Something was wrong. They were planning an attack against me. Rudolf made a noise. Männe turned away. Anneliese looked very happy.

The full examination!

I felt threatened, they were going to trick me. We had never done a full exam.

Do as you are told!

Anneliese erased me. Do as you must, as must be done!

I removed the blanket. Rudolf was everywhere. He was out of uniform. The French prisoner wore no outfit, no pants, that was the difference. This was their plan. Then my final order: *Touch his fish*.

Was it so? Was it inevitable?

Do as you are told, as you must! She erased me again. I was nothing. Nothing in their eyes. Worthless, I touched his fish. I touched it for them. It was stuck to his little bag. I pushed it around with my finger. There was no life in it. Rudolf breathed slowly in through his nose. I flipped it over. I hated him. Then I lifted it up and I squeezed his fish in my fist, to show them. To show them what I could do.

They were unprepared!

I took it by the neck and held it in the air. Here you are! Here it is! Try to grab it from me!

Männe and Anneliese were speechless. Rudolf looked at Hermann Hans, Anneliese looked at Rudolf, but my brother had nothing left, no orders to give, nothing more to say.

Rudolf pulled the blanket over himself. Enough. Männe woke up. Get out! Out of here! Hermann Hans was thunder. Out of here!

The door shut. I ran. From then, for months, I was taboo. Anneliese couldn't cope. She went to her pastor to be cleansed. Pastor Kohler with his cleaning power. Father was next to know. By then the story was famous. Männe was furious—he turned deep red—absolutely enormous, silent for months. He said no word to me. Because I was taboo. I was not forgiven. I was forgotten. Until finally much later, when Hermann Hans was fifteen, sixteen, he suddenly, in a very shy and strange way, turned to me and told me that I have the same hands as our mother had, same skin, same eyes, same hair, and that he loves me, he really, really loves me after all.

He stroked my hands. He rubbed my knee. After years of nothing but the silent treatment he suddenly showed his deep affection. All at once, he turned it against me.

HEIMAT

The girl's father was a saddle-maker. This was his specific trade. *Emil Steinmetz—Sattler.* His name was set in bronze lettering above the storefront. He was a proud tradesman, wonderful at his art. His leather creations were visible behind the glass in the front display window. Once a month he closed the shop, forfeited business, and invited one of the children to come along to act as his little assistant.

On Saturday it snowed. The girl travelled by carriage into the city, across the Oder, drawn by horse over the gentle bridge. Her father's leather workshop was on Leiterstrasse, near the Ring. She looked in the window. Travel bags, saddles, bridles, handbags. Her father made the traditional accessories until the First World War came and he combined leather with willow wood and rubber and became rich by that alchemy. He hired more personnel and the shop began to manufacture prosthetic devices. Artificial legs and arms. From the eastern border with Poland, westward to Pomerania, he became known as an expert limb-maker.

Often it was at this time, on a Saturday morning, that her father met with a man named Pohl. Pohl was the cutter. He was special. The girl's father boasted of his skill. Pohl was *Der Lederschneider Gott*, the Leather-cutting God. Without the distraction of customers, the two men spent hours examining sheets of leather. Stock arrived monthly from the tanner. Pohl carried the hides, rolled up like maps under his arm, from the storeroom. He then unrolled them on the large table, tacked the corners, and along with the girl's father studied the leather's texture and its toughness, both men sitting on high stools, smoking.

The girl took her usual spot by the street window. In the main workroom twenty tables and stools were paired and set in rows like school desks. She had homework. In the far wall was a recess and here the two men were involved in their own affairs. Pohl wore a cotton apron looped around his neck and tied behind his waist, her father a full frock buttoned to the collar. After assessing the quality of each sheet independently, Pohl took measurements and laid out stencils. He marked the borders of a pocketbook or a travel case, offsetting the patterns, tightly rounding the bend of an artificial leg. Her father watched; the white frock lent him an air of uneasy forbearance, a formality of spirit of one both detached and devout.

Outside it was snowing heavily again. It had kept up throughout the morning, collecting on the window ledge. Shoppers passed, couples arm in arm, in both directions. It took Pohl half the morning to finish planning the divisions for one hide. The trick was to eliminate scrap. Using the round knife he cut the leather without leaving flat spots or jagged edges. He worked with a naturalness, immersed in the childhood dream of being able to unfurl the peel of an orange with just two or three turns of his thumb. The girl was mesmerized.

She attended to her composition assignment with diminishing interest as the morning wore on. The table at her side was fitted with tack hammers, a glue pot, a harness and stitching needles. Everything here was organized, in its spot. Her homework was silly: to invent a dialogue between her favourite animal and a human child. She had chosen a capuchin, an organ grinder's monkey, and a small African boy. She named her monkey Bimbo and the boy Marcus. She stared out the window.

The snow and the passersby accompanied the ticking of the workroom's standing clock. The girl watched the men at work. When Pohl was finished making his cuts he presented the pieces to the girl's father. Her father examined the cuts, comparing each item with its template, while cross-examining Pohl with questions about workmen and timelines. In the years since she had been coming to the shop the girl had picked up on friction between the men, a disparity that was exposed especially during a transaction like this one, when experience was taught to yield to authority. It was difficult to understand. On the one hand her father was never shy to compliment Pohl, to reward good craftsmanship. Their partnership was successful. Both men were the richer for it. But there were signs of social awkwardness, as if some trouble simmered beneath the surface.

It was the oppression of a covenant.

Astride her stool, swinging her feet, the girl watched the scene outside the window with growing interest. Of those who passed in the street, quite a number carried signs and placards. And these ones were all headed in the same direction. Men, labourers, steel workers, miners, they now outnumbered the shoppers.

Periodically she glanced over at her father and Pohl, still engaged like army generals poring over a battlefield map. While they disputed, they displaced the stencils on the sheets, pinning and unpinning them. Taking turns, one listening, now one standing, now the other sitting, they argued and debated.

Just then something happened. The girl lifted her head. One of the sign-carriers had stopped. He was standing at the display window, hands cupped to the glass. Face enclosed, he shifted his line of vision side to side, manoeuvring like a man at a periscope. He studied the insides of the workroom.

When the girl moved the man swung his attention towards her. They locked eyes and registered a pulse before the girl turned and looked away. But then she realized—a boy! She broke into a laugh. What relief! A blond-haired scoundrel. In his badly fitting, heavy coat, she had mistaken him for —who? An admirer? Was she so egotistical to think that … that she was as attractive as her grown-up sister? Everything had happened quickly. Now she felt foolish. Was she vain as well?

Before she could analyze it further, another figure—this one was an adult, a man, the boy's father perhaps—came up from behind and whispered something into the boy's ear. What is it? What now? The boy filed it away and turned once to verify the sign above the window. And then he began shouting at the girl. She immediately felt reproached, although there was no sense in that at all. He was name-calling, this much she comprehended. But it wasn't her name.

The girl was sent out on an errand. Sent out to buy notebooks from the stationery store and cigars from the tobacconist. 'And don't take long! And come straight back …' Her father's sing-song, the chastity of his instructions. He designed everything with love and severity. It was about time: she was anxious to get outside, leave the smoke-filled workroom, and put to rest her composition assignment.

By now in the street it was snowing harder. Already it had snowed more than usual for December. The sidewalks were covered. She ploughed through the powder, making arcs like an ice-skater as she set out towards the Main Square wearing her boots and heavy coat. Her father had tightened the belt at her waist and cinched the ends. While doing so, on the doorstep of the shop, he had touched his nose to her nose.

This embarrassed her. She resented him for how fond she'd grown of his gestures—yes, for how soon she would outgrow them completely.

The girl was often sent on errands alone and whatever it was, she always completed her mission on time, without any deviation from the plan. She was dependable. She had proven that again and again. But it was always exciting to her to be sent out. Leaving the shop, she immediately felt a shift inside herself. Out on an errand she inevitably acted older than she was, she played a part for the whole city to see. In fact she was flirting, and who better to proposition at that age than oneself? She could learn much from watching the crowds, from eyeing strangers, who might give her a clue as to if she were better off this way, or carrying herself that way. What harm in pretending, when she knew she was *niemand*. No one. Nobody's rose. Did anybody at all care if she was thirteen, fourteen or fifteen years old? What difference would it make to them if she had one sister instead of two, three brothers instead of the one?

She passed Hotel Monopol on Wallstrasse, a grand hotel with the first mechanical lift in Breslau. St. Elizabeth's Cathedral and Blücher-Platz were next on the route that took her around to the shopfronts on Dieterstrasse. The next lane abutted the glowering face of the Dresden Hotel. She knew the way. It was not far to the Rathaus and Market Square. Her father had taken her there sometimes, along with her brother and sisters, for a festival in the summer, a market day in the autumn. From the first excursion she had savoured the experience of merging with the crowds, tucked up close to her father, holding his hand.

It was the same in every town and city in Germany. The city hall kept watch over the public square. Breslau's Rathaus resembled a dollhouse. She admired the revolving clock and brickwork facade. Once, on a snowy day, when she and her

63

father came alone, the square was transformed into the setting of a fairy tale. Blanketed in white, the expanse seemed miniature. Like a world that could be contained in a glass ball, peered into as it rested in her palm.

Whatever the season Market Square provided a surprise. It was cloistered by buildings. The girl remembered passing through the city streets, arriving for her first time at the square. That day the square had lain open to the sun. She had been exultant to find it serene as a meadow, a clearing in the forest. There were spaces inside her equal to this. It might take her a lifetime to discover them, but sometimes she caught a glimpse and the half-knowledge sent tremors through her spine.

She was disappointed.

This Saturday the 'quiet meadow' contained several hundred men. A rally was in progress, some kind of demonstration. Agitated and massed together, the men beat the air with their hand-held signs. Clouds of white breath hovered over them like steam lifting off a lake. Shouts pounded the cold.

She knew who they were. Her father and Pohl had discussed the protest—against unemployment and *the inflation*—sizing up the sheets of leather while men like this passed by the storefront. Doing her schoolwork, she'd overheard bits and pieces of their conversation. Her father talked just like a school professor. He described history as a book. He explained to Pohl about the heavy register. The register was closed. Germany had 'lost its place in the world'. It was difficult for the girl to follow what he was saying. Pohl, himself, equated history with an ocean liner. 'A ship passing above the Proletariat.' These men holding their signs, and shouting, were they proletariat? Were they trying to reverse the direction of an ocean liner by pulling on shadows shot through the water?

She decided on a route along the border of the square where the people were not packed in. More of them were watching than were participating in the demonstration. But still it was slow going. She made headway, nudging as she could. One man after another stepped aside. 'Why are you here, little girl?' They were without exception men. Surprised and annoyed, they looked at her as if she now reminded them of something they'd rather have forgotten. 'Hurry up!' They helped her along. Gripping her coat under her arms. Hands on her ribcage. They hoisted her up stiffly as if she were a box of soot. And placed her down again.

Free at last on the next street over she purchased letter paper and pencil lead in the stationery store and immediately set her return course. She had completely forgotten about the cigars. She was already delayed and wanted to get back to her father's shop, but now, as she approached the square again, she heard them, unified in the cold: 'Juden! Juden! Juden! Juden!'

For a short time she stood and watched, listening, unable to pull herself away. She thought of the boy again, shouting at her through the window. She was seized by the sawing of syllables, the to-and-fro working of sound. If history could be described as a ledger or a ship, why not a tree? Yes, a forest.

In one of the lanes leading out of the square, street vendors had set up the Saturday market. Instinct led her in this direction, away from the crowd. But just as she turned the corner into the lane, the demonstration swelled, the chanting and the noise: higher, higher, and then it disbanded in a roar.

She increased her pace, involuntarily at first, and then as she could. The men came running from the square. Bottlenecked, they charged and the girl was overtaken. She held her hands to the side of her head, trapped in the current, bounced between vendors' stalls and the makeshift tables, set with jams and handicrafts. From one moment to the next she was pushed and then—run down. 'Ah! Bitte!' Her left leg bore the weight. The bone twisted without snapping from its cartilage.

A good Samaritan came to her aid. One of the street vendors. He pulled the girl to her feet and sheltered her, while he managed to move her along. 'You should not be here alone.' He pushed her against the wall. Wool scarves and ceremonial hats from an old battalion lay on the table. Beside these were some antique medallions spread in a fan like cuts of meat.

The man held on to the lapel of her coat. 'You shouldn't have come …' 'I am as able to take care of myself as you are, old man.' On impulse she grabbed a medallion off the table and threw herself into the crowd. She could hear him hollering, cranking out his disgust. 'Thief! That child is a thief!'

By then she was caught up in the second wave of demonstrators. Many of these were bloodied. Noses, ears, caked and smeared. Some limping. They had been trampled. In pairs, they hobbled. The worst off were carried, limp, swung between the arms of men like hammocks.

It was a matter of two hundred yards. Not far to go. Surrounded, disoriented, she was toppled inside by disgust. She slipped on some ice and landed against the base of a lamppost, taking the impact on her left hip. The demonstrators rushed by. Even now she was worried that the old veteran might be following.

She cleaned herself off, wiping snow from her arms and legs. Her stockings were soaked through. Her left side ached. Her leg tingled. The numbness was receding. She clutched the medallion in her pocket. It was for her sister. To impress her. She was aware of a tear in her coat under the armpit. Her father was waiting and so she forced herself to keep walking a little farther, then just a little bit more. He would be worried. She carried on, straight ahead, the orientation that demanded the least effort.

In this state she noticed a vaguely familiar doorway and headed for it. When she entered the shop, bells rattled on a string. 'Guten Tag.' The tone of voice was friendly but she didn't return the greeting nor even acknowledge the storekeeper's presence with a glance. Her arrival had been punctuated by a stronger association than the subdued rattle of bells and the subliminal familiarity of the shopkeeper's voice. Upon stepping in she was overwhelmed by the moist bloom of fur and feces and straw. She rushed past the counter to the back of the shop. Here, by the cages, the ripe animal smell was strongest.

She was safe now. But shaking. From the cold, and from exertion. *That child is a thief!* She was trembling. Trembling and shaking, because of the medallion. She'd snatched it from the table. She'd acted on impulse, but whose? It was as if she'd taken the medallion from herself. Before her very eyes. She'd stolen her own heart.

On the wall was a sign. *Afrikanischer Affe*. Aha! An African monkey. She recalled the voice at the door: Herr Krusemark. Krusemark's pet store was on Valentinstrasse, only a couple of streets over from the workshop. Above the monkey's crate hung a row of cages. Tropical birds, colourful shards, querulous things. They fidgeted, alive to her every movement. What a disturbance she must have made coming in!

'Shush-shush.' She reassured the birds, then moved up closer, undoing the buttons on her jacket. She rested her chin on the top edge of the crate. 'An African monkey in Breslau?' She put the question to a canary. 'Is it true?' She peered down inside the box. A bowl of water, sawdust. The black monkey crouched there at the base.

Poor thing, she thought, the poor thing is bewildered: he

is alone, bewildered, and frightened. *He has no clue, not a clue what this is about. Everything must be new to him. He has no idea what all the fuss is about.* She undid her scarf. 'This is Germany,' she began, letting the scarf unfurl in the box. 'And here in Germany we have winter and snow.' She paused a moment before carrying on. 'My name is Marcus.' She giggled. 'In this story I have a brother and two sisters. Our mother is dead. But no one believes me ...'

She stretched out her hand, reaching into the box. The monkey crouched lower, away.

'All right,' she said. 'All right. That's normal. Yes, you're right, I am a stranger. You should not trust me.' She ignored the monkey then, paying subtle attention to the birds, blowing on their feathers. No great mischief. She could pretend. She was thirteen. Soon she would be an actress.

'This is Germany. Here in Germany we have snow in winter. Winter and snow. My real name is Eva. I have one brother ...' This is exactly how adults spoke to the girl when they had something urgent they wanted her to do, or anything important they wanted her to remember. They repeated themselves, the same words over and over and over. Slowly she led the monkey into her story, speaking her mind hypnotically, soothing him with repetition and always maintaining the even tone of her voice. It came close to a physical gesture.

It seemed to work.

'Eeolk.' The monkey stared up at her without raising himself off the floor. Chin set, chest puffed out, he barked again. 'Eeolk.' His tail launched itself and he tugged the scarf right out of her hands.

'That's for you,' she told him. 'Keep it.' He is a juvenile, she thought to herself. A macho. With that tail, he must have been a tree climber. A real athlete in the jungle.

Mother was shot. Out from the bushes, poachers surprised us.

I am sorry.
I clung on to her back.
She was dying?
Yes.
And you clung to her, you didn't think of escaping?
No.
'Don't give up! I'll come back and get you! I promise.'

On her way out she stopped to talk with the shopkeeper. She had a birthday coming. She wanted the monkey.

Herr Krusemark put his hand in his apron and offered the girl a candy.

'No.'

'Ask your father to come,' Herr Krusemark said. 'Tell him the monkey is imported from our old Tanganyika. Tell him that this is my first monkey since the end of the war.'

Crossing the street she had already made up her mind. She would not tell her father about the monkey, not immediately. She was returning late and first off he would demand an explanation. He might never discover the medallion in her pocket but the potential for it to cause trouble was a burden, so she tossed it away. When she turned the corner onto Leiterstrasse and saw her father already standing in the street, she knew he would be angry with her, not only disappointed. There was nothing to do but confess.

But to her surprise she recognized Pohl by her father's side. Pohl was nailing a board into place, he was busy with a hammer. Pieces of glass littered the ground under their feet. Neither man was aware when she approached and saw for herself the damage done to the display window.

So she had escaped.

The girl spent the rest of the afternoon in her usual spot. One section of the window was covered over with wood; however, her view of the street was not completely obstructed and after so much excitement she was willingly entranced by the snow that continued to fall from the sky. It was ages now since she had returned from her adventure. At last her father was ready to return home. She slid off the stool with his help.

'My little soldier,' he addressed her, 'lucky for you. No prosthesis. Just a bruise in your case. A purple star.'

SCHOOL

My schooling went badly. By mistake Father had put me in the same *Gymnasium* that Anneliese had gone to and the teachers there expected another little fanatic. Anneliese absorbed structure. She belonged in school, at church, she set the perfect group example. She was eager to conform. She studied very hard and impressed her teachers, and when the headmaster came to fit handcuffs on her wrist, she only smiled and asked, what should I do next? She was the great conformist!

I was the opposite. I would not connect dots. Whenever possible, I took the negative image. I already knew that I wanted to join the theatre. This was clear. I wanted to be an actress, a cabaret bad-mouth. A blonde Satan. I wanted nothing less than to stand right in the middle of the action on stage, in a place where everything is possible.

Theatre was the only solution for me. Off stage, I had no idea how to proceed. I was powerless.

In school, I became the clown, a schoolgirl clown ready for the circus or theatre.

Meanwhile Frau Hess was my French teacher. This woman started class by ordering the students to stick their heads on the desk, down on the wood.

Quiet! Your head on the wood! Everybody, dead quiet.

Frau Hess then explained: we were supposed to concentrate until it hurt.

Close your eyes and stop thinking. Concentrate on nothing. Total concentration! Until it hurts. If that didn't do it—if we were not able to concentrate on nothing—then she said, imagine there is a candle burning inside your empty head.

Imagine the burning candle, said Frau Hess. Watch the flame. Let it grow. Then blow it out!

That was a trick. Blow out the candle, then move along into darkness. Into the space that hurts.

Every morning I found myself in the same situation. Every morning I was supposed to concentrate until it hurt, then raise my arm: hold up one arm, the right arm, and keep it raised in the air until every student, in pain, was saluting. It was Heil Hitler, before Hitler's time.

Classics. German language. History. Geography. Girls and boys. Our house of education was divided. The boys were sent into the woods. They were sent on nature walks. Shit. The male intellect unfolded like a picnic blanket on the ground, harmoniously, square by square: a boy turned into a man through contact with nature, rubbing together his senses to start the fire of individuality.

Meanwhile *die Mädchen* were taught the special tasks for women within society, and within the family: boiling potatoes or setting the table or slaughtering chickens while giving birth to the superior race. We learned our tasks, grade level by grade level. In school if you didn't play the female role to perfection, you were thrown back into the pile and the difference was, the next year, the teachers expected less from you, you were given a smaller part, less and less was expected from you every year. From Gymnasium you were then sent to *Realschule*, a step down. After Realschule, the last resort was

Volkschule. In Volkschule young women learned the spirit of citizenship. Finally they joined the league of housewives.

Boys unfolded their intellects while girls played in the doll's house. We were the national treasure chest. From one end, from our wombs, the new nation was waiting to be born, and at the other end, on our bosoms, the new nation was eager to suck. That was *Schicksal* for us girls: our fate, in the hands of a male intellect.

After the first day of school I couldn't race home fast enough to tell Father that in fact, for me, nothing hurt. When *I* concentrated it didn't hurt, as Frau Hess had instructed it should. Therefore in my case there must be some mistake.

The next morning Frau Hess ordered us to close our eyes and concentrate, hard, this time, on a black hole.

Forget the candle, she said, and imagine a hole, a great void.

Do so right now! Find the hole!

We were supposed to imagine the hole and then find our way down to the bottom, without asking any questions—by thinking our way, we were supposed to arrive, through the darkness, without the candle, without a single flame, and without Frau Hess helping us.

Quiet! Your head on the wood! Everybody concentrate.

I lowered my head. Sideways, I watched the group.

Raise your hand when it …

Day after day, I couldn't do it because nothing hurt me. I never found her black hole. But in the end to be safe I raised my hand just like all the others.

As Father said: that school worked for Anneliese, *but it doesn't work for you*. Since I was different he was going to find another solution for me. Meanwhile I had to be patient.

So I waited: head turned, my cheek flat, stuck to the wood. I had to imagine the void or something else in its place. Each day was a struggle. Unfortunately French was my first subject.

One thing worth doing was holding my morning pee at all costs. If I could hold on until class then I had an excuse to exit.

One day when Frau Hess appealed for silence, I closed my eyes and counted to twenty. Then I raised my hand. Frau Hess was surprised.

It hurts.

So much? Already?

Yes. My bladder hurts.

It should hurt in the head, said Frau Hess. Eva, put your hand down. Drop your arm. Drop it now!

Please, it hurts. Please let me out to do my water.

So: she had no choice. She had to let me go. I had found the black hole. I had slipped through the void. Outside, I used time. I slowed myself down. When I returned from the toilet to class, the exercise was over. Row by row, my classmates were done. Arms raised, hands tipped forward.

Frau Hess pointed to my seat.

Finally in school we were taught the Greeks. I remember the day. First came Aeschylus' *Oresteia*. Then came dead babies in a burning carriage.

I was stunned. Now I know, I said to myself. Now I know why. Of course. Why I want to become an actress. I remember feeling pulled from oblivion ... I was turning thirteen or fourteen, and here I came before Agamemnon, king of Mycenae, son of Atreus. Iphigenia. Cassandra. Queen Clytemnestra. I realized there was a very old family structure before my own family, a framework that belonged to the world of art.

I took part in the classroom play. For weeks we worked

on one scene. Cassandra was my first amateur role: *Clear vision, dark speech!*

I stood in the middle of it and watched that wonderful scene unfold: King Agamemnon returns from Troy. Queen Clytemnestra sits him into the bath.

King Agamemnon: A woman who fears nothing—is she a woman? What can you fear? Surrender just a little, for me.

Clytemnestra throws the net on Agamemnon. She drives a pole through him. He splashes around in his own blood.

Agamemnon cries out: Help! Help! They have killed me.

There, you see. They *have* killed me. Wonderful. His horror crosses into death. Horror echoing from the afterlife.

It was a profound moment.

One day Father gave me a limb. An artificial limb. The *Sonntagsarm*. I had lied to him. I had told him I needed a prop for my part in the class play. He fixed the limb and made it smaller, perfect for my situation.

In the morning he shoved the Sonntagsarm up the sleeve of my school jacket. So off I went to Gymnasium loaded with a prosthesis. I was already focused, thinking of the void on my walk to school. I was excited, rehearsing in my mind. And then I realized I was late for school. I had been daydreaming. Walking slowly. When I reached the church on our corner, I held my breath and started my run. I was scared. I started running faster and then the prosthesis fell out of my jacket. I panicked: there I was in front of the cemetery. It was our game! I was not allowed to breathe! I had to run forward, breathe in, then return, to pick up the Sonntagsarm.

By the time I made it to school I was burning hot, red through my cheeks. I lay my head sideways on the desk. *Everyone, head on the guillotine.* I counted, then I raised my arm. My Sonntagsarm.

That day the others had difficulty finding the painful void.

I waited for them. One by one, arm by arm, they woke up. Meanwhile I had to support the prosthesis. The piece of wood. It was heavy. My shoulder started badly to hurt. Finally my classmates exploded. When they realized what I was doing, when they saw my arm, they lost concentration. They realized and burst out laughing.

What is funny? Frau Hess asked, Why are you laughing?

My fellow students went pale.

It hurts very much, I said. It hurts me! My arm hurts now!

Frau Hess crossed over to my spot. She charged without a horse between her legs.

Eva, what is it? Eva! ...

She took one step back, then rushed at me again.

Take it off! Stop it, take it off!

It won't come off . . .

The other students—really only children—kept waving their hands. They made a laughing forest of swinging arms:

It hurts!—

Frau Hess!—

Over here, in the black void, it hurts me too!

At last the French teacher had had enough. She pulled the Sonntagsarm from my shoulder and held it in the air, over my head, to crush me.

The children went dead quiet.

By the neck outside, outside by the neck Frau Hess dragged me off like a goose.

THE MISSUS PUTS IT ACROSS

Eva's account of her acting years is unfailingly and uncharacteristically matter-of-fact.

Brecht and Weill play bit parts. *Nebenrollen*. She glosses over Brecht, confiding, in German, her trump suit, that the poet-playwright had 'the potato head of a peasant.' She remembers that upon introduction Brecht said Hallo, very softly, gave his hand, and at the same time took a step backwards. The peasant from Augsburg wore a boiler shirt with multiple pockets, blue workman's trousers, and his socks, always, were rolled down around his ankles. His laugh, unpleasant, was sharp and staccato.

Eva dismisses Weill with equal economy. 'His fame came later.' Very well. 'On Broadway.'

Whereas I see the curtain opening, and history assembled on the stage, Eva, uninterested in turning the trick, is done with Brecht & Weill over the course of one conversation, in just under twenty minutes.

She went into acting to hide, she told me, not to shine. And from the moment she entered the theatre, she never stopped acting, or hiding. Max Ophüls, at that time the artistic director of the Lobetheater in Breslau, took on the inexperienced Eva for an apprenticeship, and, not long after, rewarded her with an engagement. *En-ga-ge-ment*. This term, meaning a contract with a professional theatre company, she repeats often during our conversations. An engagement is something she had only once. She chews the word carefully.

When Ophüls took Eva on, her mother was dead and her poor ape, Bimbo, was long extinct. Her brother was a menace and the household maids were older, and colder, still. At her first audition Ophüls must have apprehended the fury of that being, panic-packed into a ball, racing toward him. Eva was ready for the theatre. She was loaded with energy—but would she explode or implode? Ophüls, for taking her in, deserves some applause.

Eva sighs. She pauses, then introduces Erich Kästner.

'Kästner was from the Berlin avant-garde.'

It is early afternoon. Eva is smoking and I'm sucking on a yellow highlighter, good as a cigar. Kästner is a new addition to the cast. He is something special to her. She reaches for her glass of water, and, with freak swallows, ingests. I pull the highlighter from between my lips and stop the tape recorder. Eva's sigh, her pause, her swallowing: a quotable gesture. Walter Benjamin observed that the movements of the Brechtian actor are measured to the point that each gesture is made the way a typesetter produces spaced type. In Epic Theatre the actor is instructed to pause on stage, not in order to express feeling, but to disrupt the action, and give the spectator time to reflect. Gestures, arising out of context, are noticed.

Eva, likewise, brings attention to herself and she interrupts herself. She would also interrupt all others at the dinner table. She told and retold the events in her life, major and minor, and every retelling was an occasion for Eva to bring order to the present and spring meaning from the past. No matter how banal the incident, she would imbue it with shape and form. She would leave the house for a ten-minute walk with her borzoi Natasha, and return with sixty minutes' worth of storytelling. I've witnessed Eva get more excited describing the crinkling sound fiddleheads produce when they naturally unfold in the field at dawn—a story she liked to repeat when served asparagus—than she ever became when discussing her connection to Brecht et al.

Eva almost certainly met Kästner in Breslau. Kästner was a poet and novelist, a satirist renowned for his juvenile novel *Emil und die Detektive*, about youths tracking a thief on a train. Eva parted with her own autographed copy of *Emil* in 1933. She told me she lost it in 'the move' to Austria.

While Eva escaped Germany, Kästner was present in Berlin's Opernplatz on the night of 10 May 1933 when university students, under the spell of Joseph Goebbels, the Nazi "Minister for Popular Enlightenment and Propaganda," burned upwards of twenty-five thousand "un-German books," including uncounted copies of *Emil und die Detektive*.

On that night public book burnings were staged in university cities across Germany, including Munich, Breslau, Dresden and Cologne. Examples of "degenerate art," including the works of Brecht, and "decadent Jewish intellectualism," were thrown on the bonfires while university students shouted their 'fire-oaths' prepared by the German Student Association. '*Against* class struggle and materialism. *For* national community and an idealistic lifestyle.' With this, they threw books by Marx onto the fire. '*Against* decadence and moral decay. *For* discipline and decency in family and state.' Herewith went Erich Kästner's novels. ' *Against* soul-shredding overvaluation of sexual activity. *For* the nobility of the human soul.' Let slip the Freudian School. '*Against* literary betrayal of the soldiers of the World War. *For* the education of the nation in the spirit of standing to battle.' Erich Maria Remarque. '*Against* impudence and presumption. *For* veneration and reverence for the immortal German national spirit.' Kurt Tucholsky.

Eva was married, already, in 1930. I must prompt her for a description of Karl Paryla, her husband. 'He was already a famous actor when we met.' From their first meeting, Eva says, Paryla sought to own the means of her production. I understand from her tired delivery that this is an awfully old joke. I also understand that Eva's leaving Germany in 1933, after the Reichstag fire, had a lot to do with Karl Paryla's being a renowned Communist.

While Eva recounts the avalanche of events that took place fast on the heels of the Anschluss—Germany's 1938 occupation of Austria—I watch the magnetic tape wrap itself around the spiky wheels of my recorder, like a tank track powered by the drive wheel. It was in Vienna, before the Anschluss, that Eva first met Manès Sperber, the Austrian-French novelist, essayist, Marxist, and psychologist, a disciple of Alfred Adler. Sperber reappeared in Eva's life, in Zurich, in 1942. When she speaks about him now—what is it, nearly sixty years later?—her words are fraught with feeling.

Sperber volunteered for the French army in 1939. After its defeat, he had sought refuge with his family in the *zone-libre*. In 1942, he'd left his family and reached Switzerland from France, after swimming across the Rhine. In his three-volume autobiography, *Until My Eyes Are Closed with Shards*, he remembers:

> *Without knowing where I was going I reached a railway station and without any further incidents an express train took me to Zurich. In the telephone book I found the address of a friend; his wife told me over the phone that her husband had left her. Half an hour later I was in her house, where I was welcomed with touching friendship and given all the food, drinks, and cigarettes I wanted as well as a hot bath and a good bed.*

Eva and Paryla had separated soon after arriving in Zurich from Vienna in 1938. Paryla had left Eva to follow a promising theatre career: he appeared in the world premiere of Brecht's *Mother Courage and Her Children* at the Zurich Schauspielhaus in 1941. And, in the world premiere of *Life of Galileo* in 1943. Meanwhile, Eva lived in an apartment with her son Michael, a child of four or five.

Although it was dangerous to do so, Eva safeguarded Sperber while he recuperated from pneumonia. During the war years it was illegal to harbour refugees from the cantonal police, and Eva knew this. Eva was by definition a refugee herself. 'The Swiss set up their own camps for immigrants and displaced persons,' she told me. 'They did it all with Swiss precision.' So they did. While convoys of trucks carrying Nazi gold crossed the Swiss frontier at Basel, bound for the Swiss Bundesplatz and the National Bank, more than a hundred thousand Jews were refused entry to the country. Jews who managed to breach border security were placed with other refugees in displaced persons camps for the duration of the war. Switzerland was eager to maintain its face of neutrality. But the government showed its stripes when it levied a special tax on its own Jewish citizens in order to cover the costs of keeping Jewish DPs.

'Acting is a process within the framework of becoming.' A quotation from Sperber.

It appeared in an interview in *Gestalt Theory* in 1983. I try it out on Eva on a subsequent visit. She is unfazed: either she doesn't understand, or she doesn't think much of the connection I am trying to make.

Herr Sperber, you might remember Herr Paryla, a fellow party member ... Guten Abend, Herr Brecht, may I present to you an extra from the original workshop ... Herr Kästner, would you be so kind to explain your interest in a young lady from Breslau?

I suppose by superimposing their lives on hers I was steadily erasing Eva. Eva wasn't interested. Her final words to me on Bertolt Brecht et al. were typical: 'These men are famous and dead. You can find them in the library.'

At the library, I stand at the kiosk and interrogate the catalogue, face to face with the bland monitor, casually baffled by the number of references and cross-references each search question spits back at me. Using the wood chip pencil I scribble down a list of titles along with their catalogue numbers and then wander off, into the stacks, where, in a matter of seconds, I find myself utterly lost amidst the tombstone data of the Dewey System. Eventually, I make my selection, and then carry my bundle of titles that handles like firewood back to my seat. I think of Eva's comment about the condition of Berlin's Tiergarten after the war, how, when fuel was limited and winter came, the citizens denuded the parks.

Historical research is a positively proletarian activity. The long hours represent the donning of a kind of hair shirt—for research is reparation, penance, licence. It reeks of a lumpen imagination, perverted by puritanical desire.

Once ensconced in my carrel, behind its three walls—chair pulled tight to apron, making for me a miniature proscenium theatre—I begin reading, elbows planted firmly in the action.

WORKSHOP

LOBETHEATER, BRESLAU, 1928

Paryla watches a man downstage right rigging a sheet to the steel line. This must be Caspar Neher.

Paryla's first introduction to Brecht came two years earlier, in Darmstadt, and he remembers Neher's work in the production of *Man Equals Man*. 'Precocious.' 'Ruthless.' 'Brash.' 'Depraved.' The critics reacted favourably to the raw power of Brecht's material and the original set design, but they condemned Brecht for the kind of directing that led his actors to perform rape and murder with the ease they'd take to shit and urinate. The critics were part of the show now, weren't they? Well in any case Brecht, once a theatre critic himself, had been noticed. His brand of parody and his penchant for the naive and the droll set him apart, afloat in that lush amoral universe his characters typically inhabited.

Now Neher is at it again, same as in Darmstadt, steering a course between sparse and barren. Nothing here for the cult of beauty. Exposed lights. A table, a chair. And then the steel line and sheet. In Darmstadt the stagehands had operated a similar contraption. The sheet was whipped across the stage between acts by a runner. The runner sprinted from right to left, then left to right, dragging the half-curtain, which sometimes caught on the overhead wire. When it did, the runner paused and performed a clumsy pantomime, ridiculing the premise of a virginal *mise en scène*. Behind him, the other stagehands would be busy rearranging props and furniture in full view.

Originally Brecht had wanted to replace the curtain for this production with bedsheets. Neher had resisted. Paryla heard the story last night from Ophüls: 'The grand curtain replaced by laundry out on the line: class divider replaced by grand equalizer. If Brecht had his way, there would have been spots of blood on the sheets, as the not at all vague symbol of sex and ritual. Domination, subjugation, exploitation. Blood on the sheets! Yet another sign of the class struggle ... Women! Rise up from under your men!'

But in the end Neher, Brecht's childhood friend, triumphed. There is no laundry on the line, today. Neher gives the divider a tug. Paryla notes a refinement: a pull cord is being used, instead of the runner, to tug the sheet along the wire. The cord is haphazardly functional: noisy, at odds with its purpose. Perfect. The stage hands test it. After its screeching success, the runner reappears to return the sheet to the other side of the stage. Apparently no one thought of attaching two pull cords, one at each end of the sheet. Paryla laughs out loud. Neher, looking on, seems duly satisfied.

Something else is new. For this production, Neher will be using the curtain as a screen. He plans to project captions and maxims onto the curtain. He tests a few slides:

Jonathan Jeremiah Peachum's Outfitting Shop for Beggars.

It Is More Blessed to Give than to Receive.

Give and It Shall Be Given Unto You.

This obviously is the reason Neher has ruled out transforming the set into a laundry yard. Blood on the sheets would not do. The taboo of that would distort Neher's projections.

Paryla is impressed. He is beginning to think there is more to didactic theatre than meets the eye.

HAPPY END

Coincidentally, Eva was not the only Brechtian refugee who took up residence in the Eastern Townships near Sutton, where my father kept a farmhouse. The other was Oskar Kuper, director and puppeteer—like Eva a native of early twentieth-century Breslau. It was a fluke that they ended up neighbours: but then there were quite a few émigrés in that area—including, in some sense my father, my brother and me.

My father must have decided early on after Mom died that his boys needed to get away on weekends. Stephen and I were crammed with frustrations. So Roland found the old farmhouse on Robinson Road, just a year after Mom died. It was derelict: two storey, green-shingled, with a wraparound veranda.

That first summer, we slept on the veranda while the insides were being gutted, day by day and room by room. It was an adventure for Stephen and me, boys from the suburbs: destroying an old farmhouse with our bare hands, sleeping in the fresh air, toughing it out a bit. The farmhouse in Sutton became our summer commune, our winter ski chalet. We spent all our free time there, with any combination of our friends, cutting trees and splitting wood, seeding the vegetable garden in front of the house, and playing badminton along the side. In one respect we became more industrious than ever after Mom passed away. But at bottom I would always feel terribly guilty constructing or building anything new, adding anything solid to our lives, carrying on with projects after she was gone. Eventually I withdrew from the outdoors to do my digging upstairs, lying on my side in bed, head supported on my palm. Reading left no visible mark and it soon became my favourite pastime: a studied form of malingering, an expression of my loyalty to Mom.

In 1974, the year Roland found the house, I was eight years old and Stephen was ten. 'The boys' mother, Katherine,' I more than once caught Dad explaining to dinner guests, 'died from *a* meningitis.' The indefinite article was adopted from the funeral forward by the whole family, to render something both specific and general about Mom's death: as if to state, that if the natural history of her disease was common or classic, in Mom's case the cause and effect were creatures both spontaneous and unique. No one accepts death, certainly not their mother's. I couldn't, still don't, and perhaps that is part of everything now. Roland, cruel fate, Roland, only just retired, was a neurologist. But he also, to this day, says 'a meningitis,' as if he of all people could be agnostic about such a thing.

Eva moved into the area from Niagara-on-the-Lake, years later, around 1978. After living temporarily in our farmhouse—where she immediately started a business, running a dog kennel—she built the house on the hill, beside the goldfish pond, which was visible from our kitchen window. We watched it go up over morning tea and afternoon coffee.

Her split-level was designed and constructed by the Czech Marian, a one-time hippie to whom Stephen and I sometimes referred, adopting Eva's husky voice, as Martian—or, The Martian. He was not an architect, nor even a builder, but better, someone Eva had met playing contract bridge. His qualifications were that he had learned the game before emigrating from Czechoslovakia to 'this refugee camp' (Canada).

The Martian lived in a geodesic dome near the ski hill. Upon discovering this, Eva immediately expressed her (apparently long kept) secret desire to live in her own round house, one without corners in which dust and sorrow *do* gather. Eva had been on the move since arriving in Canada. Living first in Ottawa, then in Sault Ste. Marie, she moved from shared house to shared house, and from living arrangement to living arrangement. At last she seemed eager to put down roots near her nephew and his family.

Marian and Eva installed themselves at our kitchen table and drew diagrams on the back of a square Benson & Hedges pack, marvelling at the empty lot out the window where her house was going to be. They planned and smoked, and later played Czech Army Bridge, and usually finished off a bottle of Magyar plonk between them, a wine whose consonant-dominated designation, out of endless possibilities, became known to us as Szex-on-Sar-Day. My father's coinage. He shared an occasional glass with them.

Though it was not, ultimately, round or even domed, Eva's house was to have a special roof. Marian's flow diagrams with coloured arrows depicting the air circulation, looked a lot like the print of the Kandinsky painting Eva had hung in our washroom. At the peak of the house, one slanting wedge overlay another, and there was a gap between them. Marian claimed that with this design 'everything was free': space, air, heat, everything went its way.

Eva was impressed by the Martian's contempt for the traditional, and by his 'very rudimentary' means of roof ventilation. His irreverence—if not his architectural acumen—had struck a chord with her.

But the house did not have an attic. In the winter the heated air rose to the apex of the cathedral-ceiling and escaped through the gap between the wedges. The winter heating bill was enormous. Hot air was *meant* to escape through the roof, 'if it so pleased ...' —Eva parroted her Martian—but time and again the snow melted up top, until eventually the entire concept iced over and capped itself. The house was uninhabitable three months of the year, and in springtime the ice cap melted, sending drips, then torrents, directly into the room below.

Despite its obvious shortcomings, I slept over at Eva's house as often as I was allowed to. I remember the living room with its twin foci: a circular fireplace at one end, and an Asian-style indoor fountain, at the other. The fountain, with its black bowl, ferns, water plants and constant murmuring, anchored the east windows. The fireplace was by the west-facing windows which themselves drew flames from the setting sun at dusk. The inside of her house was idyllic, calm and thoughtful, though instead of tastefully coloured pillows arranged on the couch, there were never any less than five or six dogs. Staying overnight meant sharing the warmest corners and horizontal surfaces with them: kennel dogs, who spent their sojourn at Eva's anywhere they pleased. When Eva went out walking, pulled ahead by a good handful of hounds, each on its separate leash, each sniffing and spraying its purebredness in the tall grass along the side of the dirt road, one was never sure which were hers and which were on loan. She certainly didn't differentiate—with one exception: Natasha, that old borzoi, held forth on the leather armchair reeking of general decay, but swollen with pride, knowing both her special place in Eva's animal kingdom and the supremacy of outrageous halitosis. When it was her time of the month Natasha wore a red thong, a bikini bottom stuffed with cotton wool. Natasha had an awful thingness about her. She easily could have been a family heirloom, handed down from the mantelpiece onto the chair, and brought to life only from time to time. Eva invited Natasha up to her own bedroom at night.

While Eva was constructing her Czech retreat, Oskar, down the road, built an atelier. It was the first I'd heard of this word, *atelier*, and I was certain it involved some amount of delicate effort with string and leather.

Stephen and I were on hand the day the cement truck arrived, however, breaking off branches as it lumbered down the narrow drive, and we stayed to watch as the foundation was poured. There were troubles here as there had been with the construction of Eva's house. The footings, whatever those were, had not been properly fastened. The poured cement expanded like porridge, overflowing, rising from the ground and eventually ejecting the boards meant to contain it. There was a lot of shouting and running around, and grim expressions were exchanged between Oskar and the truck driver. But in the end Oskar got his atelier.

Oskar was a "dramaturge," which sounded to me in my youth like a terribly sad thing to become. 'A dramaturge in his atelier.' What next? Oskar staged plays that used man-sized puppets instead of actors, a concept so alien to me that I at first dismissed it as a compromise born of amateur ideas.

But Oskar was accomplished. He made these puppets and masks using great care, and, I was led to believe, by manipulating strong natural light. His atelier had windows on three sides. During the day when the interior was awash with sunlight the air was set aglow like water in a swimming pool. The room was essentially empty except for a black iron wood stove in one corner. The wooden floor, however, filled the space as if it was furniture. Oskar's workbench and tools were organized along one wall, and Mozart violin concertos were broadcast from a pair of speakers hung, half-hidden like hornet nests, under the ceiling beams. All in all the atelier *was a space*. That much I understood. Everything, including Oskar's leather apron and clogs, had been hand-picked: everything there was set up to engage a creative process.

In the seventies Oskar's theatre company frequently toured in Europe. He was in demand. I witnessed him at work in Sutton, during the production and early rehearsal stages, as he elaborated his interpretations of major works: *Woyzeck*, *The Magic Flute*, *A Dream Play*. I was a teenager then and dazzled by the mere mention of Büchner or Strindberg.

In principle, Oskar worked alone. Certainly for the pre-production phase: first researching mask-making in the South Pacific or reading about the burial rites of the Aztecs, assembling background material, making telephone calls; then adapting a script; and finally affixing his storyboard to the cork-lined wall in the atelier. When I entered adolescence, I began to wonder more fervently about Oskar and his occupation, never quite sure if it was the demands of discipline or merely his indifference to society—an unfeeling lump at his core—that kept him going out there in the country, preoccupied, working alone, for months at a time.

There were exceptions. I remember one summer my brother and I, as well as miscellaneous neighbours, were conscripted into the company to help Oskar take press photos for an upcoming show. It was *Antony and Cleopatra*. Oskar had Stephen and I and some others dress up as Roman imperial soldiers. We wheeled a homemade trebuchet through the grass in the field bordering his property. I remember the disappointment I felt, after the photo shoot was done, at having to pack away my sword and shield and return to our farmhouse, and carry on with the predictable course of the afternoon.

During the final production stage, Oskar would assemble a team of young people from the city to collaborate with him.

In the weeks leading up to their arrival, he would attend to their future work environment as if it was an actual *mise en scène*. Then, for up to two months, the team would work with Oskar running in its midst, from early in the morning into the night, humming as they consumed his vision. On Saturday night, the eve of a day of rest, the company would hold an extravagant dinner party. It was always an improvised affair—but the more formal for its impromptu nature. Oskar's youthful collaborators, many of them anyhow, were exaggerated characters, motivated by a Gothic egocentrism which I took to be the counterpoint of their restrained puppeteer personas. After dark on Saturday they would make speeches and perform soliloquies at the table, to thunderous applause and hollering. Then off they went outside, carrying instruments—usually a guitar and banjo, sometimes an accordion—and danced close to the roaring bonfire, to music of their own making. Eventually they'd strip off their clothes to go skinny-dipping in the pond. This, I admit, suited me. Stephen and I would wander over to Oskar's pond the morning after, our imaginations easily stolen by ripples in the water. Usually, we came across the picnic table sitting out in the field like an amusement park ride in a deserted fairground. Candle butts stuck in wine bottles.

I telephoned Oskar after nearly twenty years of silence because I had just begun work on my book about Eva and I needed background. I stood by the kitchen window watching the snow fall out of the night sky—it was winter then, in Montreal—as I listened to Oskar talk about Germany.

When I repeated that Eva was dying, he told me something I hadn't heard before. 'Eva probably crossed paths with my father in the twenties. I'm quite sure. He was in charge of radio drama in Breslau. He put on the avant-garde *th-tuff*.'

Oskar spoke with a lisp. He had intermittent problems in English, mispronouncing sensitive consonants. I'd unconsciously put it down to a combination of his mother tongue and the referred pain of a childhood trauma (if this often implies child sexual abuse, in Oskar's case it was probably the Allied bombing of Berlin in 1945). The lisp, combined in his later years, with his particular brand of emphysema, produced sloppy sounds: *Avant-garde th-tuff. Woy-th-eck. Imbethilic.*

Oskar was the first artist I'd known and his ideas and opinion meant a great deal to me. I did not have the confidence then to tell him I was writing a book, per se. Instead I told him I was working on 'a project' … I was reading and researching … making an outline, hanging a structure, chasing some ideas and an aesthetic, and so on. Callus-making procrastination, actually. For from the outset I had neither stamina nor willpower where research was involved—though the activity girded me against the disheartening prospect of committing to paper another famished family blah-blah. So, after a fashion, I was reading. But even as I transcribed passages verbatim, from, say, *Living for Brecht: The Memoirs of Ruth Berlau,* or from *The Life and Lies of Bertolt Brecht* by John Fuegi, or from Brecht's own *Little Organon for the Theatre*—even as I read and noted page numbers and assembled a bibliography, I did so with little conviction that I would ever return to peruse these items again, let alone use them. How? 'Use them' how?

When I asked Oskar a question about German theatre, or about Eva and Breslau, he reminisced about himself.

'Eva turned out better than moth-t of us. Those years were disasters. My father had moved the family to Berlin. We lived through the bomb-bing. I grew up in ruins. During the air raids we hid in the basement and my older sister Hannah read to the neighbourhood children. She read to us about Mowgli and Bagheera, and Rumpelstilzchen. The bombs hit our street, above us, not very far away. We played with puppets and my sister read fairy tales.' He got these last syllables out before he coughed. 'By the end of the war the stories had no emotion, the puppets had no emotion, but I was always fascinated by them.'

I watched snow fall into the alley. I decided to ask him again about Brecht. I was curious to know if his opinion of the playwright had changed in recent years, perhaps in light of a recent biography that portrayed "Poor B.B." as a plagiarist and misogynist. Allegedly, Brecht had not only exploited, but stolen from his collaborators, most of whom were women. Apparently the grand socialist, like Paryla, had wanted to 'own the means of their production.'

'That's an old story,' Oskar said. 'Alfred Kerr, the theatre critic, called Brecht's *Happy End* "Happy *entlehnt*," or "Happily Borrowed." That talk started in 1929.' Oskar—like Eva—was tired of the Brecht fad, which had dogged his own work.

Rather than pursuing my question about Brecht, Oskar offered another childhood story. It was April 1945, not long before the fall of Berlin. He had gone on a bicycle trip with his father. They had set out under the moon. There was a refugee camp near Prague, a half a million marks, advancing armies …

The snow was really coming down, now, heavy flurries. It was as though a massive feather pillow had exploded high above the street in Montreal. Outside, in the alley, the telephone lines looped from pole to pole, weighed down by the wet snow. As we conversed, my eyes travelled the trail along the wire.

The line faltered. Oskar lost his way.

To my surprise, Oskar called a week later to invite me for a visit to his house in the country. He wanted me to meet "Carola." I accepted the invitation and went to stay the night in Sutton.

Carola was someone Oskar had met on tour in Austria. Just the word 'Austria' tainted my first impressions of her. Eva had fled Germany for Austria in 1933. Fresh in my memory was Eva's comment that, after the Anschluss, Vienna had 'sunk into animal life.' It was the proving ground for the apocalypse.

When we met the first time, Carola was wearing a black sweater and a pair of loose slacks: a mature relaxed look that courted her half-hidden curves. Her skin was pale, her hands veined: they seemed almost tenderized. Freckles were sprinkled under her eyes. Her face was friendly, but in a brought-up-to-be way.

'She's another theatre person,' Oskar said by way of introduction.

I smiled at this. Were these theatre people really any different than the rest of us? *She could be his nurse, a caretaker of sorts*, I thought, *concierge of Oskar's old house*. But perhaps I was wrong. Certainly ambition had not released him. Oskar and Carola were preparing a revival of *Happy End*, Brecht's musical comedy set in 1920s Chicago that pits organized crime against the Salvation Army.

He showed me the atelier. Here, the signs of industry were remarkable. The storyboard was tacked to the far wall. The puppets and props had been completed, including a police cruiser made from plaster and papier mâché, which was parked by the wood stove. Mock stained-glass windows—a massive triptych of Saint Rockefeller, Saint Henry Ford, and Saint J.P. Morgan—leaned against the eastern wall.

I left thinking *they really are making things here...*, feeling a combination of excitement and envy, the primordial sap of plagiarism. I so much wanted to do something similar.

It was late April, a premature summer evening—not unlike the one fifty or so years before, when Oskar had pulled out of Berlin by bicycle—when I drove the highway to Sutton a second time, returning to Oskar and Carola. *Happy End* had been put aside for reasons that were never explained to me. We shared a meal on the lawn, an event for which the two were overly prepared. They seemed ravenous for my company. Carola was wearing a velvet and tartan bodice with fitted puffy sleeves; dressed as some game Lolita, she acted whimsically opposite Oskar's thickening chest and prolonged exhalations, which were now more noticeable than ever. We talked over the tops of our wine glasses, anchored by the heavy picnic table. Oskar wheezed after each breath. Gradually it cooled down and then, suddenly, they both went off to bed. A little early, I thought, to blow out the candles.

After cleaning up some dishes in the kitchen I went back outside to smoke one of Oskar's cigarillos. They'd invited me here and prepared, obviously excited, then quickly tired of me. Was that it? Strange.

In the old days when Oskar returned to Canada from on tour he brought home boxes of Dutch blended cigarillos. Over the years he'd built up a healthy reserve. Even though he'd quit decades ago, he kept a humidor and entreated his guests. His favourite brand bore a red seal. I lit one up.

It was total blackness in the field. I wandered away beyond the reach of the house lights, irritated and out of sorts. My eyes decanted their own darkness. Tables had turned and I was feebly jealous of whatever Oskar and Carola had together. It was no good feeling this way. I stood for a long while listening to the crisscross of animal and insect sounds. When I approached the house after a half hour, my shadow shot out behind me. I walked around the periphery, three or four times. One way around, then the other way around, mumbling gibberish.

Finally she came out of the house and stepped into my path.

Oskar telephoned the following evening.

'Carola missed you in the morning,' he said. 'She apologitheth …' Quite simply, the word crumpled in his mouth.

I reassured him that it was I who should apologize. Otherwise, yes, I'd had a good drive back to the city, and, of course, I'd taken many things from the night before. This was neither here nor there, and he said nothing in response.

I told him I was eager to get down to business, ready to begin assembling my research into a "body of work."

'I remember the feeling,' he said.

Momentarily, I felt awkward. During my visit to Sutton there had been no word about a new production. No tour planned. *Happy End* with Carola was never going to be. But they had worked on a dream together. The proof was in their blatant industry—*that was the production*—the atelier itself. They'd made a show of it when we toured the house together. Perhaps that's why I was asked to visit in the first place.

Oskar died several months later, that same year.

'Eva could have been anybody,' Oskar had told me on the phone. 'One of the Whores of Turnbridge. A pickpocket, maybe. A petty thief. She knew her way around the theatre. I know that for sure from all her stories. Father was very involved in radio drama in Breslau, and we agreed, the last time that I thaw him, that they might have collaborated … anyhow I only have the one special memory of *him*.' Oskar was breathless. The effort demanded was almost too great. 'There were no trains or cars or schedules. We left Berlin with all those armies coming at us. Mother was outraged. But anyway we pedalled south through a narrow corridor, it took us weeks, along past Dresden. I straddled the back of the bike. We rode through the night, night after night, under the moon. *Der verfluchte Mond!* Father kept repeating this, although he warned me not to whisper a word. At last we came to a checkpoint. There were th-t-ol-dierth. My father had a leather bag. My ass was thitting on it! Th-t-ol-dierth! Check point! So we need to hide. During the war it was a nuisance, hide, hide, again and again, hide. So we climbed off the bicycle and hid in the next field. We lay shivering until it was morning. There was something fantastic, I don't know ... was it gold coins or Swiss francs or American dollars? I am looking into it again right now and I can't remember. Was it ours? Who were we working for? Was it counterfeit ... Do you hear me? Can you understand any of it?

Who are you working for?'

2

FEDERAL BUREAU OF INVESTIGATION

File No. 100-18112

Report made at:
LOS ANGELES

Date when made:
3/6/43

Title:
Bertolt Eugen Friedrich Brecht, with aliases Bert
Brecht, B.B. , 'Poor B.B.', Berdat

Character of Case:
INTERNAL SECURITY-G-ALIEN ENEMY CONTROL

BRECHT is described as follows:

Age	45
Height	5' 9"
Weight	130
Eyes	Brown
Hair	Dark brown
Complexion	Dark
Scars and marks	Scar on left cheek

Marital Status:
Married; wife—HELEN; daughter—MARIE BARBARA, born
October 28, 1930, Berlin, Germany; son—STEFAN, born
November 3, 1924, Berlin, Germany.

Synopsis of Facts:
Subject, registered German alien, was born in Augsburg,
Germany, February 10, 1898. Leaving Finland, he entered
United States at San Pedro on July 21, 1941, with wife

and two children. Declared intention to become United
States citizen December 8, 1941. Subject alleged to
have been a Communist in Europe, where he engaged
in Underground activity. Subject recently acted as
Technical Adviser concerning the Underground for film
HANGMEN ALSO DIE. Subject's writings, some published
as late as 1939, advocate overthrow of Capitalism,
establishment of Communist State and use of sabotage
by labor to attain its ends. Translations of pertinent
excerpts set out.

PROOF

I put a tape in the cassette player and my father's voice, re-
corded six months ago, returns to my ears. There is no trace
of sentimentality, his register is clear, he speaks his mind. Roland wants to tell me the truth, simple, as it should sound,
and he makes every attempt to maintain the trained ambiva-
lence of a tenured scholar. Overall our conversation is civilized, if at times forced, spotted with chivalrous hesitations
as we hold open the doors between private life and "History."
We do our best to preserve the formal tie between an event
and its calendar date. Birthdays, declarations of war, wed-
dings and deaths are important fixtures. But there are not
nearly enough of these to light our path, and along the way
we concede as much ground as we cover. His careful recounting calls attention to the fragile architecture and narrow av-
enues of fate: it is a labyrinthine descent from the high hilltop,
along the escarpment, to the sea. It is almost hypnotic, how
at every turn his voice threads another square of time, with
measured pauses and counterbalanced clauses, switchbacks
mediating between contradiction and hyperbole, the Scylla
and Charybdis of biography.

*During the summers, during earlier years, the family
went for vacation to the Baltic coast. Along the beach the
conditions were perfect for flying gliders. Gliders became*

Papa's passion. He had trained with boys in his youth group, and then went ahead with private lessons. He was fantastically gifted at it. Still later on, the Wehrmacht became aware of his talent and sent someone to inquire if he might want to become a flight instructor. He turned them down flatly. It wasn't in his plans to serve the military. Apparently they upped the bid, promised him a new identity, he would get new papers, a brighter future ... but again he declined. He wanted nothing to do with the army and for a brief intermission the authorities forgot about his kind.

This was before my parents were married. Papa was a medical student. He was done with classes, but had yet to complete his clinical training. He shuffled back and forth, in and out of Breslau, finding it difficult to land a position. Ultimately he was seeking a residency to complete his medical degree. This wasn't easy. Instead around this time—or perhaps beginning even earlier, sorry, we are now jumping from the early 1930s back to the late 1920s—my father became involved in two extraordinary projects, and let me now tell you about these.

I am calling these our Proof Sessions. After listening to the first tapes I made with Eva, I decided to interview Roland. I knew that fathers are as complex as brothers. And Roland's father Hermann Hans—Männe, who in his adult life went by HH, like an element from the periodic table—had many reactive properties. I wanted to get a better sense of what had made Eva's brother turn from "the authority" into the Süßigkeitsgangster then into Männe, and then into this irreducible conundrum, HH.

It is the weekend and we are at the old farmhouse. I arrive from the city and we sit outside in lawn chairs set side by side, here at the summit of August. The tape recorder is positioned between us on a low table. Roland smokes a cigar. I sit and stare forward, looking out at the gentle spread of fields and forest. The house next door—Eva's "Czech retreat"—is now empty. Eva left Sutton for Elliot Lake years ago, planning to join a retirement community. A retirement community? This was not her style. But apparently she'd grown bored stiff with Sutton—ennui had set in like gangrene—and, anyway, she and the Martian 'were splitting,' whatever this meant. Who knew the two were connected? How so?

As Roland's story lurches forward from year to year to year, he loses his train of thought and, realizing this, makes only a half-hearted attempt to continue. Three years after arriving in northern Ontario, Eva pulled up stakes and folded her tent, again, this time leaving for London. Here she met Pavel. It was whippets and borzoi at first sight.

Temporarily we grow quiet. The tape recorder, slithering on its own insides, devours our breathing. The afternoon light begins to golden. Roland, elbow bent and chin in hand, flicking his teeth with one finger, is thinking.

From early on he was impressed by psychiatry—the art nouveau of the sciences—and interested in academia and research. In fact he had done preliminary work for a dissertation on hallucinogenic drugs, which he was forced to abandon in due course. But then he got involved in a research project at the university and again hallucinogenic agents were the main item on the menu. Cocaine and mescaline and whatever else. From what I recall, which is what Papa told me, the principal investigators had settled upon an especially elegant experimental design. This is the trend even nowadays, of course, to have an elegant design, few variables in play, more certainty.

The methodology was simple. 1) Put X in the room.

2) *Serve X a drug, say a pinch of cocaine. 3) Observe X from behind the window.*

Wonderful.

4) *Take notes. And finally: 5) Draw your conclusion.*

The subject ingested these agents, and the investigators observed the effects on the subject. Simple as cause and effect.

Don't you laugh. It remains a perfectly modern way of looking at things. An inquisition, a trial by ordeal. Superstition tempered by doubt. These things never go out of style. Remember it was not the day of the randomized clinical trial. It was the day of eugenics and accelerated euthanasia. Medical school in the 1920s and 1930s was quite different. Clinical experience and actual patient contact were limited. Case reports were everything. The patient was rarely encountered in the flesh, not until he or she was cut open and lying under surgical lamps on a table right in front of you. It is well known, for example, that Freud graduated without ever having examined a patient. Sure, he might have looked a number of sick people straight in the eye—and the eyes are the mirror of the soul, don't you forget. And without being invasive in the modern manner of bronchoscopes and sigmoidoscopes, Freud, understand, did not shy away from embarrassing questions: Does that man's moustache remind you of your mother's vagina? When you touch something cold, like a steel bar, do you experience self-hating thoughts?

Doctors in training shared living space. Papa roomed at the hospital before it was found out he was hosting a virulent bacterial strain, at which point he was expelled from the university. He managed nonetheless to keep contact with a certain professor who took pity on him. They collaborated on projects, and developed sev-

eral studies and experiments, like the one I have already described. Papa was the guinea pig in this one, taking cocaine orally, by injection or by drops in the eye. Impressed with psychiatry, I believe his thinking at the time was that participation might bring him academic favour or at least promote his standing. With his situation he was ready to try anything. Why not cocaine? Europe was singing its praises. The scientific community was still playing on about muscle strength, stamina, and its place as a cure for heat exhaustion. Physicians applauded its vigour and thought nothing of experimenting on themselves. Indeed the informal practice was addictive and, finally, commonplace. New knowledge tore through the faculty and spread like wildfire. Physicians experimented on surgical colleagues, on their students, and gave no thought to sharing secrets with their wives.

As was typical of him, HH persevered longer than any of the other participants in these trials. He wanted to demonstrate to his supervisors and superiors the stuff he was made of, the power of his will, his force of spirit: the very things that were in fashion. So he gave of himself, not just one organ, but the entire organism. He was raw material. Here, pollute me. Here, bend me. Here, try to change me. But if his demonstration of willpower was in harmony with the fascist aesthetics of the day, for the university department it was all too much. Contrary to his expectations he was well thanked for his sacrifice, but never again would he be looked on seriously as a candidate for academic promotion. Most likely, this professor, as well as other colleagues, came to regard him as a specimen for study—certainly he was a fit subject for clinical trials, but as materials go, he was not of the pedigree to become a scientist. After all, the department recruited neither athletes nor savages. The whole experience was *character-building, yes, but my father, if he had anything, it was character, and building more of the same was tantamount to creating a monster.*

The experiment lasted several months. Really there was no need to pose a question, or set a hypothesis. Addiction carried on where prediction left off. The data was in. The results were obvious. The subject became an addict.

But meanwhile, the 'study' having run its course—it was time to put away the drugs. The subjects were free to go. But go where? To a nightclub?

Papa, in time, escaped Germany to South America. Perhaps it was this habit which served him best when he surfaced in Colombia.

Roland has again stopped speaking. A swallow swoops down and enters the barn through a broken window. Where did *that* come from? I ask myself. Roland is drifting, it seems to me: rehashing lecture notes from the History of Medicine class he taught for over a decade at McGill University, and working his talking points into this crash course in family history. I feel the warmth of his physical volume, pragmatism radiates from him. Fathers and sons do not co-exist easily and I wonder why this is so. One generation after the next self-corrects the last, for a net loss. It seems for a moment as though Roland and I have come to the end, right here, quietly admiring the quality of dusk. But then he shifts a leg, begins again, and I pursue him, eager to do my bit. I am here to keep him on course even if all I am doing is listening. But I'm doing more than that. Sometimes we may try to remember more than we know. It is as though we are reading the past from our minds and making sense of it for the very first time: speculating and making hypotheses, assured that we are reporting, if not facts, then data as clever and perhaps closer to the truth. My father does most of the talking while I listen and look out for the fiction in all this.

> *The second project, at first glance, might seem rather strange. He worked with prostitutes. Again I don't know details but the plan was to educate street-walkers about infectious diseases—rehabilitate them. Public health, I suppose. He and the pastor—this man Kohler—went about their actions with missionary zeal.*

Strange—but again, not entirely out of sync with the spirit in the machine. Since the turn of the century the *Prostitutions-frage* or Prostitution Question had been *the* social problem of urban Germany. With industrialization more women were asked to work outside the home. Already by the late 1800s, the *Sittenpolizei*—the morals police—had been created in the cities to keep a watch on "errant females." The morals police was given the authority to register any woman of no fixed abode as a prostitute. Such women would be brought in, processed, registered, then taken to a state-run brothel. Wild rumours circulated regarding this practice. Stories about women lifted from their own neighbourhoods, one or two put on a leash and dragged through the streets, before being taken to serve in the brothels. I ask Roland about this.

> *Of course prostitution was regulated in the name of disease prevention. The policy was intended to contain the spread of contagious diseases. Treated first as criminals, prostitutes were nonetheless made available twenty-four hours a day. It was business as usual. Prostitutes have always provided an essential service like the fire department and the police, haven't they? In addition to giving the state another income source, state-run brothels conveniently served as an outlet for the middle class, the*

very men who were in charge of driving the economy forward. Where else was a gentleman of that era going to learn how to properly treat a lady?

Even your friend Brecht made good use of the sex worker, didn't he? Enlisting class-war courtesans to do the dirty work on stage. She was easily recognized as an outsider, yet she carried on with intimate knowledge of how things work within the inner circles. She understood, but did not condemn, hypocrisy. A symbol of tolerance on the one hand, a victim of intolerance on the other. Beautiful stuff.

Roland is right about the sex worker being as useful on stage as she was off, and as fascinating to Brecht and his brethren as was the clown or fool to the Elizabethans. Meanwhile, outside the confines of avant-garde theatre houses in places like Berlin and Hamburg, German public-health agencies were busy producing films to warn prospective clients of the dangers of prostitutes—and these D-movies, depicting streetwalkers as slim nomads of the metropolis, showed to packed houses across the country.

Meanwhile academics were in on the game as well: busy making an inventory of the physical characteristics of the prostitute. Narrow forehead. Abnormal nasal bones. Enormous jaws and so on. If any of these men of science had cared to look under their subject's flimsy clothes, and more closely examine these 'creatures'—and I'm sure, more than once, this was done—they would have seen that these girls were essentially undernourished, that their ribs flared when they breathed in, their cough was productive, gums swollen, because poverty, hunger and squalid living conditions, and not genetic or eugenic components, were the root cause of their advanced disease.

Even if it was in step with the times, HH's project was peculiar. If it was in Papa's self-interest to avoid attention in the 1930s, then he was going about it the wrong way. My feeling is he had already forfeited private ambition, already given up hope and meanwhile he sought some kind of static or fundamental redemption—his own, not for these women—through community service. Perhaps he merely wanted to act, to carry out that very natural and healthy impulse—to act, plain and simple. Move things forward. Then again maybe he decided on this particular project because of his sister. By then, Eva, as part of her work with The Threepenny Opera, was involved in a parallel world. Brecht's world of prostitutes and petty thieves and beggars. His choice to carry on this work is theatrical enough. It is also in character when you reflect on the stories Eva used to tell about her brother, the sufferings of young Männe, the Süßigkeitsgangster, the boy who was carried away by his youth group to be brought up in the black forests and steeped in myth.

The detail I remember about this period is that he and the pastor became quite popular with these women and throughout Breslau strangers came to greet him on the street, in shops, everywhere. On a humorous note, Mama told me the story of one evening, while she and my father were seated in the town theatre waiting for the show to begin, a decorated lady, brightly made up and quite visibly of the underclass, turned around in her seat ahead of them and blew my father a kiss.

Presumably he later explained the phenomenon to Mama. But it was soon after that she made him stop his night duty. Pastor Kohler, she concluded, was a bad in-

fluence. They were not yet married. Mama threatened to end the courtship. Only then did he change his habits and put an end to his public-health work in Breslau's red-light district.

I am sure the devil was missed.

DIE MORITAT VON MACKIE MESSER

Driving up Stanley Street in this blimp of a rental car, I listen to a 1930 recording of "The Ballad of Mack the Knife." Our Brecht is singing the lead. Vocal range limited, he thrums on the olfactory organ. Nearsighted, self-important, the great one is reading, merely reciting lyrics, blinded by the occasion. His voice harries the melody and your character, Oh Mackie, falls victim.

The occasion! Any time is right for a Brecht & Weill revival. Amen. And if any place needs one this provincial hub, this middle-Canadian flub, this little London, is ripe for one.

Macheath himself I have set strolling along the streets, inside the urban planner's imagination, up and down the sidewalk, opposite gangs of power-walkers who march, buttock-bunched, working the elbows like bellows. Is it plague or is it cholera? Or a sign Macheath's in town? Mackie, Mackie Messer, Macheath, Mack the Knife—protean and proletariat, prowling alongside housewives and golden-agers, bobbing, in high spirits, flicking his cane with the ivory handle, wearing white kid gloves and spats, scar on his left cheek. He should do damage here. Set the town on fire. Real damage right here in this London with its own Thames and turbid waters. May he join the parade—alas 'tis not the Queen's Coronation!—but a pageant, nonetheless, of the prim and proper, the up-standing members of the stay-at-home-and-eavesdrop-and-gossip society (a crime-stopper umbrella organization), out in scores in neutral outfits. No liberty in their leisure, there is no relax in those slacks!

It is a respectable neighbourhood, an old part of town with mature trees and irregular houses.

I pass the diamond Neighbourhood Watch sign on my right and lift my foot off the gas pedal. The sun glances off the hoods of cars tucked into driveways like loaves of bread. July heat. And more of the fat bubble cars. This year's models—in tan and copper and silver, corporate colours. The hues of hubris. Suffocating pods. The baking plastic inside leaks its poisoned interiors.

Approaching Eva's house, I lower the window. Punch-drunk on driving, I sing along in English translation the best I can, stroking B.B.'s lyrics with put-on opulent depravity: *And the ghastly fire in Soho / Seven children in a go / In the crowd stands Mac the Knife, but he / Isn't asked and doesn't know.*

Brecht and Weill's signature tune from *The Threepenny Opera* was a hastily added piece of the puzzle, dreamt up late during rehearsals in August 1928. It remains a classic example of that cliché, the 'Inspired Afterthought'. Ernst Busch played the street singer on opening night in Berlin—to him fell the honour of the first live performance.

The crimes listed in this quasi-medieval murder ballad, which serves as a prologue to the play, are serious enough to have Macheath put on the scaffold in the final act. In verses one and two, Macheath's knife is contrasted to a shark's fins but the real trouble begins in verse four, when an anonymous corpse turns up on the Strand. Schmul Meier is reported missing in verse five. Macheath allegedly acquires his cash box. Poor Jenny Towler is discovered with a knife in her breast in verse six. The cabman Alfred Gleet is the victim of verse seven. Then the ghastly fire in Soho. The child-bride in her nightie, violated in her slumbers in the final verse, is the last straw. The ubiquitous Macheath is involved in these crimes, one way or another, but verse to verse he remains a nonchalant observer, unmoved and still at large when, following the prologue, the play begins.

§ § §

Actors are the pits! Actors are useless! When I broke the news to my father that I wanted to be an actress … he was horrified. Degrading! Immoral. Foolish!

But I was lucky. At that time Max Ophüls was in Breslau. I wanted a theatre life very badly and so I pleaded with my father. Finally he crumbled and agreed to meet Ophüls. When he returned from the meeting, he had changed his mind. *All right. Go ahead.* He was not convinced, but go on. Permission granted: If you take acting lessons with this man, if you work hard … then I suppose … there is a chance … a valuable experience. In the end, if you have discipline …

But first I had to pass the audition. So I appeared on stage. I had no technique, no control, no picture of myself. Ophüls and a group of senior actors were seated in the auditorium, in one of the middle rows—comfortable—with their view of the stage. I wanted to impress them but how and with what—my meek Cassandra? My old, wrinkled Clytemnestra?

When I arrived I still had my monkey movements imprinted—and so swinging on the rope, wild, I dropped in front of their eyes. I crouched this way, that way, preparing my attack. They peed their pants. One of the men yelled, Stop it, Eva. Stop! Again. *That has to stop. Stop it.* Get rid of the monkey movements.

Next they asked me to audition 'properly'.

What was I to do? I stood there, blinded, in footlights powerful enough to spot Spitfires. I didn't move.

Read! One of them yelled from below. Oh yes, I had to read. I stood in front and read, stage centre, while their eyes rolled over me: my figure, my voice, even how I breathed, fast, then slowly, slow, more slowly ... better, much better. It was a courageous moment. I did not pretend, I created nothing. I left all the doors open. I placed myself bravely before them. I met the moment. And that was it. That was my technique. I wanted so badly to serve the theatre that I met the moment, which was thrilling.

What a catastrophe. I read the script without making monkey signs, exposed, fully exposed to the outside. No way—I waited for the response, a long, warped moment. Then came some applause.

For whatever reason—Ophüls invited me in. He decided I had talent. That was wonderful. It was really magnificent: Max Ophüls, this famous director—Ophüls expressed to my father that he wouldn't change a thing about me. Not a single thing. He took me whole, and just as I was he threw me onstage.

I had lessons for nine months, for a year. I worked very hard in the new world. One day I went on the streetcar alone and a man recognized me.

What kind of work are you doing? He was one of my father's associates. He had come by the house once or twice.

Proudly I answered, I am training to be an actor with Max Ophüls. I have my lessons every day. I'm studying now. Voice, movement, history. I perform with a group at the Lobetheater.

Well, fine, he said. Interesting. You should come to my office. He looked at me more closely. Did you know, he said, I am the radio director? I am in charge of programming here in Breslau. Since you are such a big success, you can audition for us.

Suddenly it started. My radio career. Work fell into my lap. Radio plays were scheduled month by month. There was a demand for actors. I wasn't very interested in that at the beginning because radio is blind and I knew what I wanted. But anyway, I went for my second audition. I knew that radio would pay better than theatre. But really I had no clue what they do there in the studio. Stare at the microphone, and blow into the holes? Bang shoes on the table?

After the audition, five minutes afterwards, the radio director—I forget his name, though I should know it because there is a connection, later—the director came out of the booth to congratulate me. Right away he offered me the contract. I was an exciting discovery, after all. But what did I know? Again I was thrown in. I met the other actors at the radio hall and I realized that for many of them, that was their living. Radio. They made their living on nothing but radio and here I came and I was given a chance to sign a good contract. I didn't even understand. There I was and I earned a lot of money even though my whole interest was somewhere else.

I worked in radio and studied for the stage. Even with the beginning of my radio success, I stayed focused on theatre. That was my goal. To step into a live performance, to feel the audience shift as each member takes you in.

Radio is blind. I wanted the total experience. The total exposure of theatre.

At school, I never had a boyfriend. Boyfriends didn't exist back then. I hadn't been kissed, except by the old family lips. Then it all started. Sixteen, I landed on the love market.

Meine Herren, I supply, if you demand.

I had no rights, because in Germany there was no such thing as a girl having rights until she was eighteen.

When I turned sixteen and joined the theatre then all the brave knights stepped forward out of the forest onto the stage.

I had to figure it out: how to run my business.

Marriage. Like carriage. Can you hear the horses? That is the wife and husband sitting side by side in the horse-drawn carriage.

Marriage was a three-act play.

One. Permission and consent. The groom requests permission from the young maid's father. Consent is given, good as a ticket: admits one only.

Two. The licence. The groom requests a permit from the pastor, a licence from the church.

Then, in Act Three, everything could be done, and would be done.

It started. Men wanted me straight away. Actors from radio, and some actors from the Lobetheater. I didn't know how to handle it. At last I was in the spotlight, I had my suitors, but I didn't have the maturity to handle all the forces of nature.

In rehearsal I became known as The Nervous Bride. It was my stage name, taken from the tale of a young bride on her wedding night:

The bride is anxious, and wants her wedding night over with, because she's frightened of the adventure that's to come. She's scared of the bed. Hysterical.

Not to worry, one of the actors—a boy from the Lobetheater, one of the extremes—reassured me: You're on solid ground, my dear. He was sure my father would select a gentleman. And anyway—so he believed, this actor: In your case, by the time you are given, dear, you will be done.

On earth, on earth as in heaven.

I had my suitors, and tragedy took up residence at the villa. The front door opened and in they rushed: actors, suitors, men. Hat in hand, pressed jacket, formal, ready to meet Father, prepared for the final audition.

The salon was arranged. Our maids prepared the *mise en scène*. Father seated on the chair with the gold cushion. Daughter beside him, lower, white bosom flaring, pumped with fire. And the man on one knee steadying himself for the soliloquy.

Father, daughter, suitor on one knee. A scene every girl must experience once in her life.

Father snapped his butterfly and the players performed—it must have been difficult. No amount of rehearsing could prepare them for the inevitable.

No, said Father. I won't permit your entry.

News travelled. Rumour spread—about that old fart who hated actors. And about the beautiful daughter without any education or know-how. Our family theatre: word travelled through Breslau about this father and daughter pair. Finally the competition was born: Who dares be next? Who will take the bride? Even actors who had no intention of taking a bride entered the running. They were curious! It got to the point when one of the very extremes, this boy, this fragile creature arrived at the house to have a closer look at the situation.

He was one of those feminine men with no use for a nervous bride. He had no wish to gain entry: but he too wanted to experience that father. The boy came to the house and spoke with a lot of courage. He was a great speaker in the oral tradition! Father listened to the boy and he didn't notice any difference between this type and the other men. He did not discriminate. Father responded, No. Danke, Nein. Thank you, but Eva is not ready.

In fact, my father threatened to send me to a finishing school in Switzerland: because it was not acceptable to have a daughter, so popular, so terribly happy and popular like me.

In Witchesland, there they finished girls—waxed the surface, polished their tops and their bottoms—in private houses run by the Sisters Without Mercy. I knew there was nothing worse than a Swiss nun. The Swiss were the experts. They made ladies who made the house more comfortable. Ladies with no scratches, with no visible sharp edges. The kind who make the male world sing!

It was well known that once you arrived in Witchesland the nuns took charge of you, from underwear to fingernails, they left you nothing. So when my father hinted that it might be a good idea to send me off, I understood a serious threat. If I did not do as he asked, if I did not behave, if the circus did not stop, he was going to take me out of the theatre—by the hair on my head—and drop me in the middle of Switzerland!

I had just started to find myself. Who am I and what shall I do now? I was halfway through growing up, between acts, and already the furniture on stage was being moved around, and the set was different when I reappeared. I was thrown into the adult world and I had to watch my step. At home I never had anyone to show me the way. I was raised by the maids on their glass stick. I had no word about the future, no warning, I learned about the present after it happened to me. Splat! Boing. Ha! Ha! Ha!

The show went on.

One afternoon I stayed behind at the Lobetheater after my lesson. The theatre was empty. I took off my shoes and skated over the floorboards in my socks. I wanted to shine, alone. I needed to play myself out on stage. The open hall thrilled me. My first steps ... before the rows of seats, the slanted floors, the back lights. My body was hungry and I followed its lead.

During rehearsal the opportunities seem endless. First you work on positioning. Where to stand on the stage. Where to place your foot. Not there! Here. Yes, right here! No. The opportunities seem endless, but be careful. Acting finally uses every nerve and muscle. It invades you. It takes your full attention. Like terror does, or fear. But you don't let yourself panic. Discipline is the only way forward. I searched for the line. I was a natural in their eyes, but I felt dull and thick inside. I needed sharpening. All the private lessons, our rehearsals and the workshops, all the work was aimed at a single point in my mind.

Meanwhile the old joke about The Nervous Bride. Before the wedding, the bride is uncertain what to repeat at the altar: 'I Do,' 'I Will,' or 'I Have'? Which is the right answer? What does the groom expect? The bride's in a state because she's uneducated. To prepare for the honeymoon she practices alone in bed at night. She pretends to have a piece of chalk stuck in her backyard. She hoists herself up, down, up, down, up and down on the bed. She concentrates on the piece of chalk and writes *Ich liebe dich* on the sheets. By the end of two weeks—in time for the wedding—the bride is self-taught. During their first night together, bride and groom, she is a hit.

But the groom—he's upset! On one hand he is happy, but on the other hand he wonders, who did she graduate from? Where did she get her education? The bride tells him everything. Fascinating. But of course he doesn't believe her. At this moment he is too jealous to think properly. So what then? The Nervous Bride then takes out her lipstick. She fits it into her backyard and she crawls like a crab into the wedding bed and she begins to write *Ich bin Breslauerin, und willst du mit mir* ... She writes a very long Teutonic sentence and then hides under the sheets. At last, the groom understands her better. He appreciates the trouble she went through and he admires her handwriting. Very proud and excited he crawls under the blanket and they do it twice-over-twice-over. The wedding night is an adventure!

I had the story in my mind ... but I was prepared to make a serious effort. I wanted to experiment. The theatre was empty, the floor was smooth as I stood at the lip of the stage. I walked along the edge where the stage dropped to an orchestra pit. I imagined myself as one of those cabaret badmouths, one of those nomads from Berlin, a woman with tempo, real tempo. I placed my hands on my hips, defiantly. Nonsense, I made nonsense. Pure delightful nonsense.

Click. A side door. *Who is it?* My throat went dry.

The door closed, it then opened. Who?

HH was standing by the wall. He said nothing at all. He hesitated, I thought he was going to say something nasty, but then he left.

I was critically wounded, again.

For the next lesson, I want you each to return with something from nature, choose something from the world. Whatever it is, let it define your character. Let it describe you.

This was the exercise Ophüls gave us.

I arrived back carrying my artificial limb, the Sonntagsarm. All right Eva, Ophüls said, show us. I asked for a table and a chair to be brought on stage. I unbuttoned my blouse, and withdrew my left arm. I inserted the prosthetic into my sleeve and I asked for quiet, for it to be absolutely quiet. There was a group of five actors seated on the stage with Ophüls. Quiet they were.

I folded forward on the table, head turned sideways. I concentrated. I tried to imagine a candle. Then a black hole. Then the moon, then stars. But no use. I couldn't concentrate. I opened my eyes, and closed them again, tightly. Then I burst into tears.

What's wrong, one of the actors spoke up. Does it hurt? No, I said. It doesn't hurt. Then I told them the whole story, how my school experience was shit.

Interesting that you chose the prosthetic for this exercise, Ophüls said. It was only a prop for you then, I wonder if it means...?

Right then I knew what Ophüls was getting at.

He was right. I was crippled inside.

In theatre the director tells you to forget you're on stage, while outside they tell you you have to try to act like this or that even if you don't feel like it. It's almost the same thing. When an actor has difficulty playing a role, the solution is simple: become the character, you are told. Be the character and stop acting. In life, when you feel bad, friends tell you: Try to at least act as if you're happy. And finally: Believe in yourself.

Art and life are two different worlds that share the same stage. The world is a stage, yes. But art is not life, and life is not art. From early on I was in a hurry. I ran straight onto the stage, then continued in a line, off the stage, without expecting there to be any difference. That's how I got called a natural.

§ § §

I park the car behind Eva's and go around to unload my bags. One turn of the key and the boot springs open, like some sort of spastic defence shield. Standing in the driveway already I feel that I am being watched. Eva stands behind the screen door, her essence rinsed through the purple-grey mesh. I wonder how on earth she ended up in this house on Stanley Street all the way from her internship at the Lobetheater? But I do know she's earned her oblivion.

During the drive from Montreal I thought about how I should approach this the second time. While listening to Brecht & Weill's *Threepenny* collaborations, I reviewed as much as I knew about Eva's life, returning again and again to the play's structure, its three acts and nine scenes, which by now I query like components of a powerful relational database. Unlike other forms of bibliomancy, however, Sortes Threepennianae divines not my future, but Eva's past.

I duck back into the trunk of the car to reach the carrying case of my laptop computer. I loathe the word aura but Eva has one. She maintains eye contact even when I am turned away. Eva maintains this dialogue which has been ongoing between us for years, even though we live apart in cities as different and as far away from each other as Breslau and Berlin, way back then.

THE THREEPENNY OPERA

Act One. The play opens in the morning and we are at Jonathan Jeremiah Peachum's outfitting shop, The Beggar's Friend Ltd. Beggars in London are required to register with Peachum and pay for a licence. Although Mr. Peachum has a monopoly he laments that the callousness of mankind has made his business difficult: for his business is arousing human sympathy.

Mrs. Peachum arrives at the shop and upon being questioned by her husband about the whereabouts of their daughter, reveals that Polly has been courted by the notorious criminal Mac the Knife. Indeed, the two have plans to be married in a stable in Highgate in Scene Two. A group of Mackie's lumpen criminal mates are the wedding arrangers. Tiger Brown, the police chief, attends. Tiger and Mackie served in India together and are old war buddies. Together they sing the infamous "Cannon Song" (that set the audience on fire during the 1928 premiere):

The troops live under
The cannon's thunder
From the Cape to Cooch Behar.
Moving from place to place
When they come face to face
With a different breed of fellow

Whose skin is black or yellow
They quick as winking chop him into beefsteak tartare.

Peachum is devastated because 'the defection' of his pretty daughter to Mackie is again bad for business. As it is, Polly often spends time in the shop. Therefore Peachum goes off in Scene Three to demand that Tiger Brown arrest Mackie (he provides a list of Mackie's crimes). Meanwhile, Mrs. Peachum heads off to the brothel where Mackie is a regular, to bribe one of the women into turning him in should he show up. To finish off Scene Three, Polly and her parents sing the "First Threepenny Finale Concerning the Insecurity of the Human Condition." (Remembering Brecht's admonishment that *nothing is more revolting than when the actor pretends not to notice he has left the level of plain speech and started to sing*, these actors take precautions not merely to sing but to show themselves to be singing.)

Act Two. Polly finds Mackie at the stable in Highgate. She tells him that under threat from her father, Tiger is going to arrest him. Mackie's crimes on record at Scotland Yard are considerable: over thirty burglaries, twenty-three hold-ups, arson, forgery, multiple murders, the seduction of underage girls. Upon reciting the list Polly states, matter-of-factly: You're a dreadful man. Mackie concedes he must run away. Unemotionally he turns his ledger and control of his gang over to Polly, who proves more than able to run a tight ship. However, the Queen's coronation day is fast approaching and Mackie's gang mourns his first-ever absence. For them, pickpockets and petty thieves, the Queen's parade is usually good cause for celebration.

During the Interlude at the end of Scene Four, Mrs. Peachum offers Pirate Jenny a bribe. Jenny is Mackie's regular girl. Jenny feels that with all of London on his heels, Mackie won't be returning to the brothel any time soon. But shrewd Mrs. Peachum knows otherwise. She proceeds to sing the "Ballad of Sexual Obsession" (a tune the cabaret singer Rosa Valletti, replacing Helene Weigel on opening night, refused to sing because of its raunchiness):

There goes a man who's won his spurs in battle
The butcher, he. And all the others, cattle.
The cocky sod! No decent place lets him in.
Who does him down, that's done the lot? The women.
Want it or not, he can't ignore that call.
Sexual obsession has him in its thrall.

In Scene Five the coronation bells sound. Mackie visits the brothel and Jenny, taking his palm, reads his fortune. Mackie begins "The Ballad of Immoral Earnings:"

There was a time, now very far away
When we set up together, I and she.
I'd got the brain, and she supplied the breast.
I saw her right, and she looked at me—
A way of life then, if not quite the best.

While Mackie is performing, Jenny beckons to Constable Smith and Mrs. Peachum. Betrayed, Mackie is taken to the Old Bailey.

Scene Six: Tiger commiserates with Mackie on the latter's arrest. Mackie applies for a more comfortable pair of handcuffs and writes Constable Smith a cheque for fifty pounds. While doing so, he worries aloud that Tiger will find out that Mackie's been horsing around with Tiger's daughter, Lucy. Mackie then sings "Ballad of Good Living," in which he concedes it is not for him the simple life—to him the only comfortable life is a life of wealth. For verily,

The search for happiness boils down to this:
One must live well to know what living is.

Lucy arrives at the Old Bailey. Through the bars of the cage she lambastes Mackie for marrying Polly. Ach don't worry, he tells her—she's nothing. Then Polly arrives. Lucy and Polly sing the "Jealousy Duet." Singing, Lucy informs Polly she is pregnant and therefore has a better claim to Mackie. Mackie supports Lucy in the argument, wisely, since her father is the police chief. Mrs. Peachum arrives and takes Polly away after boxing her ears. Lucy exits, Constable Smith enters Mackie's cell—burlesque manners take over—and Mackie escapes!

Tiger is relieved by these developments, but Mr. Peachum soon after arrives and threatens to disrupt the coronation the next day with his army of beggars—if Tiger does not go out and re-arrest Mackie. At the end of Act Two both Mackie and Jenny step out before the curtain to sing the "Second Three-penny Finale: What Keeps Mankind Alive": *For once you must not shrink from the facts*, they reprove the audience: *Mankind is kept alive with bestial acts*. In the second verse this duo (with Brecht pulling the strings backstage) addresses the hypocrisy of the ruling class:

You say that girls may strip with your permission.
You draw the lines dividing art from sin.
So first sort out the basic food position.
Then start your preaching: that's where we begin.
You lot, who bank on your desires and our disgust
Should learn for all time how the world is run:
Whatever lies you tell, however much you twist
Food is the first thing. Morals follow on.

Erst kommt das Fressen, dann kommt die Moral!

Act Three. That same night inside Peachum's Outfitting Emporium for Beggars. Peachum prepares his campaign. He plans to disrupt the Queen's parade with a demonstration showcasing the five basic types of human misery. The demonstration's cast will include The Merry Paraplegic, from the Victims of Vehicular Progress and, representing Victims of the Higher Strategy, The Tiresome Trembler. The beggars en masse are painting signs for the demonstration when the seventh scene begins. One inscription reads 'I Gave My Eye for My King.' Another, 'My Two Legs for Your Kingdom.' Jenny enters with a group of ladies to demand her reward money. Peachum refuses to pay. In an emotional outburst, whilst defending Mackie's character, Jenny accidentally reveals his whereabouts. He is with Suky Tawdry. Tiger then arrives at the shop. He plans to arrest Peachum in lieu of Mackie—and hence scuttle the demonstration. Peachum ignores Tiger outright. He commands his army to march in his absence and warns Tiger: with his men standing outside the Abbey on parade day, it won't be a pretty sight. Tiger backs down. Peachum sends his army to the dungeons of the Old Bailey to await Mackie's arrest.

In Scene Eight Polly visits Lucy at the Old Bailey to find out where Mackie is. Both have been stood up. Voices are heard in the corridor. They think it is him. Mrs. Peachum arrives and asks Polly to change into her widow's dress.

The next day—Scene Nine—is the day of the coronation. The bells of Westminster ring. It is five a.m. Mackie is shackled and brought into his cell. He is scheduled to be hanged in an hour's time. Mackie offers Constable Smith a thousand-pound bribe. Smith makes no promises. Some of Mackie's underlings show up. He tells them he needs money. They reply that it will be difficult to lay their hands on so much so early in the day. Polly appears next. She comes to the cage and tells Mackie that in his absence business is thriving. Are you very nervous? she asks him. He tells Polly to get him money. She replies she needs more time. Smith inquires if Mackie has raised the funds yet. Tiger arrives, and Mackie and Tiger sit down to settle their accounts. *The accounts, sir, if you please, the accounts. No sentimentality.* They do business: strictly business—payback and kickbacks—no bribery, no escape plans here.

For the finale, all the characters arrive at the side of Mackie's cage. Jenny and some Turnbridge ladies. Constable Smith. Mr. and Mrs. Peachum. Polly in tears. They do now grow sentimental. The ways of destiny are cruel. Six o'clock and Constable Smith leads Mackie out of the cage. Mackie gives a last speech in which he claims that small-time crooks like him—lower-class artisans, as he calls them—are being run out of business *by corporations backed by the banks. What's breaking into a bank compared with founding a bank?*

Mackie is led along up to the gallows. At the penultimate moment Peachum speaks:

> *Dear audience, we are now coming to*
> *The point where we must hang him by the neck*
> *Because it is the Christian thing to do*
> *Proving that men must pay for what they take.*

But then, abruptly, in a reversal, he tells the audience that since this is an opera and not real life, justice will give way before humanity.

Tiger enters on horseback as the *deus ex machina*. He brings a special order from the beloved Queen. Macheath is reprieved, set free!

PAVEL AND THE REVOLUTION

His brush moustache is a museum piece. Polish like Lech Walesa, he has the tired eyes of that famous unionist and politician. Pavel is that rare chip off the Eastern bloc, a dissident even here in a culture of processed bread and bottled vitamins.

He grips my hand. Forearms like hams. 'Very pleased to meet you.'

Pavel wears multiple rings, each inset with precious stones, and around his neck are strung linked clusters of white coral, each fragment the size of a small mammal's vertebrae.

Pavel is the unlikely prototype of the middle class suburban male's propensity to wear jewelry around the age the voice breaks.

He is a theatre type.

Roland accepts Pavel as a platonic ideal, in relation to Eva: happy hybrid of the Good Son and the Loyal Husband. They're good for each other, Roland likes to say.

For years I had fancied a special bond with Eva, but seeing them together, Eva and Pavel—talking dog-shop, drinking wine, dealing cards—has put me on notice. I don't know who adopted whom originally but for the past ten years Eva and Pavel have been inseparable.

These days there are no more flights together to Chicago or Cleveland for the International Kennel Club Annual Show. Instead Pavel accompanies Eva by taxi to the oncology outpatient clinic to have her medication adjusted. Pavel does her laundry. Pavel walks the dogs. Pavel understands Eva. Pavel makes her smile.

Eva and Pavel have a number of inside jokes and set routines.

Eva inquires, naively, her face half-hidden behind playing cards: Pavel, how is it upstairs?

Pavel answers: You will find out soon enough, my dear. Play your cards. Soon enough.

The designations of East and West Berlin for the upper and lower halves of the house, respectively, are only for the default *mise en scène*. Otherwise they are into far more wide-ranging role-playing.

Another set dialogue goes:

EVA: It hurts me.

PAVEL: Already?

EVA: Yes. My bladder hurts.

PAVEL (twirling a finger by the side of his ear): But it should hurt in the head, dear. In the head.

There is another gag, a dialogue set in a Viennese ballroom, so I have come to understand. At an elaborate state function, a pair of diplomats, German and Austrian, spar over which land is the more highly repressed, and which cradles a greater horde of uncultured peasants; meanwhile, both dignitaries submit to the silent subterfuge of foul odours. One ambassador must be constipated; the other, it is said, stepped in cow dung on his way to the ball.

I knew there must have been something personal but no longer private about the oft-repeated marriage scenario involving Eva's namesake, The Nervous Bride. In their remaking of the original skit, involving today an obvious role-reversal, Pavel is happy enough to play the bride, and Eva the priest, or, as she called him, Pastor. Pastor Kohler, whom, one imagines, given Eva's performance, was a rather wan master of ceremonies. A no-frills, no-thrills spirit.

§ § §

The revolution started in 1928. Ophüls received news from Berlin. The circus was coming to Breslau, a whole caravan. Without tents, without lions, elephants, or jugglers. But with Bertolt Brecht, Kurt Weill, Erich Engel, Helene Weigel, Lotte Lenya, Caspar Neher, Carola Neher and Elizabeth Hauptmann. They were outsiders who travelled from town to town, idea to idea—misfits, but a family. They were the avant-garde and, of course, the avant-garde was always in a hurry to get something done.

In Berlin the avant-garde showcased fresh ideas. Berlin had culture. It was the centre of activity. But before a play opened in Berlin it was given a trial in the provinces. The trial for *The Threepenny Opera* was in Breslau.

I met Karl Paryla during the rehearsals. Karl was born in Austria but he made his name in Berlin at the Deutsches Theater. He'd also been part of the Breslau theatre world. Karl was communist. He was known as 'the revolutionary-communist actor.' He was only twenty-three and already recognized as a leading actor of his generation. Everyone loved Karl. Popular and political, Karl Paryla was on top.

You know in those days to be a communist was an intellectual choice, a decision that meant, You better watch out! For the hammer or sickle behind you! Coming to crush your skull.

I continued with my lessons. I studied voice and movement. Gestures. The way to walk or pass your hand through the air. Dance, and also the history of theatre. *Here is your Achil-*

les' heel. Here is your blind spot. Here is the forest. Here is a Roman legion. This is the path into the dark.

A total school for the body and mind.

I had my every movement measured and at the end of the lesson Ophüls explained what I could do differently, what I should forget and what I should remember, and what I should practise again, again and again.

Here is your beauty spot. That is the hand of fate on your knee.

I never in my life had so much attention. Acting starts in the mind, Ophüls told us, and that's where all the attention went: to my head.

It was an exciting time. I went to my teacher and told him I wanted to become more involved, somehow I wanted to help. Ophüls spoke to Brecht. The leading roles were taken but there were beggars, constables, criminals, prostitutes. *Nebenrollen.* Many opportunities to play a minor role.

Brecht presented himself, 'Hallo.' Features of a farmer. Cap and cigar like a peasant. A hooked nose and a potato head. Kartoffelkopf. Like Kartoffelsalat, potato salad.

I felt very moved by it all. It was a wonderful project. It was not just acting. It was not only theatre. It was something new. Brecht was surrounded by his gang of collaborators. Hauptmann, of course, and Erich Engel, the director. Weigel, his wife. Caspar Neher. Artists surrounded by other artists. Writers, actors, musicians. It was make-believe and Brecht was the magnet. He was a strong force. Epic Theatre was his invention. He called our old theatre a circus robbed of its magic. Performances by torchlight. That was what we offered the modern public, he said, performances by torchlight.

He took me to an apartment in the morning before rehearsal. He arranged the music, wrote the script, he prepared everything.

Karl Paryla took the bride.

At long last I passed the final exam. I was done, as those extremes had promised, done on earth before marriage.

Practice and discipline made me perfect.

Hard legs. Sour mouth. I was given the part. One of Jenny's girls. There is the domestic scene in the brothel. The girls are darning socks and discussing underwear.

Shoptalk. Underwear first and last. Silk underwear. Wool underwear for winter. They go on gossiping about the trade, discussing the virtue of different materials. Silk. Wool. They rate their results with customers. The end which justifies the means. What works, what doesn't work.

It was sensational to be in the group. Ironing my shorts on stage. Listening to one old whore talk about money. Then she says she wouldn't wear silk because it might make the gentlemen think you've got something wrong with you.

Another girl declares that wool underwear really puts men off. Then it's Vixen's turn to say that she's had good results using homespun underwear. It makes the gentlemen relax. *It makes them feel they're at home.*

This was my favourite line of Brecht. It makes the gentlemen feel they're at home. Just marvellous.

It was a good year. In the winter Karl took me to that secret hideout. It was an apartment where two extremes housed together.

We arrived in the morning. Karl brought the newspaper. *Permanente Revolution.* The two boys were eating breakfast.

Hallo. Greetings.

Then at once they tucked us into bed. Das Kapital and The Nervous Bride. We had no other place. I felt full. I already had an engagement with the Lobetheater. This was an important step. I had a contract to act in the next three plays. And I had Karl Paryla. Popular and political. The revolutionary actor was on top.

WORKSHOP

The overhead lights have been lowered so as to obstruct the audience's view. Substantial as automotive parts, the lights let off a subliminal hiss. It is this white noise that plays harmony to Pirate Jenny's frank rendition of "The Ballad of Immoral Earnings."

It is not often that Paryla is a spectator. But generally, after about thirty minutes—the smirk gone from his face—he succumbs to the velveteen notion that he alone occupies a higher echelon of consciousness. They, down there, actors. Me, up here, comprehending everything. They, mortals. Naive. Cumbersome. Entangled by star-crossed destinies. Blind. Me, omniscient. Sympathetic. Understanding. Now what is Brecht doing to this tested and fine arrangement?

'A thing that has not been changed for a long time appears to be unchangeable.' Ophüls knew his stuff chapter and verse.

What Paryla so far grasps about Brecht's Theatre reminds him of Party propaganda; the difference is that the pamphlet of pseudo-Marxist ideas by this dissolute poet has been pressed and folded along the edge of the stage. The synthesis, the synthesis is pure dissonance. Another playwright stretched on the didactic rack, awful to watch.

Especially dubious to Paryla is Brecht's new and 'scientific' theory of acting. Brecht's Siamese twins of alienation and detachment. How did Max Ophüls put it? 'The new detachment.' 'The new detachment is designed to disrupt socially conditioned phenomena.' Correct. 'New.' It is certainly going to be 'new,' and therefore 'modern'—or, vice versa.

Already Ophüls could recite verbatim much of the doctrine, but over dinner, he had dismissed a number of Paryla's ideas and assumptions about Brecht: 'Forget his politics, *oublier* his Marxist orientation. For now he is a man in one hell of a hurry. He's got less than two months, only forty days to get ready for Berlin.'

Paryla was astounded. Brecht and Weill had first been approached in March, Ophüls said. Brecht was passing time in a café in Berlin—out of work, but not ideas—when his friend Erwin Piscator entered from the street with Ernst-Josef Aufricht. Piscator and Brecht had recently completed a production of *The Good Soldier Schweik*. Piscator introduced Brecht to the equally young Aufricht. Aufricht was an actor, but more importantly he had recently come into his inheritance of one hundred thousand marks. Wanting to make a name for himself as a producer, he had booked a set of nights at the Theater am Schiffbauerdamm. At this first meeting, Brecht had promised Aufricht not any old production, but an aesthetic revolution. Aufricht's lucky day.

As Ophüls related over dinner the particulars of Brecht's theories, feigning the commitment of a true disciple, Paryla imagined that first encounter between the out-of-work genius and the impressionable Aufricht. Brecht almost certainly told Aufricht that he had a role to play—but forget acting, who needs more actors? Become a catalyst for change! Aufricht's first foray into the theatre could be instrumental—decisive!—in overturning the old cult of beauty.

The play Brecht offered Aufricht was not his own; it was in fact only a rough treatment from a translation of a play in

English. The provisional title was *Scum*. *The Pimp's Opera* was an alternate. Kurt Weill was working on the songs. Lyrics recalled, at various points, François Villon and Rudyard Kipling. In other words, Brecht and Weill were cooking up a *potage*. Whether Aufricht considered the script, in its submitted form, stageworthy, or whether he merely scanned the pages while replaying in his mind Brecht's heroic narration of aesthetic advancement—well, Paryla has little doubt about that. Aufricht had listened to his heart, not his mind.

Most astonishing to Paryla is that Brecht and his collaborators were given only six months to get their act together for Berlin. Six months to adapt, arrange and produce their street opera. It is July already. The proceedings are in full swing.

But are they preparing a drama or a demonstration?

HOMESPUN

I reported for duty. We worked in the factory. I was eager to fit in. Brecht instructed us to throw away our old methods. Everything Ophüls ever taught us went out the window. Alienation took the place of identification, detachment took the lead from empathy. And theory took over from story.

Brecht wanted no part of the old school. No part of naturalism. For naturalism, he told us, go into the forest: wade into a stream, gaze into a pool of water! For the trance of things, for the reflection in the mirror—walk up into the mountains and stare at the clouds.

He was right.

Art is not a mirror. *Art is not a mirror to reflect reality, but a hammer with which to shape it.*

There were many teachers in the group, actors, artists, friends of Brecht. One weekend Erich Kästner came visiting. After rehearsal I was invited to Hotel Monopol with the group from Berlin. The Berliners never split up. I went along with Kästner and we dined at a long table. Wine, cigarettes, coffee, laughter, waving hands. It was important to see this side. The next night everyone was invited to a private home. It turned out that it was the house of Resi, a university professor who taught drama. Her daughter Suzanne was an old friend of mine from the swimming pool. Resi was separated from her husband and on top of that she taught the Greeks! What an incredible mother to have! A mother who held parties. A mother who taught the Greeks, who followed the avant-garde. Imagine this woman. Then imagine Erich Kästner and Kurt Weill at the same table. Hauptmann and Weigel. Brecht with a guitar in his lap. Everyone at the table. Brecht strums his guitar. He wants to sing. He plays an old patriotic song. Then he sings some ballad about roses and about springtime and about youth. Next "Mack the Knife." Weill begins to sing in a shaky voice. Bravo! Brecht stood up from the table and mimed the interlude. Bravo!

Speaking slowly upset Brecht. He asked you to speak quickly, and get on with it. He would bend his head toward you so that he received each word, separately, as a word to itself, and a short time afterwards he put the words together into a sentence and broke the code.

Immediately when he understood you, he waved his hand for you to stop talking, *shush, shush,* because now he has something of his own to say and he wants your attention, he needs it, because what he has to say is important, very, very, important, quite different from anything you've heard before.

Just like Männe.

All day at the theatre Brecht was surrounded by collabora-tors. All day he was surrounded by women. All day he sat with a witness at his side in case a crumb fell from his lips onto the rug. Then one of his women would bend down and pick whatever it was off the floor and place it in a bowl on the table beside his elbow.

Nothing of Brecht was wasted.

I was not a Jenny, but a Polly. Not from the streets, but from inside the villa gates. Homespun. I was a Breslau girl, and there was a big difference between Breslau and Berlin. Berlin was our Babylon. The street cafés, the theatre, the cabarets and bars and *kellers*. Hauptmann, Lenya, Weigel. They *were* Berlin. Each one exceptional. They wore silk underwear! I observed these women closely. Lenya of course—when she tapped her feet or drummed a finger on her knee. Lenya lived by the city tempo.

Berlin women. They gave me my break. After the last rehearsal we went out to celebrate, cast and crew at a café. This was a rite of passage and a farewell party. It was after midnight when it ended. We poured out of the café in one swoop, leaning on top of each other, that way, this way, each went their own direction. Kästner took my hand: he said something formal—which totally surprised me. Then he presented me with a copy of *Emil und die Detektive*. What's this? I thought. A great moment. Kästner interested in a Breslau girl? Me, homespun. I had to warn him. I was saving my opening for Karl. My opening!

§ § §

The doctors want to put a shunt in Eva. Why do that? Pavel doesn't understand. I don't like the sound of it either. *Shunt*: Pavel pronounces this word with disdain, as though it's a typical Canadian concoction—not something that would fly under communist system, this shunt, which I imagine as a rubber piece, short and blunt.

On this, the third visit, Eva's nights are short. She is jaundiced. I see it in her eyes, especially, but also in her hands and neck. She retires to her room with a glass of wine by seven o'clock. The wine is for show. She sleeps four hours at most, and then to snack and take her pills, she is awake. During the night she rotates between the bed and a chair at the kitchen table. Before she goes off (this evening, dressed in a black kimono) she selects, from among the four whippets, the one to keep her company for the night. Klee, Davenport, Rachel or Gould. Tonight she chooses Rachel, her special darling, with grey and tan spots: the one I find most resembles an anorexic rat on steroids.

Pavel and Eva: dog people. She lived with a miniature donkey for a spell at Sutton, but monkeys, donkeys—these were exotic exceptions. She was a dog lady. By matching winning mates, she and Pavel have bred their share of prize whippets, borzois and Salukis. Organized by kennel clubs, their own dogs competed, in elaborate tournament-like structures, for Challenge Dog and Challenge Bitch. The judges looked for a combination of innate and learned traits, and dogs had to conform to published breed standards. The animals did not compete against each other so much as against ideals.

Eva herself was once a professional handler. The handler's job is to present the dog to the judge—to stack the dog: to position the canine in a proper stance, so that the judge may view all its parts at rest. I imagine Eva here, as one of Oskar Kuper's puppeteers: on stage but in the background, holding the strings. Given her showmanship, her success is not surprising.

Dog breeding is a science, or a pseudo-science. With every litter Eva would threaten to destroy the runts, the undesirables, if she could not otherwise discard them to friends and neighbours. I have always seen an irony in this. Not because I am a dog lover. But because these two card-carrying eccentrics, Eva and Pavel, seemed to me to be committed to their own brand of eugenics: breeding their darlings from a 'founder group,' arranging marriages, in the same spirit of the Nuremberg Laws.

Dishing out natural selection. Eliminating the weak. Practising race science on man's best friend.

Wineglass stem in her fist, Rachel at her ankle, Eva says goodnight. *Gute Nacht!* She leaves me in her kitchen with a plate of cheese and a book. She closes the door to the sewing room, which Pavel has converted into her private quarters. The room is bare, furnished only with a cot and dresser. It shares a wall with the toilet. So close to death, Eva doesn't want to make trouble. She is cleaning up behind herself. Sweeping herself into a corner.

THE PRETTY ASYLUM

Just when I was beginning to soar, HH showed up again at the theatre. I had had hardly any news from him. Contact had been cut between sister and brother since the time he left to live with the pastor. He lived such and such a place. He was studying at the university, and he was involved in a research project. He volunteered to be the mouse. A research mouse. That's what we had heard. I understood. At home we were only three witnesses. Only three sisters. At the University of Breslau he found a whole department to impress. He thrived under scientific observation.

He stood by the stage watching us, without saying a word, not even *Hallo*. Hands in his pockets. He observed the rehearsal. A couple of the girls thought he was cute. They put on a show for him. They kicked their legs into the air. He checked his watch. He left. The next time he came he confronted me. *Here I am and now you listen.* He didn't want me working in the theatre—I had no business there, or here. Ruff, ruff, ruff. *It is not for you to do it.* Stop it, Eva. Stop it now. He is my brother. Enough is enough. He forbids me to continue on like this or that. Father asked him to come. He and my father were in it together.

It became the routine. I would not stop, he would not give in. Very short visits. Crude interludes. The blind meets the deaf. *This is not right for you.* Finally he threatened to take *all my freedom away.* He gave me his final warning and left, in one door, and then out, in one door, out, like a bird from the clock. Cuckoo! Cuckoo! *Eva, I forbid you.* No more. No more of this. *Eva, this has to stop!* Quit your radio work. Quit theatre.

His voice was flat. He was only the messenger. *Act like a person of your upbringing.* He was reading the incoming news from China. *It is now forbidden.* He reported on fertility experiments in Tennessee. *It is not for you to stay here.* And if I dared ask him how things were going ... O Gott. That was none of my business. I had no right to ask. *He hadn't come all this way to get involved in a conversation.* There was no relationship.

Act like a person of your upbringing. HH and Father demanded that I act like them, that I act like my upbringing. But I had no upbringing!

Both were furious. I had broken their code, their suffocating code of honour. HH came one day and pulled me off stage. He was rough, he twisted my arm at the elbow. *From now on ...* He told me if I wanted to join the real theatre, then I should go ahead and walk the streets and be like the others. Bravo. He delivered the message, which was a puzzle. Afterwards he bowed, and left. Bravo. A stiff Prussian. That was part of his sickness. His upbringing. HH never would explain himself. When we were children it was the same: everything he said was carefully presented to us in a way that made it difficult for us to understand. The prophet with the parable. The puzzle all along was him. There was no other meaning. The mystery was him. He chose his words carefully to make *that* absolutely clear.

It went on for a month. The grand show. Conflict. HH came to the house. He interrupted my work on stage. He disappeared, then reappeared though another hole. It continued like that until one day—something had changed, something in his favour—and he returned to tell me that he still has the power, he and Father have the absolute power, together they can stop me. They have the authority. They have the power and the means to cancel my contract. My engagement. They can do it.

So now it begins to unravel. HH and Father go to see Max Ophüls and they tear up my contract. Then I am put in a car. This was no joke.

Now we will consult. Consult for what? You will see. How far is it? You will see. Where are we going? You will see.

We drove into the countryside.

It turned out to be a clinic. A clinic in the woods. A pretty asylum. My father had made an appointment with the doctor. They sat me down in a chair. The doctor walked into the room and right away, without an exam, I was supposed to swallow a pill.

No! I won't. I won't swallow. I want to leave!

You're hysterical.

I won't cooperate.

You're excited.

Next thing I woke up in a white room. I lay sideways on the cot. It was no dream.

The doctor pinched the bottom of my feet. He listened closely to my breathing. He opened my shirt. He looked deep into my moral fibre. My loose moral fibres.

Where were my long braids and my embroidered folk dress? Where were my rosy cheeks, where my smile? Why this frown?

Diagnosis: I was hysterical and depressed. I was dangerous to myself and to others. I had damaged the family reputation. I did not listen or obey. I was doing everything I wanted to do. I was enjoying myself. I had talent. I had the same soft skin my mother had. I loved my brother. My brother loved me.

He hated me. I was lost. I had too many boyfriends. I was a socialist. A true communist. I showed pity. I had opened my heart to society.

This isn't true, I told the doctor. I am not depressed. I am not hysterical. I'm an actress. I'm learning to be. I'm happy.

Rest, he said, you need to rest.

I don't need to rest.

Take your pills and go to sleep. Soon enough you will behave like the others here, who sit in the garden in striped pyjamas, who fart on the benches and laugh at the butterflies.

I don't need to rest.

Shush. You're excited.

Yes, I was angry. My father cancelled my engagement. My brother betrayed me. My sisters deserted me.

You're hysterical, the doctor reminded me.

What could I do, there was no way out. There was no escape from the Freuds of that time. By the third day I broke down. I lay on my bed and I cried and I cried until the doctor came and found me.

Good, he said. You see, you are upset. See how upset you really are.

No visitors came. Karl searched but could not find me. I had been taken to the clinic at night and my friends didn't have a clue where The Nervous Bride had gone.

She was sleeping in the woods. The doctor had knocked her out. She was having a bad dream. She was brought to the zoo and put in a cage with all the other monkeys: pregnant monkeys, promiscuous monkeys, monkeys with bad social hygiene. There was a whole colony of apes. The place was shit. There was no mercy at all.

At the clinic we shared one birth defect. Missing a penis!

The chief doctor wanted me to sign a paper, one of his forms.

A declaration of dependence. A legal contract with depression and hysteria. But there was no way I would sign. After weeks went by he sent for my father. Well, the doctor declared, we cannot keep your child here forever. She will not sign this form.

At the same time I was supposed to mark something that said I would not go back to the theatre.

I will never sign your treaty, I told them. You cannot make me sign!

Very well, said the doctor. We cannot keep you here forever ... since we have already taken your dignity ... we have drugged you already for one month ... since we cannot rape you in good conscience: You're being discharged.

But discharged to where?

My father walked out of the room.

At that moment I knew where to go. The clinic sent me in a car. I told the driver, take me to such and such a place. Suzanne's mother, Resi, the teacher, opened the door. I stood there, this disturbed person. She took me in her arms and brought me into the house.

OLD NARRATIVE SYSTEM

Eva settles for the night and very soon afterwards I hear Pavel's footsteps on the inside stairwell at the back of the house that connects East and West Berlin. Pavel knocks softly and enters the kitchen. I've been reading an article from yesterday's newspaper, it lies open on the table. I pour him some wine. 'How is the book?' He glances at the article, then pursues his line of questioning. 'Have you put me in it?' Indeed. His part is undecided. 'It's going fine,' I tell him. But meanwhile, I wonder if I've gotten the chronology half right. Probably this whole mess, for Pavel, is Verboten slash Not Accepted Under Old Narrative System.

The newspaper article is about a social program ongoing in Dortmund. Prostitutes are being 'retrained' in geriatric care, then employed in old-age homes. Pavel came across the article last night and left it for me. I've just gotten around to it having spent half the day with Eva in The Pretty Asylum and the other half with Eva and her son Michael in Zurich. The program supervisor (a reformed prostitute herself) relates a simple social equation: there is a growing aging population in Germany and there is a dearth of nurses and caretakers and hospital orderlies; on the other hand there is a surplus of sex-workers walking the streets. For this supervisor the math makes things self-evident. In addition, she is quoted as saying, prostitutes are not bothered by human contact and are familiar with bodily parts. They are not put off by intimacy.

No, I think, they are not. They are obviously great communicators and, of course, working late hours on the night shift is not unknown to them. The only caveat mentioned in the article was that, with old men being what they are, the staff will need to be even more vigilant than usual in ensuring that undue expectations are not put upon these workers.

Germans, says Pavel, reading my mind, pragmatic as always.

On previous visits Eva avoided the subject of her son Michael. It was as if she had written him out of her story. Thirty years after his death the subject was taboo. Today she talked around the subject: about blackmail in Vienna, about the kind of mother she became in Switzerland—how she didn't want her son to grow up; she wanted Michael to 'keep small' and hide under her breast until the end of the war. Pavel believes Eva has a need to reconcile herself to Michael's death now, at the end of her life. According to him, Eva needs closure, and our talks are doing her good. All right, but closure? For closure she comes to *me*?

Michael was an actor. He died in Hamburg in 1967. He had left Canada for Germany in the early 1950s to apprentice, because at the time there was no place in Canada to study acting and Eva couldn't afford to set him up in New York. So off he went back to Deutschland. His choice. Eva was mortified. But in Munich at least he could board with relatives. Eva's sisters in fact. In time Michael's theatre career took off. He earned an *engagement*. He acted in several films. He met an older woman. He fell in love.

Eva disapproved.

The relationships soured: between Michael and his lady friend, and between Michael and Eva. No one knows or is telling why.

Then one night in Hamburg before a performance Michael's heart gave out. The theatre staff grew anxious. They called the authorities and the police broke down the door to his apartment. They found a bottle of pills, a bottle of whiskey, on the bedside table.

An overdose. A broken heart. Something else?

Michael exited the stage for good at thirty-two years of age, but not before securing a walk-on part in John Sturge's World War Two adventure film *The Great Escape*. In this Hollywood classic, featuring the likes of Charles Bronson and Steve McQueen, Michael—ironically—plays a Gestapo agent. His character is responsible for identifying the allied POWs, who are posing as civilians on a Breslau-bound commuter train. But for this role, Michael was never given a film credit. I have checked this on the special edition (two-disc collector's set) DVD of *The Great Escape*. The credits tumble down at the beginning and end of the film—for the American, British and German actors—but there is none for Michael. He is unidentifiable unless you have what I have: family photographs and oral family history.

I can understand what an audience appreciated about Michael in 1963, the year the film was released. He was chosen for the part for his good looks, which are quantifiably Aryan. He wears a stylish homburg and a tan trench coat, unbuttoned. His fashion bespeaks his casual flair as a fresh-as-the-breeze fascist. He's been historicized all right—which means what? Restored to size or true dimension? His behaviour is staged and scripted, surely, but watching the DVD I am the one spellbound. Acting is a type of self-hypnotism, yet I'm the one mesmerized. Why is this? Because Michael is convincing. Damn convincing. Blond. Of course he is blond. The boy is positively plagued by his blondness. I understand this is a counterfeit version of my uncle once removed, but close enough, close enough to the real thing.

My head is spinning as I stare at the photograph of Michael which stands on the mantel in Eva's cramped salon, where Pavel and I have moved to continue our conversation. Michael, in the photo, is again blond. He is handsome, pensive, smoking a cigarette, casually insolent in a tight collared shirt. The moment is burning him up. Beside Michael on the mantel is a photograph of an equally young man. This is Damian. Pavel's Damian.

I understand that Pavel became a caregiver a full decade before Eva fell sick. Damian died of AIDS. Pavel has had practice looking after a faltering loved one. He's seen close-ups of human misery before, and reacted with human decency.

3

FEDERAL BUREAU OF INVESTIGATION

File No. 100-18112 (LA)

SUBJECT: BERTHOLD EUGEN FRIEDRICH BRECHT-INTERNAL
SECURITY- R
Berthold Brecht is a German refugee writer employed in
Hollywood freelancing for various movie concerns.

May 29, 1946
While BRECHT is undoubtedly a Russian and Communist
sympathiser, investigation has failed to reveal any
present activities on his part in connection with any
Communist groups or organizations. Furthermore, contacts
with Soviet personnel have been very, very rare. BRECHT,
of course, continues his work as a poet and undoubtedly
endeavors to inject his political philosophy into his
work.

In view of the foregoing, this case is being closed at
the present time but will be reopened in the event BRECHT
becomes active.

WORKSHOP

Ernst Busch holds the accordion, cumbersome as an x-ray machine, to his street-singer's chest. *See the shark. Teeth like razors. Macheath. Has got a knife.* Overnight Brecht has written "Moritat von Mackie Messer" at the behest of Harold Paulsen. Paulsen, playing Mackie, demanded something like this murderous ballad as an intro piece to bring a bit of shine to his character. A razor's edge.

Midway through Busch's solo performance, Weill joins on the piano, stamping on the foot pedals, and the conductor, Theo Mackeben, begins dusting the air, twirling his fingers, taunting the street orchestra (banjo, mandolin, harmonium, cello and Hawaiian guitar) with a series of cat calls and animated gestures. Paryla is enjoying the music: *sehr kapital.*

Hauptmann is again working with her group of whores, repositioning them on the set, and Brecht has left the scene for an instant. As he left, Paryla noticed, Eva re-entered. Here she is again, the new girl, standing to one side, deep in concentration. She is practising pantomime—a mother consoling her child?—and repeating the same gestures over and over. Eva is something to watch, but mime is pedantic, it is fussy and finicky, it reeks of perfectionism: it is irritating. Brecht, no surprise, adores mime. It is his specialty, Ophüls had said so.

When during the morning session the entire group practised mime, as a kind of warm-up exercise, Paryla suffered through their incoherent and bland ballet. It was claustrophobic to watch such a thing. Worst of all he knew what their message was, the message he tries to ignore: that sound is a prosthesis for those who like him are, on a profound level, deaf to human experience.

Brecht returns just as the whores and also now a group of beggars seat themselves on the floor inside Jonathan Jeremiah Peachum's Outfitting Emporium for Beggars. The company is already well-versed in Peachum's basic types of misery. Manikins, to illustrate them all, are set up on stage. One dummy in a glass case, on a modest pedestal, has been fitted with a pair of dark glasses. Its fingers clutch a walking stick. The Pitiful Blind Man is touted as the cordon bleu of beggary. Paryla uses his spyglasses again to make out the pickets and hand signs stored by the side wall. *I Gave My Eye for My King.* Tacked to the interior walls of the set are some inspirational notices. *You Will Benefit from the Interests of a Powerful Organization. Close Not Thine Eyes to Misery. If You Are Satisfied Tell the Others, If You Are Dissatisfied Tell Me.*

Brecht begins the lesson by establishing general principles. He compares Aristotelian Theatre to Epic Theatre. His neat comparison belies a standard script. It is obviously the very script Ophüls paraphrased to Paryla the night before. Action is the lifeblood of Aristotelian Theatre; narrative argument is the essence of Epic Theatre. The Aristotelian involves the spectator in the stage action, and through the catharsis of pity and fear destroys the spectator's own will for action in the world. The Epic form of theatre is designed to make the spectator an observer of the stage action, and arouses the spectator's will to action in the world.

The comparison continues: Emotional experience on the one hand, the awakening of a conscience on the other. Class instinct versus class consciousness. Suggestion versus argument. 'Man given as a known quantity' versus 'Man as a subject of investigation.' Organic development versus collage. Feeling versus intellect. Paryla shook his head.

Brecht is enthusiastic and delivers to the house with conviction. The actors nod, several of them ask questions. But ultimately there is no dialectic. No true learning here, not just yet. Everything could have flown directly over their heads and not mattered much to the company, that much is obvious to Paryla. The local actors had no need to go to such depths to play the bit parts of petty criminals. All this would be more a hindrance than a help. Obviously the session has been held on diplomatic grounds.

But when Brecht starts to explain his new technique of acting, they grow a little more interested. This is about them, now, about acting itself. The goal of the alienation effect is simple enough: to represent the familiar as unfamiliar. And why? The motivation is political: *to free* the spectator from the dead-weight of old habits. Ophüls has already done a first-rate job explaining this. But if the goal and motivation were clear, the means are more difficult to grasp. In turning away from habit and tradition, the actor is being asked to discard the old methods. Brecht wants them to act as if in a trance, and to speak in a voice free of magical cadences, or saintly syncopations: matter-of-factly, that is.

'The actor, first and foremost, is not his character.' Ophüls had reiterated the mantra to Paryla the night before. 'The actor knows more than his character; he knows the beginning, middle, end, before the character, and maintains a calm independence throughout ... that is one reason ... his foreknowledge is claustrophobic and manifests itself in detachment.'

Paryla defended the spectator. 'Where does that leave me, on my night out at the theatre?'

'The character shouldn't grow on the audience,' Ophüls ignored Paryla, 'this, again, is part of identification. Rather the character should strike the audience or leave them cold.'

'I see. Where exactly does the character strike, on the head? With a heavy hammer, I suppose.'

'The character,' Ophüls reiterated, '*should strike the audience.*' He said so adopting a peculiar accent which Paryla took to be Brecht's own. 'On stage, in a trance, self-aware, the actor may openly observe his own movements. Naive, ironic, fable-like. The character should arise out of the ordinary. Like a sculpture coming to life out of air.'

Wonderful. The theory is exquisite, like ballet almost, with ideas coming to life out of nothing. But Paryla has heard and seen enough. The rebellion against the old theatre is really a rebellion against the idea of fate. Every rebellion is the same. This is what he concludes. It is a rebellion against providence and lot and predestination and destiny, in favour of human judgment and intervention. In favour of man. Not bad, this. But how will the great rebellion be waged? Using the alienation effect? Fabulous. Using the spectator's detachment?

Estrangement, disharmony, detachment. These were the main ingredients. The actor's distance from his own character. The character's detachment from the drama. And the spectator's detachment from 'the conditions of life' set before his eyes on stage. All an analogy for man's out-of-sync being in the modern world. His utter disorientation. Man out of step with the music of his own times, applying friction against forces of historical progress, economic reality, and so on and so on.

Man reduced to an absurdity, observing his own absurdness.

Man as a mime.

And what of the removal of estrangement, the elimination of alienation, the closure of disharmony?

Lights. Action. Revolution.

DREAM ENDS

Eva is taking a rest so Pavel and I take a quick trip out to do some shopping. He is wearing the black sailor cap I brought from Montreal, the original Greek rendition of the Freddie Mercury special. When she is awake Eva keeps Pavel on a short leash. Recently unemployed, Pavel complies, playing endless games of Scrabble and cards, and seeing to it that she has everything she needs, which granted isn't much right now. When she goes down for a nap Pavel heads straight for the door.

Leaving the house, I am reassured by the sound of Eva's voice emanating from the side window. She's in character, reading to Rachel the whippet from a picture book. This is something she started doing ages ago. It has roots in Breslau, when she and her sister Romy would sit themselves on the floor beside Bimbo's cage and read to him from his favourite, *The Grimm Fairy Tales*. Eva was a little Jane Goodall or Dian Fossey, who, before the Second World War even, had assimilated the lessons of beauty and the beast. Standing by her window, Pavel dryly observes that Eva spends more time reading to her dogs than parents nowadays read to their children.

The story she is reading tonight is 'Rumpelstilzchen.' In Sutton Eva had an Italian greyhound called Rumpelstilzchen. I always had difficulty pronouncing that name, which pretzelled my tongue: Rumpel-stitching-chen. In those days Eva, just like the miller's daughter in the story, was hard put to spin straw into gold and yet her life always seemed to depend on making magic happen or on selling illusions. When initially she declared her intention to leave Sutton for the frigid temperatures of Elliot Lake, we assumed it was a financial decision, and Roland offered help. But Eva didn't take handouts. She liked to make things happen her way.

Arriving in Canada in her late thirties, Eva had never been financially 'sound,' and was ever in want of advice on money matters. She came to Roland for this, which he dispensed, trying not to get too involved in her private affairs. She regarded him as a second son. But Roland eventually grew tired of the scenario: having her come to him, the supplicating aunt, bewildered by bank accounts, confused by the categories of chequing and savings. Her poor business decisions were a source of constant aggravation for him. At one time, she'd thought about opening a dinner theatre business (she was prepared to run it out of her home that reeked of dog). She proposed to import actors from Europe, presumably former bridge partners of The Martian. These two were going to form a private company. Marian and Eva had even chosen some obscure plays to produce (unknown, minor and, probably, un-entertaining, plays) from the old country (her old country, not his). This was neither corporate level 'blue-sky thinking' nor was it 'visioning' on her part; it was quite simply daydreaming, the stuff that Eva lived on. At a sensitive juncture of the financial planning for this venture, Eva had come to Roland to ask how she could incorporate herself. She was frightened by the prospect. Incorporating oneself, did it hurt? Was it invasive? What would it all cost, and what was the correct procedure? Understand, she didn't want to do anything wrong, she wanted to do this the right way, she was going about it cautiously, you see. These were not business decisions at all. She was attempting to spin gold from straw.

Pavel and I are gone twenty minutes. When we return with milk, Eva is smoking a cigarette at the kitchen table. She has no ashtray in her room. She no longer inhales her tobacco but she likes to light one up occasionally, and sip from the end. Pools of smoke spill from her mouth. Her breathing is so shallow that a cloud forms in front of her face, and lingers, and eventually she has to wave it away with her hand. In her day Eva was a consummate smoker. Especially, she tells me, in post-war Berlin. But now smoking is forbidden for her. Her supply is my packet. When I leave and return to Montreal, she will have to climb the stairs to East Berlin and buy her own on the black market.

I have a dream that Eva dies in her bed, having fallen asleep holding a lit cigarette. The cigarette rolls off her fingertips and lodges itself against her thigh. I understand this in my dream, I understand it is an old story. I understand that Eva was unconscious long before the smouldering fire burst into flames. In case I do not 'get it,' the phenomenon is explained to me and Pavel by several nightmarish firefighters in succession (one of them resembles Michael, one of them Damian). When the fire caught and the flames erupted, they tell us, at that moment the heat was so great it probably blew the glass out of the small window. One of your neighbours called us, and we managed to save most of the house.

Two things about this dream strike me as strange. First, as it progresses—as the dream cycles and turns back inside itself—I feel better and better about Eva, not worse. The longer the dream the better I feel. Is this because I begin to understand and thus come to accept her death when it is repeated?

167

Or is it simply that, as each successive firefighter has his turn at the pump, time moves forward? Time moves forward even in my dream, and with time moving forward the forgetting begins. Although I will remember *the event* forever, the news begins to sink in after ten dream minutes. As long as time keeps moving forward, even a fraction of a second, I feel better—because time itself is good. Understanding is secondary. Living is primary. Necessity is the first thing, morals follow.

Secondly, the dream is peculiar because in it Rachel survives the fire. She's discovered in the kitchen, rescued by one of the firefighters. Eva must have let her out of her bedroom before the flames caught. Perhaps when she snuck out to steal a cigarette and the ashtray from the kitchen table. There is a note on the table, the paper was slipped under the pepper grinder. The note is from Eva. It is addressed to me. It reads differently every time: 'Pity is that which you decide to give those you have decided not to help.' 'If ownership is theft, what are intellectual copyrights for?' 'The collective unconscious is *the* Marxist ideal.'

'I see that you also are cooking your soup on a burning house.'

Then the dream ends.

UNTIL DEATH DOES ITS PART

I'll never forget what Resi told me the night after I arrived from the asylum. After dinner she took me aside and whispered in my ear, Suzanne has to find a husband *now*. Why? Because she will be so ugly later in life. I looked at Resi. *She* was ugly. But how could she say such a thing about her daughter? And then it dawned on me ... Oh yes, now I know why, now this makes sense. I'm given shelter, I'm allowed to stay in their house as long as I help Suzanne meet the man of her mother's dreams.

It was straightforward. It was business.

I was bait. I was the slice of cheese on the floor. My job was to lie still on my back by the front door, inviting men outside to have a look—then spring to my feet, slam the door, when the time was right to introduce Suzanne.

But to make things complicated, Suzanne liked Karl. Obviously. She enjoyed his company. When Karl came over to visit, she had no idea herself how out of tune she was—how see-through she could be. Karl teased her. He performed a waltz. He copied Suzanne from head to foot, and she stood by laughing, watching him. *Pinguin*. She had penguin feet. Suzanne waddled with pointed toes. Karl walked and talked like Suzanne, and Suzanne always thought that was great, but I felt cornered. I had no family, they had deserted me. Suzanne's mother was depending on my contacts, but how long could I lie there in a crack under the door, snapping my legs to gain their attention? I was welcome as long as I wanted to stay, Resi told me. So long as I could supply the demand. But what were my choices in the end?—I had none.

Think now, Eva, concentrate. Stop now and think. I sat on the bed and I closed my eyes. Think now of the black hole. Think now of a candle. Concentrate. A candle burns, a candle burns. Fly into the void.

What else could I do of course in a situation like that, but get married?

I would not return home, so then I had to ride in the marriage carriage. Rise and fall, in sickness and in health, I had to marry my way out of that place.

All right. Calm down, I told myself. You can marry the communist. You will ask him to marry you. You know what to say and how to say it—what to do and how to do it. Now is the time. You will marry Karl Paryla.

Married. Married, up, up, and away.

It was airlift. My first airlift.

Karl was in love. He was ready for love. He was already waiting for me on the corner of the street with a ring in his pocket. Me? I was unknown. Unknown! I was supposed to meet him at the altar, that's as far as the plans took me.

We were married in the Lutheran chapel. Our theatre friends attended, all together, in the front row. Many had come simply to see my fantastic father figure again. Father walked me down the aisle, gripping my hand before throwing me to the wolf. I was rolled under the wheels of the stiff Prussian-Silesian show. Pastor Kohler was at the altar and Karl and I repeated our lines after him. He then declared us man and wife, for better or worse, until death does its part.

After the ceremony the two head families staged a meaningless dinner party at a restaurant in Breslau. The dead supper. Both sides behaved coldly.

Outside the restaurant, after our meal, Hermann Hans *demanded* a cigarette. What is this about? He didn't smoke cigarettes. Has life run out of paradoxes? It was odd behaviour for him. We were sitting alone on a bench in the courtyard. The brother and the sister. He had summoned me. He was preparing to … to tell me, what? I could see he wasn't up to it, the dinner party, the wedding, none of it. He was a miserable mess.

What's wrong? I asked him. Is there anything wrong, brother?

The moment had come: Once you made me a picture, and I didn't want your picture …

I didn't understand. I never understood him. Running red eyes, trembling lips. He was talking about ages ago like it was just yesterday. He said he would never let anything like that happen to me again.

But Hermann Hans! I had to remind him: It was you! It was you who hurt me. You were the one who hurt me so badly. You!

No! You don't understand … I will never … I will find … No! Again, he was enormous. I can take care of you. I can fix it. Then he turned his back to me. He turned around. *But you know they have those long arms—they can stretch across trees.* And he was laughing. Laughing to himself, right into his throat, which sounded like he was vomiting. He was laughing and choking and throwing up into himself. He wanted something. I knew he wanted it badly. He knew it was forbidden. We all knew and we all said nothing. He put his arm on my shoulder and then leaned forward and his face touched my face. His salty tears on my cheek. And again he told me as he had said once before, Eva you have the same hands, same hair, the same white skin.

Bells. Flowers and bells. I came out with a new family. Karl's mother was Austrian. And so there with that Austrian mother-in-law I got plunked. It reminded me of a joke.

There is an important diplomatic dinner party at the embassy in Vienna. Chandeliers the size of motor-car engines hang from the ceiling. It's a crowded event and the diplomats are doing their best to behave. Every whisker is polished.

A German diplomat and an Austrian diplomat begin a conversation.

The Austrian diplomat points out to the German diplomat that there is cow shit pressed under the German ambassador's shoes: For you see, there is no way to hide the fact that the ambassador is a peasant, a Weimar farmer.

The German diplomat answers, directly: The stink in this chamber is not cow shit. Definitely not.

Austrian diplomat: What is it then?

German diplomat: You see the Austrian General standing there, twitching his moustache?

Austrian: I do.

German: What stinks is high culture.

Austrian: Our culture?

German: Yes. High rates of repression exist in your country and don't you see, the General has held a turd too long in his backyard. See there! Again! When he twists his moustache, he twitches, and each time he lets a little bit go. A little cloud of gas escapes. Pouf!

I knew that Austrians had one way of doing things and that their way was the right way to do it, and there was no other choice. When I arrived at the Paryla house in Breslau, Karl explained how the mother-in-law worked her magic. Everything is under control, he assured me. You should rest.

My help was not needed, so in the beginning—*for now, please*—I was told to stay out of the way and rest because of my condition.

My condition? Karl was worried about my health. He knew what I had gone through, sleeping in the woods. I was angry, upset, I was tired. But there was no danger. I wasn't about to faint.

Well you should not overdo it, said Karl. Rest until you feel stronger.

I got the message: I should not help in the house. I should not tire myself out. I should maybe stop theatre. I could quit radio. The list went on. I Should Stop.

Was this special treatment again? Here, a glass thermometer. Child, don't move. Take these pills, lie down on the bed. Sign the paper. Here is the special treatment room. Lie flat. Rest your head. Open your shirt. Let us have a look inside. I see your moral fibres are loose. Here and here. These ones are very loose. Let me tighten this one. Let me support your back. Stick out your tongue. Push down on my arm. Now push against me!

Everyone believed I deserved something.

Before the wedding when I was at my lowest Karl accepted me for who I was. But after we were married, and after I had had my rest period, and he had helped me, he expected to see an immediate improvement. On the count of three, sit up straight and open your eyes: he was tired of the old me and my pathetic performance by torchlight. He slipped on white gloves, he was ready to saw the woman in two and take her better half, leave the other half in the box. He expected some change in my mood. He expected me to finish what I had started and stop my playing around. Get over it. Move forward. For Karl, it was this simple.

Karl changed, I could not change.

Below the surface, he couldn't see.

He grew impatient.

He paced the rooms downstairs. After All I Have Done for

You ... Why Don't You Change? He waited at the bottom of the staircase, and he drank too much, staring up the banister. When could he expect me? At what hour would I descend in my long dress and slide, laughing, into his lap? *He* wanted special treatment.

Meanwhile one day disaster struck. We were sitting for dinner. It was Week Two or Week Three in the household of the mother-in-hell. The grey-eyed Ursula would sit on Karl's side of the table, me alone on the other. She had prepared the veal, and she watched Karl put it into his mouth. When he chewed, she smiled. When he spoke to me across the table, she rearranged the napkin in her lap. When I swallowed some wine, she touched her hair.

Her potatoes and the vegetables were boiled, and drained of colour.

After our meal I stood up. I said, I will make the coffee!

Karl and his mother glanced at each other, then at me: they stared at the girl on fire.

I will make the coffee, I insisted. Please, let me make the coffee.

Well, that was unheard of.

No, absolutely not. Don't be foolish. Sit down. No trouble, this is *my* house.

But I insisted. I insisted and the Austrian froze. Karl reached for my hand. Brave and courageous wife, please, sit down.

But I stood my ground.

I marched into the kitchen, found a pot and filled it with water and I threw in the coffee beans. I put the pot on the stove. Ten minutes later, I looked inside the pot and saw the beans down at the bottom, in a pile, which looked like deer shit. The water was clear, but there were these small bubbling pieces of deer shit. How was I supposed to make coffee?

I know we made coffee like that at home, I know we did.

Grind the beans, Karl instructed. You need to grind coffee!

Tremendous.

No! I shouted. But suddenly it dawned on me, Oh yes, the maids had a machine, I was missing some noise, the machine.

This was my start in the kitchen.

I was dug up and with dirt falling off my clothes I was carried to Darmstadt. So, I left Breslau. We rented the upper half of a house. Small quarters. Karl had his engagement with the Reinhardt Theatre and I had a marriage contract with Karl. I had to perform also. There in Darmstadt we started out as The Young Married Couple. Her Under Him Until She Falls Apart.

Karl played Franz Moor in *Die Räuber*, *The Robbers*, by Schiller. His success continued. But I could not make it come—any of it. What was supposed to come from me did not come. I was numb with stage fright. We were unhappy.

There lived a family downstairs. They had two children. One on the breast and the other riding a bicycle.

They lived under *me*.

Karl was busy. He went on tour with the company. He took trips to Baden-Baden, to Bremen, to Berlin, and even back to Breslau. As for me, my career was over. My time on stage, my dream to become an actress—nothing was left of the opera.

When Karl went on tour loneliness became a fact of life. I had no visitors. No strangers walked up the path and knocked at the door. Day by day I fell into a trance. I observed my own life: marriage alienated me. The world detached and floated away from me. All I had was this family living on the first floor. They were the dirt under my fingernails. The sound of their voices, their life. A door slamming shut, the toilet flushing. The older child running and jumping and stamping his feet. I listened through the floor.

Did you know I was a spy well before my Berlin time? I devoted hours to spying. Whole days and weeks spying for the Russians.

In the morning the baby cried. When she cried, mother nursed. The mother carried the baby down the hall and into the kitchen. My kitchen was directly above their kitchen. All the rooms matched. One on top of the other. Our apartment mirrored their apartment. I lay on the floor, my head flat, sideways. My ear down. I listened for signs of life. I concentrated on the bathroom floor. I crawled under the table and around beside the bed and into the hallway, then inside the closet. I was dragged through the rooms of our apartment following the sound of their life below.

For weeks that went on. I ate my breakfast when down below breakfast was served. I slept in the afternoon when the child took its nap. I lived the same life, I followed the same recipe. A shadow play. I lived in the cave. The baby crying, mother upset, the boy running, and the man closing the door at night—opening it again in the morning.

But upstairs, I made no sound. When Karl returned on the weekend, sometimes, it was terrible. At night we heard the other couple. Our room above their bedroom. Their bed below our bed. Husband on wife. Downstairs they worked by candlelight while upstairs Karl and I rested in the dark against the wall like shadows, tired of ourselves.

Karl laughed. Listen, he said. Just listen to them.

I turned away.

Listen to them, he held my chin and turned my cheek.

No. I don't hear anything.

First you play dumb, he said. Now deaf like Romy?

I don't play anything, I said. I won't play anymore.

After one year in Darmstadt I went back to Breslau and I visited Suzanne at her mother's. I also went to see my family. To repair some damage. Father, sisters, brother. It took courage. But I was never interested in the scales of justice. Justice never helps, until injustice has been done. I didn't want to make the situation worse.

Right away I realized my brother was in bad condition. Physically he looked pale and very thin. He looked like he had been hard at work for a long, long time, getting organized, setting-up, while he prepared to welcome a great disease into his body.

I told Suzanne how I felt very bad about my brother. He lived with another boy on the rail line, a fellow student who had some form of TB. I saw how they lived in a small rented cottage. It was filthy. Sweet, rotten, alcoholic. Wild animals couldn't have created the same mess. They'd hired Vincent Van Gogh as their maid.

Please, after I leave, I told Suzanne, help my brother.

I don't understand, she said. He treated you shamefully.

Suzanne, he isn't like that. Those times are over. New times are about to begin. He needs your help.

One day we went together to visit him on his street near the Jahrhunderthalle, called Rothkäppchen Weg. Red Riding Hood Way. All the streets in this area were named after fairy tales. Rows of very small houses, families asleep inside. Their door was locked and the boys were not home, so we went around to the back and entered through HH's bedroom window. He slept on a bare mattress, a stained, yellowed thing. The kitchen was worse, the stove was splashed blue. They'd made blueberry soup and all the dirty pots and dishes were piled on the floor.

The boys were rotting on a diet of fruit soup. They spent their weekends foraging in the mountains. We cleaned everything up, laughing, disgusted, and left behind a note to say we'd been there, Eva and Suzanne—not to worry about three little bears returning in the night while you are sleeping.

HH was very embarrassed when he met Suzanne later. At the time he was taking the *Staatsexamen*. His public health exams. His first exam was Hygiene. Good luck. It was an oral examination. The oral exams were done in groups of five or six. After the exam HH and the other boys decided to make a party. In an effort to make peace, HH invited me along with Suzanne to a restaurant.

It was an underground *Keller*. A dark place with low ceilings and long wood tables and benches. A beer hall. There was music, a band playing, but it wasn't The Beatles. You could dance if both partners were careful, if you ducked your head under the beams. The party continued on late. Dinner and dancing and a lot to drink, quite a lot of beer. You know how people are after taking an exam. They feel set free. Like they've escaped through a tiny hole into a wonderful place. HH surprised me. He was a different person. He introduced me to his friends as, My sister, the great actress.

I almost fell on the floor. My brother, I had never seen him like that before, joking, relaxed.

He danced with Suzanne.

Then it was late. One of the boys lived on the train-line and so he said, since my parents are away, we should go and continue our party there, at my house. But when we arrived we all collapsed, too tired to carry on. We fell to sleep throughout the house, in different beds, one in the tub, one on the floor in the hallway. Suzanne slept on the sofa. When she awoke in the middle of the night, she was surprised that HH was lying beside her. He was awake, watching her until she opened her eyes. He then told her she had the most beautiful white teeth. In fact perfect teeth. And she responded that all the boys said that to her and he should think of something else to say, because she was neither a dog nor a horse. But she understood, he had been studying too hard.

After this Suzanne would go to HH's little house every day after work to cook and tidy up his place, so he could study for his next exams in peace.

After a month I received a letter from HH. Suzanne wanted him to come stay with her, in her mother's house. What should he do?

Go, I wrote to him.

He was gone immediately.

~~OUR JEWISH ORIGINS~~

Whenever I become unsure of my place, I play the tapes. Today is one of those days. I begin with a cassette marked "Proof: University of Breslau 1933–1935" and shortly an hour has passed, swallowed by swirling tiny plastic white teeth.

HH was finishing off his final year at the university when he got notice—someone tipped him off—that he was on some kind of list. He had been identified as a trouble-maker, the authorities had caught up with him and requested—

The black magnetic strip runs transparent and Roland's voice, cut, mid-sentence, is replaced by a neutral hiss.

I press the eject button, pop in another tape, and this time the voice is Eva's. Eva's jokes. Eva's power. Eva's acoustics:

That year HH was sitting for his final exams. There were new rules, legislation, a blood purity act. Nuremberg. Before graduating university students had to prove they came from clean stock, from a reputable race—you needed the official papers—the burden of proof—that declared that your ancestors descended from Zeus.

Proof or else there was no room at the inn.

Hermann Hans didn't have the right papers. He was

sent to a lower court and it was in this Hereditary Health Court that he found out we had the Jewish background.

Verfremdungseffekt! *Our Jewish background. The entire family had a Jewish background!*

On my father's side of the family, crouched very low, there, behind several generations, our bearded Jews were hiding.

We were raised Lutheran. Evangelisch. *We had the pastor, no rabbi. Original sin, never Yom Kippur. Dumpling, not flat bread. Schnitzel, never matzos at the villa.*

Suddenly it was a fact. There was no ritual, no ceremony, we converted on the spot. Pouf! It was written. Pouf! We were Jewish. We became Jewish instantly. Chosen and wanted people. An exceptional case.

Father was outraged. He went to see that wonderful pastor of ours, Pastor Kohler. Anneliese's pastor. Do something! Convince them to stop this!

Pastor Kohler was powerless. He like everyone was impotent against miracles of the state. Race laws and eugenics divided the sea.

We were Moses' people after all.

Germans of the Mosaic persuasion. Mosaicher. Mosaic. Moses. *Jews who assimilated. Jews who embraced Kultur. Good German Jews of the Mosaic persuasion. Jews who tried to escape reality through wish. They broke off from the old tradition and formed a movement loyal to the 'fatherland.' Jews who believed by assimilation they could avoid extermination.*

Mischlinge 2. *This was our type. Half-castes. My brother and I and Anneliese and Romy were* Vierteljuden. *A quarter Jewish each.*

Father was half-Jewish.

Early on he ignored the new reality. He followed a safe routine. Reading the party paper surrounded by a stone wall and gate. Inside the villa, he raised his voice, he shouted louder, much louder than before.

Hitler brings structure!

He is ours!

Early on there were no penalties.

Hitler brings order!

He splits hairs.

He makes lamps from skin.

Father wasn't bothered, no one attacked him in the park, nobody took the trouble to embarrass him at his business. Emil Steinmetz, Saddle-maker. Craftsman. Not yet. Work makes work makes work. He kept busy. But he must have sensed more change was coming. Fire was on fire. For sure it would happen. If it could *happen*, it would *happen*.

And it did: his business was recognized as a Jewish shop. One segment of the Judenparasitenokonomie. The Nazis invented this word. Long as a worm. The Jewish parasitic economy. A bloodsucking eel of many syllables. Father lost workers one by one. This crippled him. Some were afraid. They were scared of being seen working for a Jew, so they quit. They left, no problem. But others turned on him, they exploited the climate. They demanded higher wages, they stole tools from the shop. Little by little it started. The cruelty of children. Impunity, which was a fantasy. And rumours. Emil Steinmetz is a traitor. A war profiteer! Under our nose he counts his blood money. Over whose dead body did he build his fortune? He built on German blood.

Yes, it was true: his shop manufactured prosthetics for war amputees. World War One made him rich. Everyone

*knew that. It was known for years. But now, because he
was a Jew ... it was filthy work and dirty money and as it
turned out he was a war profiteer, a dirty greedy Jew like
the rest.*

I sit the whole day in the front room, swapping tapes, edit-
ing, splicing my father's careful testimony about HH between
longer sequences of Eva's more open narration. For once Eva
and her brother are working together. I limit myself to the
role of stenographer. The wheels start turning. Roland:

*I know that my parents lived together from 1933 on-
wards. They were not married, initially, because there
were difficulties accommodating the opposing houses,
and because, finally, they were not allowed. The state for-
bade it. Papa had Jewish blood, or anyway his father had
more direct Jewish ancestry. Marriage between Aryans
and Jews was verboten. And Papa also was not entitled
to work. The new laws decreed that only Aryans could
study at university, or become professionals. You know
this already. Students were required to provide proof of
their racial heritage, records like baptism certificates and
so forth.*

*Papa's reaction to all this was one of irritation, more
so than fear. The apparatus was seemingly set against
him putting down roots. He felt wronged by the motor
of cause and effect and no longer believed so much in
the invention of a stable reality. The circumstances only
allowed for stubborn life, and for stubborn growth. Everyday his movements were constricted by a group he
crowned the* dunkle Männer. *This was one of his inven-
tions, a neologism.* Dunkel *means dark or dumb, or uncertain. So the dark-minded, or the know-nothings. The
dumb-men. These know-nothings were intimately related*

to the do-nothings, the Taugenichts. *I know that Papa
reserved for the latter the lowest echelon in his caste system.*

Everything was FÜR POLEN UND JUDEN VERBOTEN.

*He was permitted to attend classes, it seems, but from
then on was designated a seat in the back row of the lecture hall. He would sneak around between lectures and
hide from certain people, or else he was afraid Jens or
Ulrich or Tomas or Hansel might spot him, point, grab,
lift him up by the tail, and throw him out the window.
Outside! Get out, go back.*

You there, what were you thinking?

*Generic classmates turned away. Eventually even close
friends dropped him. This must have come as a shock.
For years he had been part of that youth group and gone
travelling with them across much of Europe—hiking,
orienteering, building fires, repeating oaths and reciting poems. And now, push came to shove, and the same
group of friends, some of them yet in his medical school
class, would gladly have seated him in the campfire and
kept up their singing*—Ich hatt' einen Kameraden, Einen
bessern findst du nit ... —*full of patriotic sentiment and
vigour, teary-eyed from the smoke but nonetheless detached from the spectacle, watching him roll and burn
like another book on the censor's list.*

One for All and all For One!

You Are Nothing. Your Volk Is Everything!

*Things became quite serious. His name was on a list
or on multiple lists and he was in real danger of being
collected or confiscated by the authorities who were,
needless to say, by his nomenclature,* dunkle Männer *of
the most rudimentary sort. He struggled to complete his
exams. Apparently the University twice expelled him, let
him go, and then eventually that same sympathetic pro-*

fessor intervened and he was reinstated and then completed his exams in a matter of weeks, not over six to twelve months as was usual. This really was an achievement. All the same, diploma in hand he didn't get very far. Forty-five percent of doctors were party members, a percentage higher than in any other profession.

So he left. He got out. He took off by boat for Africa. He went to Kenya, in British East Africa, where he worked as a farmhand and as a language tutor for an English Jewish family. Something crazy like that. Mama was still in Breslau and Papa was off teaching German in British East Africa to the child of this missionary family. He was very unhappy. It turned out that this English family treated him badly. He boarded in a back house with the black servants, and was an oddity to them. And so after several months here he left to work in a German Mission hospital in Usambara. This was in Tanganyika. T-A-N-G-A-N-Y-I-K-A. *Which had been a German Protectorate. Here, he had a miserable time once again. So not quite a year after leaving Germany—all this happened in eight to twelve months, we are now entering 1936—no, that can't be—sorry, it must be earlier—he was urged to return to Germany by a powerful friend of Suzanne's mother, and promised a position as an intern in the Catholic Hospital in Oppeln.*

So in July 1934 for the sake of argument, he returned to Germany without a medical registration number or whatever it was he was missing, encouraged because apparently there existed a strip of land along the Polish border where the race laws were more lax. There was a free zone in Upper Silesia, the territory disputed between Germany and Poland. The League of Nations was involved here, and they had granted minority rights to Jews in Upper Silesia.

*Greeted in Hamburg by Mama they boarded the train
back to Breslau. Onwards and forward—he completed an internship year in Oppeln and was then offered a
position in the surgical service in Breslau, which he accepted. However, things were still dangerous, not only
because he was Jewish or part-Jewish, but also because
during his university years he had been politically active,
dumb, dumb, dumb, which in those days surely meant
that you were not in favour of your daily bread. So. Life
was compromised. His colleagues became progressively
intolerant, many refused to work alongside a non-Aryan.
He was a foul odour, you see, so he had to leave again, to
find another temporary position, on rotation, as a holi-
day replacement, as a surgeon's assistant, as a chimpan-
zee, anything—he was constantly looking in the newspaper for announcements, for any opportunity. But of
course, in time, the loopholes were closed by* Kranken-
kasse, *the medical insurance board, which finally refused
to acknowledge or pay for his services.*

By this time it was getting late. My grandparents decide to
get married, the hell with it, if not now, when? They couldn't
obtain a civil licence in Breslau but once again some friend
of Suzanne's family came to the rescue and directed them
back to Oppeln, and here my grandparents were married on
25 May 1936. By this date Eva was already in Vienna, and
she no longer had much contact with her family in Germany.
Yet she came to life, fifty years later, when, on a dull day in
London, I asked her to tell me what became of her sisters
Anneliese and Romy:

*A disgrace. The story of Anneliese's round head. My
sister never accepted that she was Mischlinge or a half-
breed. Anneliese never planned on leaving Germany.*

After all she was the perfect example of everything. So she decided to fight the Jewish background. She would not conform to that. No way.

Apparently my parents were minderjährig, *underage, when Anneliese was cooked. Mutti was from the lower class. Her father was a cab driver. Mutti was The Carriage Driver's Daughter. She was found spinning under the wheels of society: When father untangled the mess, dress from wheel axle, he found that she was pregnant. With his own child? By another man's fish? Aha. Either way one thing was certain: Anneliese was* done *before my parents were married. She was made on earth before a promise was made to heaven. I don't know how she discovered this. But right away she asked Papa to write a letter, an official letter, declaring that Mama was pregnant when he married her, and therefore he was not the father.*

Therefore Anneliese didn't share our Jewish background.

It didn't stop here. That was only her start. Step one. For Anneliese it wasn't enough. A formal letter wasn't satisfactory. She recognized this. More bureaucracy was required to prove that she was one-hundred-per-cent squeezed and seedless, Aryan. She needed proof beyond doubt that she came from good livestock. Because if there was any doubt, any question, she would end up in court, or in camp.

Court or camp.

Anneliese went to see a Doktor Katzen, recommended by Pastor Kohler. Katzen was an Africanist. He was an anthropologist, a specialist. A eugenicist. I don't recall his professional show name. He studied race and family origins and tribes and lost nations. He was an expert in

*geography and genealogy and genetics. He called himself
a scientist when in fact he made head measurements.*

*He studied skulls. Doktor Katzen studied the skulls
of the living and the dead. He then made comparisons.
He calculated the dimensions, from back to front and
around the ears and under the chin. He read the skull
like a map. After taking measurements he could tell you
if your grandmother preferred perogies to strudel, if
your great grandfather chewed his corn and if he ate fish
before the Sabbath. He told you if your ancestors came
from Silesia or Prussia or Pomerania: from which territory, from which gene pool.*

*Doktor Katzen measured Anneliese's head. He also re-
searched into our family's roots. Then he came with the
verdict.*

*Her skull was not too small, not too long, not too
round. It was ideal. A perfect example of the Aryan race.*

*Anneliese was safe. She had her letter from Father and
now she could produce her certificate that showed she
belonged in the human race. But Romy had nothing. She
was mute. Romy had no defence. She never had any defence.*

What about Romy?

*That was easy. Anneliese kept Romy as her maid. If
anybody peeked their head in and asked—Romy was an
orphan.*

*Meanwhile, things become difficult for my brother Her-
mann Hans and for Suzanne. Their names are on the list.
Wherever they go, someone follows them. They deserve
special treatment. Terror with no end or an end with terror.*

It starts for real.

Humiliations in the public square. In Breslau. Aryan maidens married to Jews are rounded up, pushed through the streets, heavy signs hanging from the neck:

I Am a Dirty Farm Animal.

I Fornicate with My Pig.

Citizens shout, spit. Mock them from the sidelines, flash their good teeth. The strong blonds throw rotten food at the fallen women: Dirty Farm Animal!

Sick parades, a carnival atmosphere. Circus excitement before the orgy.

Suzanne is in line. She must be. She is first in line to be in the parade, any day now, she is on the waiting list.

Sure enough, one day a pair of Hitler Youth come to the door of the house and ask for the dirty daughter, for the fornicator to step outside. Suzanne's time has come. Two fresh-faced children wait at the front door. Sparkling red heads. Rosy-cheeked youths.

By chance Rudolf, HH's childhood friend, is visiting that day at the house. He is back in Breslau from the military academy and visiting with HH. Rudolf answers the door wearing black. His black uniform. He runs his hand through his hair. Is it a dream? The little shits get frightened. Their smiles disappear. They hesitate, then run away.

This is a warning. They will be back. Like mice in the walls: come winter, come the cold weather, the weak become brave.

My grandparents left Germany in 1936, the same year they were married. I don't know the precise date, but one night—certainly it was summer—my grandfather shouldered his rucksack and walked over the mountains that separate Silesia from Czechoslovakia. These are the Sudety mountains, a system of ridges and massifs, stretching along the frontier.

Dense and impenetrable, these woods were nevertheless the haven of his childhood. During the long holidays he would come here. He'd never carry a tent. He bivouacked under the birches, alders, the local species. Larches, fir trees. At the river's edge he cut branches, laced them together, built himself a raft and placed it on the river. Lying on his stomach he entered Europe, paddling with his arms.

When she first met him, my grandmother Suzanne complained my grandfather was too primitive. Though no telling photograph exists, I expect she found him dashing nonetheless, sporting a bare torso and strapped into a goat skin, chomping on handfuls of nuts and berries. I see him in this role even then, carrying his walking stick, craving a neutral master, a natural religion. Breslau was too confining for him. The masonry, walls, and stone architecture. Nothing built ever supported him.

The mountains were patrolled but because my grandfather was familiar with every path and byway, he got through without any difficulty. Next he found his way into Austria and to Vienna where at that time Eva and Karl had settled into an apartment in close proximity to the Theater in der Josefstadt. It was very cramped, not very comfortable for any of them, but it was secure for the time being.

The very same night, as planned, my grandmother went to the police station in Breslau to apply for an exit visa. She already had her bags packed, but you had to stand in line, make applications, and fill out multiple forms; an absurd and lengthy process, a bureaucracy that foiled the methods of chance. Luck, chance, these things were ruled out, squashed by a preoccupation with knowing and confirming. It was mandatory that Suzanne obtain a travel permit; and the instant she received her papers—stamped, signed, folded—she returned home, kissed her mother Resi goodbye and hurried on to the railway station. And so she was off to Vienna, being afraid, very afraid, all the while that a tired clerk in the visa office would scratch his nose inauspiciously, that a pinwheel in the machinery would click, and he, this Taugenichts, would gaze at the clock to find that her husband was missing and therefore Suzanne's exit in fact was an escape.

From Vienna, my grandparents then tried to emigrate outside Europe. They made applications to countless countries, including China, which in those days must have been unheard of. But these were extraordinary times. They made inquiry after inquiry. Diligently they set to work, writing letters and registering with the embassies, but the door was closed. They were trapped.

Sometime in 1936 my grandfather sent an urgent letter, written in English, to a number of medical schools in Britain. I have a draft copy of this letter, and what always strikes me first when I reread it is the variability in the shades of type, from which I derive the weary state of the typewriter ribbon. In the letter my grandfather states his name, his age (twenty-six), birthplace (Breslau), his years of study. He notes that he spent time in Kenya, British East Africa, working as a farm-hand before returning to Germany and eventually coming to Austria. His language is functional, understated. He writes, 'I wish to emigrate abroad as there are no possibilities for me in Vienna.' Today we know what *possibilities* lay waiting for him and my grandmother had they remained in Vienna. 'The best possibility for me' he writes, 'is to try to come to England and study for one further year in a hospital in order to make my English medical diploma and therefore be enabled to practise as a doctor in the English colonies.' He is sure of that. But midway through, he must address his present situation, the entanglement with medical boards in both Austria and Germany. How to approach the Oxford Don? What to say to the ladies at Cambridge? How will they perceive him?

Should he deceive them? Over this ground, at least in draft form, he stumbles again and again:

> ... *I secured a position as medical assistant in Oppeln. After one year there, I could apply for medical registration since I had the protection of minority rights granted to Jewish in Upper Silesia by the League of Nations, and I became medically registered. But before I got the registration I was dismissed from my hospital post because* of my jewish origins *I had not the Approbation.*

And there on paper his crossed-out Jewish origins: the trademark of a scared animal, leading us through the trapdoor—by slip and slide of the psychopathology of everyday—to the shibboleth of yesteryear. Shibboleth. Who can pronounce this word anyhow? Who can say 'shibboleth' without blowing air out both sides of their mouth at once? No one.

DEUTSCHE GRAMMOPHON YELLOW

Her old records scratch and hiss: Lotte Lenya and Marlene Dietrich on the turntable in the corner while I write. It becomes winter, that Canadian foster child of slow time. Pavel telephones from London to say that Eva is in remission. After spending time in the hospital, she is outraged, What kind of country serves Kraft cheese slices to its sick? No doubt, shunt in place to drain bile, she'd have preferred her tub of goose fat.

Visitors flock in from Europe and across America to visit Eva at 10 Stanley Street. Bedridden, six months into overtime, she receives her audience. Eva is an exceptional case. But the doctors warn us not to get too optimistic. It may be a honeymoon phase. A brief remission of symptoms before the full embrace of body and disease. Aware of this, I maintain one eye on Eva now, one on Eva then, and continue to work under this heartbreaking apartheid. Brecht and his gang were given six months to prepare for Berlin. Eva was given about that much time to live back in July. On slow days, I feel burdened, beset with an urgency to finish this opera before she dies. It is not the deadline I would have chosen for myself, but as reasonable as any, and—if it is any consolation (to me? to Eva?)—I have found that deadlines are rarely respected. Dates slide, and are deflected, reprieves are handed down, sentences commuted—and all along, blind to this bookkeeping, life goes on. And art, art is still more patient.

I have pruned and preened our interviews, obeying instinct, chopping off years and changing names to protect, not family nor the innocent, nor a life, but the story. Story first, morals follow. The vagueness of the rules and the apparent power-lessness of the writer stimulate transferences and distortions of both a sexual and an aggressive sort. Amen. Everyone has their price: prostitutes, beggars, the chief of police, genius and collaborators, even the reader and especially the writer. The writer who least expects this is too firmly aligned to his or her beliefs.

Life is what happens when you breathe. A story is a life pulled through the theatrics of time and place. Eva knew the difference. She was well schooled. She could add and sub-tract, exaggerate or simplify where necessary. Eva and I meet on the high plateau where authorship is shared, where vision is everything and reality nothing. There is nothing to see, neither character arcs nor conflict and resolution—not even a Joseph Stalin or an Adolf Hitler. The process or method entails mostly waiting, absenteeism from the present tense. Loitering at a standing desk within the cathedral of the eter-nal temporary. The hours, studied at length, are colourless, transparent—pure and empty are they, and absolute as con-sciousness. She works from her living script, from memory, while I work with voice and write, locked away in my châ-teau of inexperience, on a quiet page far from anything re-sembling action or plot.

Night. I stand at the table and look out the window, nurs-ing the Deutsche Grammophon fluorescent yellow highlight-er. On her way through Montreal, Eva used to grab a taxi and race up St Laurent Boulevard to Coupe Bizarre, a salon where it was understood that the difference between art and nature in a haircut was about sixty dollars. She was into her seven-ties by this time. After each appointment, she would emerge raving about Yves, full of praise for her hairdresser's wicked eye and shampoo massage. But Eva's hair looked about the same, to me, always. It was cut short, and dyed a metallic white. It had no body, no curl. She wore it straight.

I wander over to the turntable and stare through the small opening at the optical pulse, warming to the stroboscopic effect, the orange glow. Around I go on this carousel with Eva: close to one hundred years, I realize, since Eva took Bimbo into her arms and carried him to the Breslau Zoo. But it's nothing. One hundred years is nothing. Near the end of her life everything has become 'meanwhile.'

'Meanwhile, in Vienna,' she would begin. 'Meanwhile, in Berlin.' Her opening lines were often drenched in sarcasm: 'Meanwhile, in the Third German Zoo ...'

With a statement like 'Meanwhile, in Zurich ...' Eva did not mean *at the same time in Zurich;* she meant, rather, *at the same time plus or minus five to thirty years.* Eva trumped the calendar with character. She implied that a range of thirty years, or five or fifty years, made no difference. It wasn't that her memory was failing—the opposite was true. Through memory, she was saving experience, redeeming it from time's linearity, the ruthlessness of numbers—from rigid conclusions of cause and effect. Her memory shot through every age, simultaneously, back to front and front to back, the eternal through the heart of the ephemeral. Eva spoke like a champion. The victor writes history; the adult writes childhood; and identity is something like a personal best. It survives the truth. When Eva talked to me, time glistened in her eyes. I found that if I listened to the tapes in a random sequence, it was the only way I could begin to see things her way.

§ § §

In the asphalt city, in Vienna, we were comfortable. Newspapers. Tobacco. And brandy. Every last sacrament. Espresso and chocolate. And dream analysis.

When Hitler stepped onto the podium in Nuremberg, the avant-garde took a trip over the Alps. Swept off one stage, the show reopened down the road. First in Vienna, then Zurich. At the Theater in der Josefstadt, then in the Züricher Schauspielhaus. Austria and Switzerland never had such fantastic theatre. They had no idea what hit them. The cafés in Vienna overflowed with actors, artists, intellectuals, writers, producers and directors from Germany. The circus came to town. An explosion of newcomers and strangers. Vienna flowered overnight.

In Vienna you also had the Freuds and Adlers, and their groups of disciples. Imagine hundreds of young psychoanalysts. Lost minds wandered in the street like children, dazed on their way to school. There was a mix of émigrés and refugees. To go looking for a particular branch of psychology, you only needed to find out in which café the associates made their headquarters. The Freudians at Café Siller on Franz-Josef Kaistrasse. The Adlerians at Café Elbe on Leopoldstrasse. Long hours were spent around marble tables. Arguing, debating, and sorting through the newspapers. Depending where you came from, from which region in Germany, there was a café in the neighbourhood suited to your needs: a café where you could find the newspaper from Breslau or Bremen or Baden-Baden or Berlin.

We spent our time waiting with no routine to set us straight in Eternal Temporary Vienna. Long hours in the cafés sorting through facts and rumours. I held my face in my hands and I burned cigarette after cigarette. I hovered over white cups of coffee. Blew waves around the rim. Like every other refugee I had no clue what this life was about. I was unhappy. We were unsettled. Karl and I separated for a time. We went our own ways. Not very far but in opposite directions. Kaput. Act five, scene five. To the audience: *He sleeps at the theatre or at a friend's apartment or with his mistress.*

There was already a mutual friend. Manès Sperber the psychoanalyst. He held court at the Keppler. That was his café schoolhouse. One afternoon I found him there at one of those round marble tables reading the newspaper. Drinking a coffee, smoking a cigarette. Later on, when business picked up, he was surrounded by disciples. A group of thinkers and students. Sperber was their teacher. He was a Marxist, a Jew, a psychoanalyst—not a friend of the Nazis. He and Karl, already, had a political connection.

The other dreamers respected Sperber. They gathered at the café together to discuss books and their ideas. They went on adventures carried off by their own voices. They leaned over the little round tables together like old women cooking over fires. It was the ritual of the intellectual. Marble-table talk. I came there and I felt the excitement in the air, their arguments and new ideas, terrific things, terrific things that came from nowhere, from nothing. They were beginning to build something. I wanted to be part of it.

Meanwhile in '38 the Anschluss. Germany rolls into Austria. Anschluss means 'connection.' *Anschluss finden* means making friends. Germany invaded, and Germany and Austria made friends!

German Speaking Republics as One! *Erwache*! Awake, Awake! German speakers in one house, awake!

Weg Frei für den Frieden! The Path is Free for Peace!

In the kitchen there I would sit and listen to the broadcast on my radio. My Norwegian Radionette. My one companion. My Norwegian waitress who wears burlap over her speakers. She has one green electric eye. She broadcasts Bach and Goebbels and Hitler. Weg Frei für den Frieden! Her upholstery bounces. Erwache! Hitler's voice, I had his voice inside my four walls. Karl was off sleeping with his mistress, and meanwhile I had the Führer for company. For company now for years I had him.

History. From '33 to '38 it was a slow process. But when Germany took Austria, the change was dramatic. It was instant. An orgy. Every animal in the zoo ... out of its cage. Vienna sunk. Out my window I saw: in the road, crawling on hands and knees, ancient men in long beards. Hebrews licking the paving stones. Licking the streets clean.

Everybody could see. The crowd had gathered for the Queen's parade, and everybody did their nothing. Their do-nothing.

I had to escape Vienna. Although we were split, Karl and I decided to join forces again to defeat the enemy. We had no money between us for a bribe. I stared out my window day after day. There was no escape route, there was no tunnel to the other side that I knew of. But we had to find a way to Witchesland. Below in the street was the circus. Soldiers carrying whips. I watched children break their sticks. Citizens holding signs. *Wien Judenrein.* Vienna without Jews. Ridded of Jews. That was their wish. Their dream. *Wien Judenrein.*

Well, it was our dream also: to escape.

I couldn't stop staring, until one afternoon I looked straight down and sure as I knew I was going to get out, Rudolf was in Vienna. HH's friend, the 'POW.' Now officer. In his black uniform. Proud SS. Smoking, stepping through.

Rudolf in Vienna. Sure enough. It was the usual game.

VIENNA

Irises, your irises beat like butterfly wings. While your larynx is cartilage, yes? A natural fibreglass.

The baton slips up your neck like a rolling pin.

Stop. Your tears catch nothing but his reflection: the black swan swerving above you may as well be your childhood sweetheart. Unerring, he rips the fluff from your adorable white body, rummaging, he riffles through you.

Done. You swallow hard, the wood thrums your throat.

Your larynx switches sides.

Meanwhile there is another story.

The officers wear knee-high riding boots. And Rudolf is an officer, how fitting. He wears breeches on his promenade, this spring day in 1938, strolling mindlessly through the herd of hump-backed Hebrews—a towering black shepherd he is, working the streets of Vienna. They are like rats with long whiskers for scrub brushes. There they go picking between, and polishing cobblestone.

He stops, stands still in the street. Does he pause to ponder? Is it the history of the place, the art nouveau paintings and architecture? Or the palette of these facades, the scent of burnt coffee, a childhood memory loosening from the empire of adulthood? The squeal of a frustrated mechanism as the shopkeeper turns down his awning? No. None of these. It has recently stopped raining. The air is atomized. Misting.

He rolls out of his mind and says such and such and such and such, and the old man at his heels turns upwards, his head back over his shoulder. Rudolf nods—and you, Eva, watch from your window in dismay, astonished and not astonished, when the old-timer crouches low, lower, to lick clean Rudolf's riding boots.

Rudolf pays no attention. Isn't it marvellous? Instead he stares off down the street, far as one can see, to the very end where Vienna meets the horizon.

Who was he looking for, just then?

And you already are watching him from your window.

This works out well.

He knows you are in Vienna. He has a nose for these things. He heard by letter that you are stuck in Austria, trapped with your actor-husband Karl, a communist, who cannot make anything happen: Anschluss or no Anschluss, offstage he is nothing. So it was only a matter of time. Really only a matter of gazing into the distance until he found you.

That very night, Rudolf visited your apartment. Just as soon as he could manage it he came for you, gasping for air—as if you *both* were in a hurry to escape.

Karl never knew anything. He was ignorant. *He's not a communist for nothing*, Rudolf admonished—and you were tricked by that figure of speech. Rudolf explained: Now Eva, there is an escape mechanism, a set route to Zurich over the mountains, but first of all we should play the old game. Our old game. You nod your head while Rudolf makes the preparations for tomorrow night (he does so by rolling up his sleeves). You feel dizzy as he arranges for a car (he does so by standing up from the chair). You accept on behalf of Karl his best wishes (Heil Hitler, he raises his right arm). And you faint after he leaves (he closes the door anyway).

The next day his car and driver come. He surprises you in

the car by his presence. He snickers. Could it be he is laughing at how ceremonial this seems now in the car? That the manner in which one exists is more formal than one could ever suppose? No time. Off you go through the streets of Vienna. Rudolf leans his head against the side window. He is taking you to an apartment. What apartment? Officers' quarters. Which? Never mind. Together you are going to consult. Consult who? Never mind. Vienna is magnificent. Don't ruin it. *You are the one in the car, the one by the side window,* around and around the streets, *you are this very one encased by the years.* Through interlocking neighbourhoods, you drive past the great stone houses, handsome and magisterial facades hewn from the evening itself. Gardens and trees, villas surrounded by walls.

Then you arrive at the gate. The driver opens the side door.

Here we are. Rudolf glances through the window and next you are climbing the steps up to the front door behind him. The car and driver are gone by the time you reach the decision finally, that this is better: much better to have an end with terror, than terror without end. Buoyed by that rich slogan you enter the front hall and discard your face to the oval mirror, which is substantial.

The mirror is dull as well. The frame is gold-leaved and the iron eagle is perched on the apex, its neck askew: alert, searching for prey in its frozen state. A bronze-gold monstrosity, the blackened bird. Well, the thing makes good sense. Rudolf is gone. He went off one way down the hall through your mind leading to the next room. He disappeared.

Slowly you enter the house, the honeycomb of rooms. Turkish carpets, African sculpture, a bust of Mozart, oil paintings, a rosewood harpsichord, a Renaissance sofa, a grandfather clock, a piano. Immense. This decadence. The objects soaked by a tide of semi-darkness. There is no continuity, no comparison to the apartment you share with Karl, no connection. You are alone here in these officers' quarters—or is it the house of a very rich ... it doesn't matter. No use taking notes, the dining room, the salon, the library.

Rudolf reappears from a side room, above you, beside you. He veers towards you with a glass of wine in his hand, for you, and whiskey for him.

Aperitifs.

Rudolf is in difficulty. His cheek twitches. There, you see, a tiny man inside the cavity of his mouth is pulling the rope and stretching his lips sideways, revealing his teeth. Someone is concealed inside, drawing the pull cord.

You can see over the top of the curtain: utter confusion. Those eyes are red, raw, wet with decay. He has no clue, you realize, no idea what it is all about. He is a boy, a little boy. All little boys are the same. You know how to handle them. Nothing will happen to you if you handle this right. He is injured, you are his nurse, you have the same hands, the same hair, he has the same memory, the same wounds, the same appearance as before.

But. Then. He switches places on you. He switches from past to present, from present to past. Give up. He has you. He hates you. He wants you. Kneeling before you, princess, slowly he rises. Again a trick. Again the game. Cup of whiskey, cloth, bucket. Strange. One arm around your waist and now his head on your breast. The man is injured, he is sobbing sick. He pushes you onto the chair and follows forward with his weight. Then he starts undoing you. Buttons. Here more buttons. He rips your clothing. Still more. He will get there. He will undo the past and present. He tears at them, sobbing, and then he switches again. From sentimental to sober.

He tightens his grip. He's found the strength.

He slaps the rosewood baton into the palm of his hand.

Silence.

Oh Eva, he says. I am the officer here, I give the orders. It's very, very important that you follow my instructions.

He takes you by the hair, by the neck like a goose, and leads you into the bedroom—the circus chamber, an old world—and there you see him, turned a definite angle, you see him in the mirror, you see him in the chair, but are you sure that is him? Are you sure it is you? This is not believable. What is wrong with him? You must find the spot. Find the spot where he hurts.

Meanwhile he takes you, skin and hair, by hand and by mouth. He growls. He lands on you. Play your part, he taunts. Perform, assume a virtue. He picks through your mind and memory and he turns you sideways and back and rolls you onto your stomach and pinches you and then he throws you onto the floor and forces his thing in. His fish.

He feels filthy, he tells you, because you are filth. He says he will take a bath (and he does take a bath).

Meanwhile. The instructions are in an envelope by the door. You hadn't noticed, entering, but an envelope has been placed in the beak of that eagle, an obvious place. Open, read it. The directions are simple. Go to such and such a place. Insanely simple. There is a barn, hide in the barn. Wait quietly there. Someone will come. Again wait. Someone will come and guide you across the mountains. And sure enough there is an escape chain over the mountains to Switzerland. Sure enough, the next day, you will flee Austria in a fabulous story, running through the forest and across fields, hiding in barns along the way. (Nature was: serene. Sure enough: it was obscene.) You vomited day and night, you were sick to your stomach. You knew. You knew what to do.

But now: You slip the envelope under your skirt. You open the front door, *and then you close the front door*. Half and half. Free to go but you stand before the mirror like the past looking into the future. You are the one in the house. You looking ravaged. Now you walk back down the hall. You hear the running water. You remember scene and act. No one can change your course of action; not you, not Agamemnon—and not the spectators who watch, from generation to generation, helpless as you bloody the stage.

Rudolf had those arms, those long white arms that he spread across the rim of the bathtub. He turned his head. Eyebrows rose.

The air divided above and terror entered your life.

You sunk the iron eagle into his skull.

That is art.

And you watched for the outpouring of evil.

WITCHESLAND

Meanwhile, in Zurich. I didn't want Michael to grow up, not in my exile, not in our zoo. I pleaded with him: keep small, Michi. Hide under my breast. Here between the two it's warm and there's room for you. Squeeze in between left and right. But stay out of the way. I don't want you to grow up. Not here. Not now. Not in Witchesland.

You can imagine the kind of mother I was. I pleaded with him: Return to the womb, go back to the blackboard, Michi. Hide away my son. Can you call her 'mother' if she doesn't want her first-born to crawl, if she doesn't want her son to speak, if she doesn't want him to have hair? Is she his mother or is she a witch? Keep small, Michi. Disappear. Crawling, talking, walking: none of these were cause for celebration. Not for me. On the other hand the war spread across Europe. The waters broke and it came out. War. It rolled over and the war held its head up on its own neck. It crawled and then took its first steps into Poland and Poland cried out. The war grew up under my nose and it turned into something I didn't recognize.

Karl and I had split. Once or twice we tried it again but nothing worked. I couldn't make it come, and when I was supposed to feel it, I couldn't—I was numb. I wanted a divorce. Karl wanted a divorce, too. But there was no divorce for us and no love either in the family. There was war. There was silence.

In Zurich we couldn't get a divorce, actually, because we were not Swiss. Karl and I were immigrants you see and the government refused to come between us. On Swiss soil we didn't have the right to a divorce or the right to work. We had no rights. It was a privilege to have survived. Many did not. We were among the few who escaped from Austria and Germany to Switzerland. We'd escaped—two of us to the sound of music, hadn't we? Over mountains we'd come to this island in the clouds, a floating plate of cheeses and chocolate and wines, and we had no right to a divorce. We had survived. That should have been enough.

Lucky for us, we had made it to Switzerland before the DP camps were set up. During wartime, refugees were rounded up by the border patrol and put in camps. Refugees and immigrants were not welcome. Switzerland was overcrowded. It was already overpopulated. For us it was different because Karl had his contacts at the Schauspielhaus and he immediately, against state rules, was given an engagement. So straight away we were off the street, out of sight. We were a special case: separated but not divorced and sleeping on the floor on our sides. Michael crawled over top of us, and tried to save us with his laugh or smile but the little mountaineer was too late.

Come hide, I whispered. Here it's warm and there's room for you.

Seven years in Zurich. Meanwhile I began my accordion life. I took lessons twice a week, I practised eight hours a day. Michi loved music. He had no choice. When I wanted to accomplish something, I usually accomplished it, even in exile. I lived on my old ballads and joined a quartet. Guitar, accordion, piano and violin. We performed in taverns. I was proud, I was happy with the accordion. A girl with her gift. That went on some months. Then I heard at the Schauspielhaus they needed an accordion player. It was a chance to get back to theatre so I auditioned without informing Karl. The director offered me a contract. They were doing Shakespeare. *The Tragedy of Macbeth*. I was hired to sit in the pit and squeeze my arms.

Poor Karl. He was not impressed. By then he had moved on. He had moved on to his mistress. He had moved out of my circle.

Karl played king. King Duncan. When rehearsal started the first day he sighted me down in the orchestra pit with my accordion, and he froze. He turned pale and pointed at me, one finger. I was his mole of nature. His tragic flaw. His Lady Macdeath of the Accordion.

Immediately he stepped forward on the stage, under the lights: Karl shouted at the director who was sitting in the dark.

No way, there is no way I can act, no way! Not with her squatting in the pit! Not with my wife crushing the accordion like some giant chicken!

He squawked. He flapped his arms. Karl tore out his hair. He performed.

The director didn't have a clue what the fuss was all about. He stepped out of the darkness: What's the problem? Who is the girl? A German Jew. A refugee. Karl Paryla's young wife. His estranged wife. Oh, I see. She's desperate. But she can certainly play.

Karl couldn't act with me staring up at him from the pit. He was so afraid that the music would not come, when it was supposed to come out of me. He was frightened that from my angle, below, I would look right into him.

After Shakespeare was Goethe and after Goethe inevitably came the Greeks. Romance, comedy, tragedy. The worn repertoires of fate. Throughout the war years those sessions went on, hours of practice, days of rehearsal, inside the Zurich Schauspielhaus.

The theatre was an empty box. That's all it ever was, an empty box removed from the street. But a box with the potential to explode. It was liberating, and cruel. Karl couldn't live outside of it. He couldn't survive without the artificial air. He appeared as the cook in Brecht's *Mother Courage and Her Children*. He also played a part in the world premiere of *Life of Galileo*. The world premiere! There was no point in 1943. Outside the bright day was buzzing. Inside they were working in gloomy spirits on a world premiere. Outside, across Europe, soldiers were squinting down the barrel: learning to aim and fire. Inside actors were finding their character. They were learning gestures. They were taking on voices. Karl already had years of experience in conflict resolution: in climax and denouement. Outside they burned villages. They drank black milk at daybreak. They drowned communists, skinned gypsies and gassed the Jews. Inside seated under the mezzanine spectators welcomed conflict. It was necessary on the stage. Outside they took turns killing, inside the director judged each performance and expected a breed of perfection that couldn't and didn't exist—that had no business in the mind. The critics judged performances more harshly than reality.

Outside death. Inside, the world premiere of *Life of Galileo*.

Against Karl's wishes, I stayed in the orchestra several months for the running of Macbeth. I put my head down and returned, rehearsal after rehearsal, carrying my accordion in the black box through the empty foyer into the auditorium. My footsteps echoed. I knew Karl was sitting in the dressing room, fuming. He was slumped in front of the mirror, staring at his own hands, reading his future from his own palm. I was carrying in a bomb. Down in the pit I lay the case on its side and flipped the latches. There it was. My bomb pressed in red velvet. I hung it across my chest. I played!

Instead of getting a divorce, one night I received a phone call from a man who asked to speak with 'the actor Karl Paryla.'

He's not here, I told the mysterious caller. Who is this?

Oh, he said—Hello, Eva? It's Manès Sperber.

Then I told him: Karl makes his bed someplace else. We're no longer together. He's no longer the same man. He's King of Scotland. His days are limited. You'll find him rather at the Schauspielhaus ...

Oh, I can't go there, he said.

Then come to us. Come stay here.

Manès Sperber had made his swim in the cold night through the Rhine. He'd escaped the south of France and arrived in Switzerland with pneumonia. When he telephoned, I didn't recognize his voice. He was hoarse. He'd been on the run. Manès was lost. He was somewhere—he didn't know where, but in Zurich—standing in a phone booth. He was hiding from the border patrol. I told him my Karl is gone but if you want you can come and stay with me and Michael at such and such an address.

Manès was in terrible shape. He needed to see a doctor but there was no way I could call for a doctor. That would have been suicide. That would have been the end. I had to hide him. I gave him a bath and cigarettes and a bed and he went to sleep. He lay curled on his side like a sinking ship. And Michael lay down beside him. Right away they formed a partnership. Michael and Manès. Manès stayed with us several months. He lay in bed, and in bed, and in bed. Michael thought that was so funny. To have a grown man who lies in bed all day. It was terrific news for him. He covered Manès in the blanket and carried around his pillows and brought him his tea. In return, when he got better, Manès started French lessons for Michael. That's how Michael learned a little French before going to school.

For months we stayed inside together, us three. We lived quietly. There was no opportunity for the top hat. No chance to wear a dress. I played the accordion. Manès read and wrote in his diary. You know, I told him, I once had a diary, too. What happened to it? He asked. That's an old story, I told him, an old story I would rather forget.

We put on our own plays and puppet shows and built a theatre for ourselves under blankets hung on chairs and the table. It was a children's theatre. The best world for us three. Michael loved it. For him finally there was action. And something was happening to us. It was happening under the blankets. All together we were changing. When Michael fell asleep at night Manès and I talked. I didn't have to tell him, he knew Michael never would have a father. But, he said, every human being needs love.

I broke down. Yes, I know. I cried. But what do you think? Mother courage doesn't exist around here.

Yes she does, he said. He was firm. YES, YOU DO.

Finally, near the end of 1943, I read in the newspaper an urgent call for volunteers. There was an outbreak of scarlet fever in Zurich. I left Michael with the neighbour for the day and I reported to the address, a school gymnasium. There was only one nurse and one student nurse taking care of one hundred and fifty beds. Nobody else had responded, they took me right away. They gave me a white uniform. I went to work wearing a cap shaped like a paper boat.

At the end of the first day, I said I'm exhausted. I have to go back home. I must get back to my little boy.

Are you crazy? They looked at me, astonished. You can't go

home. Now you're in quarantine. Scarlet fever is infectious. You're one of us. You cannot leave.

So I was in quarantine for three weeks. That was incredible—three of us taking care of one hundred and fifty scarlet-fever patients. It was a great adventure for me and for the neighbour who took care of Michael. There were complications with some patients and specialists were called in. Even the student nurse got sick. Then there were only two of us. We worked ourselves to the bone. And when it was all over the head doctor arrived and he and the nurse thanked me and said about the pay—you volunteered, we know—but there is a reward and we will send it to you.

I said, definitely not. I am an immigrant here. You cannot pay me. That's not acceptable. It isn't even legal.

Instead of paying me they gave me a certificate and a recommendation of my work. The certificate was my ticket into Swiss life. With my certificate I was chosen next by a Catholic group to be involved in a refugee program. All those organizations, Christian, Catholic, Jewish, worked together making plans to manage the refugees after the end of the war. We were in rehearsal, us too. They trained us as child welfare officers, and we became part of the relief strategy. It was a wonderful thing again. All the other volunteers were more qualified, but I had my certificate.

When the training program finished it was still only 1944. We were prepared to launch our relief strategy and fly into the war-torn countries. There were plans to build refugee shelters in key points and networks were ready to go to distribute food. But the war continued. The Nazis were slowly on the retreat, leaving behind only darkness. The organization I worked with was taking care of orphans. So instead of flying out of Witchesland, I was assigned to a DP camp after all, and put in charge of the orphans. Papers had to be filled out, case histories collected. That was my assignment:

to interview as many orphans as I could. To make a record for each. To find out about their past, and help them plan their next step.

Shame. The stories that came out of their mouths. Like Romy they were frozen at eye-level and could hardly speak. Pain as dry as teeth. Children robbed of magic. Shame on life. Shame on every one of us.

4

PROOF

Oh to wander again, undistinguished,
unattached and poor.
To silently walk through cities, aloof,
and to rest in the woods
and by the sea.
To live among people, unnoticed,
known to no one,
everywhere
and everything foreign,
and the ships, all still, in the harbour;
to go all places, where nobody is.

HERMANN HANS STEINMETZ, *Monologue with God*

*Their ship left from Genoa, stopped in Marseilles, then
set a course across the Atlantic, through the Panama
Canal, down the West Pacific coast, to the port of Buenaventura. Six weeks. During this time the passengers—two-hundred and fifty political refugees—were
kept down in the hold of the ship, men separated from
women by a grilled partition. They were all, except my
parents, communists. The operation leaders had picked a
mechanic, an engineer, tinker, tailor, baker, farmer—you
name it, the complementary skills and trades to lay the*

foundation for a self-sufficient community. But among their chosen class they had had trouble finding a doctor. They accepted my father only after he pleaded with them, and then offered a bribe. That he was Jewish, or part Jewish, was problematic but less heinous to them than his socio-economic standing: he was, Marx forbid, bourgeois.

Once or twice a day this human cargo was hauled on deck where my parents could breathe some fresh air. They would spend the half-hour talking while the ship continued on through the Panama Canal, then down the coast of Colombia.

They docked in Buenaventura and directly, without a stopover, they were sent in a convoy of trucks to a place called Popayan. Outside Popayan is a village which I have never seen on any map, called Totoro. T-O-T-O-R-O. Neighbouring Totoro, the operation leaders had bought land, sight unseen. Hacienda Buena Vista. The farm with the good view. Good View Farm. Home away from home.

Well, there was no farm. What was there? Hardly anything at all. An estuary of huts and shacks lay at the foot of a mountain. The land was unsuitable for agriculture. The people were let out of the trucks and the vehicles drove off. Immediately, or anyhow within days or weeks, these people started quarrelling, one incriminating the other, brothers and sisters, children and elders, comrades and mothers and fathers. Apparently, a large group split off and left straight away for the capital, Bogotá, while the majority remained behind in Totoro.

My parents stayed put because Mama was pregnant. They occupied a primitive building with mud walls, and little ventilation. The room they shared with two other families had no windows. I was born soon after arrival in

*Totoro, on 13 May 1937. Carried all this way by Mama,
I was delivered on term by Papa—I broke from his hands
into the jungle without complications.*

*Farming proved a catastrophe. Living humbly, in peace,
proved demoralizing. They were the dispossessed. There
was no revolution to fight, no enemy on hand but survival itself. Survival meant looking at yourself, it meant,
Here's looking at you kid. Here were these white folk,
traces of every lost European tribe and trade gathered
together, forming the basis for a self-sufficient community, and they were hardly able to feed themselves. They
worked on the land and planted their crops in rows but
it was useless. The jungle is limitless and jammed with all
forms and patterns of life. It assimilates you. But coming
from the first world—whatever their class or ideology—
the community clung to the notion that they were colo-
nialists of one kind, Europeans, if not Aryans then plain
Caucasians. Buena Vista Farm must have attained some
kind of subconscious recognition as an 'outpost'—as
their 'camp in the interior'—when in fact it was not at all
dark or morose as in vogue literary cautionary tales often
it is, but brilliant and brittle. The flora was stunning. The
elements were harsh. Hard and bright. Forget the incho-
ate sounds or intimations of metaphor, forget and erase a
scheming, sensual, lugubrious texture, there was no heart
of darkness, nothing but stark reality, a fierce physicality.*

*I remember because the playground threat of tropical
exotica intruded upon my childhood. Snakes, and spi-
ders, crippling sun. The sun and humidity caused nausea
in those not accustomed to it, and many were not accustomed to it. For all the colour of its plants and flowers the foothills of the Andes were alienating enough for
a couple from Silesia. There was some optimism at the*

beginning that the Indians would join our ranks; you
know, perhaps savages and communists shared the same
discontents, even a common psyche. What is more uni-
versal than human suffering?

But the Indians treated them—us—coldly. Or indif-
ferently. This land, the Hacienda, was never an out-
post to the native or indigenous people. They had lived
throughout the area for millennia; foreign to them was
this group of leftists dropped in their midst, this bizarre
collection of hunterless men and pale women and sickly-
frightened children. Between the two groups there was
bickering, but ultimately no combat, no systematic exter-
mination. But neither was there any easy mingling in the
markets, no sharing of virgins or cigarettes.

Inside the settlement, as I gather from Roland's wry appraisal, 'little Europe' began to crumble and eventually it fell apart, mirroring events across the ocean to some degree. The family was ostracized within their own community. When the doctor was useful he was useful, but otherwise my grandfather was an outcast, a class felon. The quarter-Jewish doctor and his bourgeois wife and child were a foul odour among the rest of them. Although they boasted no material advantage over the blacksmith or baker, my grandparents were steered to one side of the camp. Discrimination, even here, was a very strong force.

Eventually the family moved from the farm into Popayan, and here my grandfather set up an outdoor surgery, and my grandmother started a bakery. He went daily to the market and placed a chair under a tree. Suzanne baked bread and sold her bread in the day surgery waiting room—that is, under the shade of the next tree over. Hermann Hans pulled teeth, animal and human, whichever were rotten, but ultimately he became known for amputations.

This was the ace up his sleeve. Performing amputations was his bread and butter. He was frequently called when infection had travelled up from a green toe— they came running when an accident had left some poor labourer with one of his limbs hanging by a tendon. They gathered my father at our door and then walked him to the spot, often escorting him a fair distance into the jungle. When it was urgent, when one magic already had failed, then they came for the white doctor. And apparently, good for him, because it was not his habit to put on airs, he did really perform for them. Uncertain of what calamity awaited him, from the outset he was aware of being scrutinized. When he arrived at the cabin the people inside drew back and the patient was revealed to him, lying on a cane mat, shivering or moaning. Customarily, he said, there was some sort of mat on the dirt floor. Quite often they expected a miracle. On these excursions he came to question why human suffering time and again has been confused with the question of the existence or non-existence of God. He came to realize that human misery is human misery. It was a child with an infection with a fever with seizures with a black foot. Almost certainly suffering was the recognition or acceptance of what he found when he arrived to do his amputation.

There was no time to waste.

He unsheathed his cutting knives, deliberately doing this, while uttering German nonsense. He grasped that all good magic was finely dressed and wrapped in ritual. Over time he developed a repertoire of extravagant behaviours to inform this brutal act with the aura of the unexplained. It made all the difference. Nowadays we prefer the antiseptic—denial in a general anaesthetic—over enchantment. But over sixty years ago, newly arrived on the continent, Papa gave the people what they wanted. He put on a show for both the patient and the spectators.

I once asked him about this, about the primitive tools he was forced to use and his method, and if it bothered him to carry out amputations in those settings.

No, he responded, gruffly. It didn't bother him. The Indians were a brave people and anyway, all he had to do was to cut the whole way through. Any idiot can do it, he said, and smiled right then. Many idiots make their living doing it.

TRANSFERENCE

In 1942, after six years in Popayan, my parents moved the family to the capital. We left in a caravan for the high plateau of Bogotá. En route Papa made three amputations. On an indigenous boy my same age, on a farm labourer and—his last was on Mama. He carried the medical instruments he'd rescued from Germany in a black leather handbag. Mama's problem: a snake bite. She was wearing sandals. Hers was the left foot.

Upon arrival in the big city we had many adventures because my parents had no money. My father carved out a reputation for himself and made house calls to the European embassies; as a white doctor he was trusted, but as a displaced quarter-Jew without a medical license he was abused: they calculated how little they could get away with paying him, how much they could withhold.

We were four by then, with my younger brother Jens. In Bogotá we boarded with a succession of families as emergency guests. There was one childless couple called Ballack—also German—and we stayed with them for six months. Herr Ballack was an architect. He'd come to Colombia on a contract to design and build the National University on what was then the edge of the city. And when he finished the job, Hitler was Chancellor and the Ballacks decided not to return.

Ballack was a very peculiar man, at least that was my impression. He worked through the night and slept during the day. One afternoon, shooting marbles in the courtyard, I knocked my favourite white banja astray. It clattered on the terra-cotta tiles and rolled into the sunroom. I went to retrieve it and discovered Herr Ballack lying flat on the wicker ottoman. Black patches tied over his eyes, although heavy drapes blocked the windows. His presence faintly terrified me. Indeed there was something unnatural about this man who designed his buildings inside-out and slept counter-clockwise. My own father and my mother were always hard at work. They never *stopped* working. So when Herr Ballack jumped up from his dream with those black eyes of his, I ran from the room screaming and empty-handed.

My brother Jens was four at the time. I was at the age when you take on the responsibility of showing the younger sibling the ropes, extending his horizons, helping him to a full plate of experience. I wanted to really frighten Jens. I would hold his hand but I was sure going to show him. What could it be?

I had limited options. Our host Herr Ballack was perhaps the best bet. On top of his other oddities, there was the fact that he'd recently wrecked his left hand in an auto accident. It was wound in a pale bandage which my father applied, making it taut, ravelling it until it looked like Herr Ballack had a wasp nest on his wrist, a bloated thing that he kept buried in the sling hung across his chest.

In the evening my father set his bag on the kitchen table and cleaned Ballack's hand with iodine and told him how lucky he'd been. No infection, no amputation.

Yes, I could take my brother Jens to see napping Herr Ballack. Or, I could sneak away my father's medical bag and share a look at the insides. The sleeping architect wearing the freakish mask or father's medical bag? Papa had told me when I asked him that an amputation was easy to perform and that most people are courageous when you give them the opportunity. I'd in turn told Jens a formidable lie for which he gave me three black banjas and a bumblebee: I told him that after Papa performed an amputation he collected the pieces, and that's why his bag didn't close. The bulging base meant it was full.

Even Mama's foot? Jens, though quivering, had begged that it be true. He knelt on the terra cotta beside me and, squinting, waited; I squeezed my new marbles in one fist, making the scratch of glass-on-glass.

He has to, I replied, erasing Jens' question and forgiving Papa for something he'd never done, *in case he needs money and has to sell them*. Not counting his medical toolbox, the only item of value my father had rescued from Germany had been his stamp collection. It was lightweight and he knew in an emergency he could sell it to the right buyer. Our first week in Bogotá he'd sold the collection to an Austrian and used the money to pay back a loan—perhaps a loan from the Ballacks themselves.

Between ghost limbs and sleeping Herr Ballack, however, I chose the latter. The siesta encroached on our terrain. Napping trespassed on childhood, which was ours. Together we could sneak inside the sunroom, and, if we were very quiet, inch forward and stand above him while on the couch unawares he would go on dreaming of one of his buildings. Perhaps dreaming of the walls, the empty rooms of the university city. Perhaps dreaming of money. Money on trees. Of gold. Pavilions standing on roads paved with gold.

I'd planned this return expedition from the very day I had run from the sunroom, but there was no opportunity for the next couple of weeks, because Herr Ballack had gone out of town on a business trip. We were left alone in the house with Frau Ballack. She was a nervous woman. Urta was her name. In contrast to Mama she was mostly idle, though consumed by fidgeting. She must be so, I thought, because she is pretty and because she has no children of her own yet. She wore colourful dresses and liked to garden—flowers, no vegetables—and she smoked cigarettes using a long thin holder. Sometimes she would smoke at mealtimes and not even touch her food. My parents repeatedly warned me off staring at her full plate.

In the evening, Urta insisted that my father accompany her for long walks in the city parks. Her husband was too busy or away on business. Mama had a hard enough time keeping up all day. By evening she raised her legs and even as a child I read to her. My father could not be rude and refuse going; after all, we were guests in the Ballack's house. It was a difficult situation, but on those evening strolls Papa learned his way around the nomenclature of countless plants, their Latin, Spanish, English and German titles.

Finally one night about two weeks later we heard that Herr Ballack was coming home from his trip. He would be arriving back in Bogotá while we were asleep. Urta told us so at the dinner table. I noticed she knocked ash into her cup of coffee. Secretly I was exhilarated. Arriving in the night, after travelling, Herr Ballack would be exhausted and certainly then sleep off the day. I planned our excursion for the next afternoon.

The house was silent. Jens and I were playing marbles as usual after lunch. Up to then I had kept my plan a secret. We could crack the sunroom door open and enter from the courtyard. When I sprang it on Jens his eyes opened wide, then wider: a fine idea it was to him. Anyhow the sun was blazing in the corner where we played. We came in through the glass door without making any noise. I had already threatened Jens into submission; I taught him that the price of acting like a grown-up, as we were about to do, is keeping quiet about your feelings. You have to choke them off, swallow them down.

We were very hushed, intoxicated when we pushed the door, but the semi-darkness inside the room was in motion. In it some animal was rooting around, tearing the stuff from pillows. What was it? Even *I* got scared. When Jens tugged my shorts I reached behind and pulled the drapes sideways. Light tore into the room. A figure shot up. He turned to face us wearing the mask. Black patches, but his eyes burned white holes. And behind him we could see very well was another animal-person, Frau Ballack. Urta was pinned to the ottoman by the incoming sun. Underneath the ottoman I spotted a bumblebee and a cat's eye, but not my milky banja. Half-sprawled, Urta hurried her dress back over by swivelling her shoulders. Jens screamed in delight. I slapped him across the mouth before we both ran out. It all happened so quickly that the image of my father pulling the mask from his face to see who was there did not properly settle before my eyes until, many years later, late into my fifties, I discovered who all we were, that distant afternoon.

What is it? I can still hear his vain shout. What is the trouble with you?

PROOF

Yes, on the stage, you love the tragic.
And sweet tears warm your heart.

Fate has always struck me foul
and unexpectedly ...

HERMANN HANS STEINMETZ, *Monologue with God*

*In 1943, my father was hired for an exploration team by
an oil company from Texas. Texaco. It was then called
the Texas Oil Company. They had plans to survey the
valley of the Magdalena River, which was a watery and
malaria-infested ground. Terrible conditions. My father was anxious to leave the capital, temporarily at
least. Anyhow, for the first time in a long time there was
money to be made.*

It must have been while pulling teeth in the market, or during one of his more or less futile house calls, that my grandfather was reintroduced to the big flakes of his favourite
natural cereal. The Indians used the coca plant as an anal-
gesic for toothaches. They chewed on the leaves. There is a
photograph of HH from this era vigorously poling a canoe
along the muddy Magdalena—hell-bent on poling that ves-

sel back through the mouth of the jungle and on to Germany, where he might fix a thing or two. His expression is curious. Deeply tired, jaw strained, he is ready to persevere. His eyes are raving; a madman's stare from a week spent on the river, hatless under the sun. When you look closely at the photograph, the lump is noticeable. It's not a tumour. Nor fibrous tissue. His right cheek is rounded, squirrel-plumped. It's one of those things I've put together just recently—in fact, only since I started holding these conversations with Roland. This provides the denouement, a gentle coda of the coca variety reaching back to Germany: HH's addiction dated to his university days.

Our family set up in a camp with the exploration team. This was by the riverside. Mama, who was pregnant again, my brother Jens, and myself.

Within weeks Papa contracted an ear infection from bathing in the swamps. One ear, then the other. Pus-bloated ear canals. There was no treatment, no penicillin, and draining the interior chambers was about all that could be done to reduce the pressure. Mama did this for him in the evening beside the fire. She lay the tip of the dental scaler over the coals. She gave it some time. The metal turned black, then breathing orange at the tip. I remember watching, sitting on a stone, mesmerized by the procedure. His head on her lap, she punctured the abscess. He would ask her to please sing or at least to mumble in Spanish. Mama shook her head. This sport seemed to lighten his spirits. As per his instructions, she then dripped beads of iodine into the canal.

Nothing worked. Things worsened and Papa, desperate for relief, finally succeeded in bullying one of the company officials into flying him—and all of us!—out of the jungle. A plane was dispatched days later. My father gave up hope of ever returning to the company encampment, and the whole family, along with three other passengers, boarded the craft which was to deliver us back to Bogotá.

Now, I have to tell you that I have specific memories of that day. I was seven years old and I remember there was only one pilot, and this man reported in uniform. His headgear consisted of a leather toque, which fit snug as a condom over the top of his head. He wore goggles, from behind which his eyes, wide as saucers, were challenged, and seemed to be gasping for air. He also wore a scarf wrapped nonchalantly around the neck. All in all, he resembled a cross between an Olympic downhill skier and a WWI fighter pilot. But this was post 1919, and the aircraft, which belonged to the Colombian Air Force, must have been twice a hand-me-down. It was certainly no fighter plane. It was a shell of what we nowadays call an aircraft, very lightweight—indeed, it could not have been less heavy. Bulletproof it was not—I don't believe it was waterproof, but it was similar in design to the kayak your mother and I bought on our honeymoon in Prince Edward Island. It had some kind of wood frame, covered in canvas. In any case it did not take to high altitudes, as planes do these days—and thank goodness, really, that modesty, in humans and in machines alike, appears to be an innate feature of the overall design.

We cruised barely overtop the trees. I remember the floor was laid with wood slats, like in the old trains, and between these boards, which were loosely fitted, I could see the land, rivers, the jungle passing below us. I spent the greater part of the journey on my knees, one eye pressed between the floorboards as though looking down for a lost marble. I was in fact studying our progress, estimating distances, and, occasionally, when the plane dipped and details swerved too rapidly into a larger scale, I would shout out a warning to the pilot, who in any case could not hear a thing.

We were eight or nine passengers in all, not including the motor, which was oppressive. Loud as hell. A drone that bore into the skull with spiralling monotony. It really was prohibitive. Communication aboard was impossible. It's a miracle how the pilot coped day after day, earplugs or not—which brings me back to Papa. He was suffering throughout, even in sleep, or semi-consciousness. The only part of his anatomy that seemed keyed-in—his Adam's apple—was deranged, tensed. The drama of referred pain. Even the low altitude had put him out. He lay with his head on Mama's lap. Mama was pregnant. In my mind's eye I picture him chewing a wad of leaves, juices leaking from his mouth. Mama is knitting for Ursula. Jens too is asleep on Mama's shoulder. Papa's eyes are squeezed shut. Mama is trying her best not to disturb him, his sleeping head. Yarn and needles, she's working her fingers in cramped quarters, plying her knuckles like a small threshing machine.

Then—all of a sudden, forty minutes or so after take-off—the engine cut out. I think it would be accurate to say we all released a sigh of relief. No more drone! No more noise! There followed a brief, hyphenated interval—silence, a loaded pause—before knowing caught up with instinct. A whining, a drone, a whimper, flump, then more sickening flumping. The engine itself was undecided: it caught, then fizzled. The pilot was swearing, damning and simultaneously praising the Holy Mother. WE COULD HEAR THE PILOT.

The plane began drifting, slipping on the air, from side to side like a feather.

I pulled myself up from the floor and grabbed Ma-

ma's knees. Jens scrunched his eyes. Papa was unrespon-
sive. Saliva dripped from the corner of his mouth as he
lightly chewed and beheld, like Jens, an internal fire-
works display. These were not hallucinations brought on
by Magnon's Syndrome, I doubt that. Hallucinations of
white snakes crawling though his skin, or small animals
lounging in his calves, mice licking pointy crystals, or lice
under his fingernails. Cocaine bugs. Snow lights drop-
ping down his eyelids. More in character for Papa would
be a fascination or preoccupation with his own thought
processes—what could be more elaborately spellbinding
than this? Don't you think?

Roland plucks his cigar from his lips. There is a moist pop.
He has it in for 'Papa' today. The tape cassette is marked
"Proof: Colombia, 1936–1943."

I rewind the cassette and press play and listen once more.
Roland's plane lifts off, from out of jungle, en route to Bogotá. His storytelling intensifies:

Mama reacted quickly to save our lives, and the lives of
all the other passengers. She is the unsung hero of most
of this. She unhooked her knitting needle from the line
and in one motion guided it into the flaring red seashell
resting on her lap. My father came to, screaming, in
agony. She reached for his face, fingers extended, hands
frozen mid-air. Then, in seconds, recognition unfolded.
Apprehending our doom he yanked the pilot from the
cockpit and, jumping back decades to when he was a
child flying gliders at the Baltic Sea, he expertly brought
the plane down 'with the gentle hands of a ruffian,' one
of his favourite expressions.

None of the other passengers reacted. They each hid
their face as the plane touched down and buried its nose

233

in a field: it cut through the high grass like a car going through a mechanized wash, and the day was saved. Silence. The pilot lay prostrate, belly up like an over-turned beetle. My father and another man pried open the cockpit door and the rest of us poured out over the sides. Our disorientation was encapsulating. We disembarked into the enormous sunshine, while the afternoon itself creaked to a standstill. No one collapsed. Not one person spoke. People wandered off, not very far, this way or that way, exaggerating each footstep, just like astronauts on a cratered planet. People returned to first principles, pri-vately impressed by the benign pull of gravity, which here on earth was nothing to be worried about—reduced as it was to a play object, a kitten to be teased with a roll-ing ball of wool, or the hanging end of a shoelace. You could tame this force, you could train it. You could bring it along a distance. You could make gravity your friend. There were no injuries. We were that lucky, or we were blessed. Or perhaps Death was gorging on the other side of the globe and so it spared these ones, today, gave us a shake and rattle and then turned abruptly and crossed back over the ocean to complete its work in Europe.

If my father's memory serves him reliably, this was in 1943. The Germans had begun their withdrawal from the Cauca-sus. The Allies had landed in Sicily. Colombia had broken diplomatic ties with Japan after the attack on Pearl Harbor. The South American nation had an agreement to supply the Allies with petroleum. Hence Texaco Oil Company's survey of the valley of the Magdalena River. In the same year, a Ger-man submarine destroyed a schooner from Cartegena and the German ambassador was sent packing. German citizens in certain areas of Colombia were sent to internment camps. The plane which crash-landed in the jungle, as Roland has narrated, belonged to the Colombian military. Times were such that it was alleged that my grandfather had sabotaged this aircraft. In court, the other passengers claimed he had siphoned gasoline from the fuel tank. A ridiculous charge—considering his family was aboard—but it was his word against theirs. And since he was no Catholic, and hence not permitted to swear on the Bible before giving testimony, the outcome of the trial was predictable. Furthermore, he was accused by Colombian intelligence officers of being a Nazi terrorist and spy. The charges held, and this *Mischlinge 2* spent six months in a crude prison cell, where he suffered a nervous breakdown. My grandmother visited him every day, and watched him—quarter-Jew, refugee, alleged Nazi spy—as he got hold of his forehead, squarely, and mashed it on the bricks, into the crud of molecules. He was, for the world to see, erasing himself. At one especially despairing juncture, he beseeched my grandmother to retrieve his pistol from their packing crate and shoot him, please, through the bars. He was eventually freed, but not before he cured the warden's wife from one malady or another, and not before he was able to prove that siphoning gasoline for use in his kerosene stove (as was alleged) would leave verifiable deposits. More than half a century later—having examined the evidence—I suspect his crime almost certainly was that he spoke with a heavy accent. His limited Spanish, scarred by an unusual syntax, offended the ears of his accusers.

By the time I came on the scene, in the 1960s, my grandparents were living in the United States. HH's professional career had begun in earnest when, newly arrived in the USA from Colombia, in 1955, he studied medicine for a year and then retook his exams, passing them all. This was quite an achievement, since he'd last studied biochemistry, physiology, and pharmacology in the thirties. But he didn't stop there. He wrote to the American Psychiatric Board, telling them he'd trained abroad, and wished to undertake the American Board Exams without a second internship. This was a flat lie. He'd never formally trained in psychiatry. However, they consented, and he passed these exams, too.

He practised in a series of Veteran Administration Mental Hospitals, and my grandparents had homes in Binghamton, Roanoke, Charlottesville, and on Long Island, where they tasted nothing but isolation. Wherever he landed he was never one of the team—he was different. He used to complain that the kind of caring atmosphere inside the psychiatric wing was more of an incentive to be sick than anything else. He accepted that most human behaviour is learned, from language to morality, from sexual to work habits. He told Roland that the majority of his patients needed to learn how to live among other people without serious friction. Learning to function, he said, is a lifelong learning process. All this, he felt, cannot be taught in a hospital where people sit around smoking and drinking coffee and watching television, while waiting to be entertained by well-meaning and compassionate recreation specialists, who repeat to them, *ad nauseam,* that 'they are O.K.'—when they are most definitely not 'O.K.'

It was from Virginia, where my grandparents lived outside Roanoke, that my grandfather mailed his monthly, handwritten German language lessons, a non-credit correspondence course both Stephen and I received with *a priori* dread, but could not opt out of. Our lessons were interrupted in 1972 when HH volunteered for two years of medical service in Vietnam, where he was put in charge of the Bien Hoa Mental Hospital. This was a local hospital. Here there was no incentive to be sick. There was no electricity or plumbing and the inpatients had no clothing. HH was accustomed to 'primitive,' but not to the inhuman squalor of this pretty asylum in Dong Nai Province, no more than thirty kilometres east of Ho Chi Minh City. In a matter of months, he clothed the patients, brought in electricity and rebuilt most of the hospital, using volunteer labour. Not one to believe in talking cures—although by this time psychoanalysis flourished outside the greenhouses of Vienna and New York—he organized the inpatients into highly disciplined gardening platoons and preached something like hand-in-the-earth healing. He was a pioneer in the much-derided practice of therapeutic horticulture. His efforts at Bien Hoa Hospital were later written about in *Reader's Digest,* among other places.

Afterwards, when he returned to the VA Hospital in Roanoke, a patient under his care jumped from a third-storey window. He discovered this patient of his, heaped in a rose bush, broken-limbed, on his routine early morning walk through the hospital grounds. What happened next? I imagine him: crouching down beside her, then—he waits. At this moment, with his ear pressed to her heart, he perhaps composed lines for one of his aphoristic poems (I inherited the manuscript, *Monologue with God,* which was discovered, post mortem, in HH's study): 'I am with the trees and with the beasts who choose a free death' or maybe 'There is no one among us as he was meant to be. Much befalls us and distorts our growth.' In any case, he did not ring the alarm, nor did he call for help. In his own words—and I am quoting here—he wanted to rescue her from "the team of clumsy life-crusaders." I know this because he wrote as much to myself and my brother; it was an anecdote contained in one of his correspondences on German grammar.

At last, in 1978, my grandparents ended their years of travel and exile by buying some land and setting up a self-sufficient community of their own, several miles outside Winston-Salem in North Carolina. This was some forty years after the failed experiment at the Buena Vista Farm in Totoro. In North Carolina they formed a community of two and life revolved around their magnificent property, keeping the garden—the tomatoes, cucumbers, squash, spinach, sunflowers, lettuce and carrots—and pruning the fruit trees. Work, says one family legend, made HH incredibly strong. But did it? I often wonder about this. Strong as in stubborn? Strong as Krupp steel? Tough as leather? When Stephen and I came visiting in August—sent by bus from Montreal, four summers in a row—we were immediately put to work in the garden. It was just the thing for rudderless grandsons. We worked day and night alongside HH and "Pinguin." We'd leave their place exhausted at the end of the summer. We couldn't wait to return to school.

By the next summer the garden would have doubled in size, for when spring came he'd have planted another row of sunflowers, another row of cucumbers, another row of oriental herbs. He'd have transplanted fruit trees. They added more and more. They'd both become vegetarians. Working side by side, my grandparents always seemed to be munching on zucchini: they could not seem to get enough to eat. Eventually it became clear to any observer that their beleaguered bodies could not keep up with everything that had to be done: the watering, weeding, picking and pickling. We begged Roland not to send us back the next August, to let us stay in Sutton all summer—but when his vacation time ended and Roland had to return to work at the hospital, we were put back on the bus and sent south for another round of therapeutic horticulture.

HH treated Stephen and I, his grandchildren, as if we had sophistication and maturity beyond our years: a privilege, maybe doomed to become our burden. He taught us to play chess; nightly, we played match after match. He made us practise archery: *stand perpendicular to the target, hold the bow opposite the dominant eye, draw the bow string, pinch the arrow.* As you were squinting at the target, he'd whisper some coup de grâce wisdom into your ear: *The true marksman, fundamentally, aims at himself, to hit his own heart.* Well, that made it easier to let go of the arrow. HH even taught us how to drive, on the back roads.

And whatever the lesson or situation, our grandfather impressed upon us the importance of being able to accept pain and endure injuries without grimacing, without complaining or squealing. There was always this accent on suffering, or pain, even when there was none. Recently, I found the following typical-of-him Note to Self, on the stationery of the New York Pilgrim State Hospital, where he'd practised in the 1960s: 'One of the real important experiences of life, one of the essential experiences is defeat, the feeling of helplessness, of being confronted by an overwhelming power of nature, fate, or if you want to call it, God. The deeply felt reality of worthlessness and guilt, of inadequacy and of one's limitations is a *needed* experience.' This is the kind of thing HH would have taped to the refrigerator door, as inspirational gospel.

When HH told a joke, the scenario inevitably involved a psychiatrist and serious illness, or some extravagantly futile action—a low comedy of indecision or absurd compulsion. He liked aphorisms. Loved the Zen motto, 'Life is a great teacher, but it kills all its students.' This pleased him immensely.

My most complete memory of my grandfather dates from the summer of 1979, eight years before his death. I am in my early teens, he in his late sixties. We are sitting side by side on the couch in the living room in Winston, and both of us are staring at the black plate spinning on the turntable. We are hypnotized following the spiral grooves, which spread in concentric waves from the phonograph needle like ripples in a vinyl lake. David Lee Roth, hoarse from yelping, is singing "Running With The Devil." Eddie Van Halen's bombastic, heavy-metal guitar erupts from the speakers on either side of us. We are silent because my grandfather has inquired why I might like this music, and in response I have only now delivered a non sequitur, *I think they are Dutch*. Van Halen sounds Dutch to me, and it is my wishful thinking that Holland, being part of Europe ... well, I am hoping this might resonate with him.

HH scratches his beard. He'd driven me to the shopping centre and accompanied me into the music store and told me I could choose whatever I wanted—but this is the real price tag for me, this right now, sitting with the old psychiatrist amidst the bamboo furniture and indigenous art, listening to the new Van Halen album in its entirety, together.

That afternoon a quarter of a century ago, HH may have spoken at length and made some obvious references to *Civilization and Its Discontents*—if so, they were lost on me. I remember only this: that he was neither aghast nor horrified by my musical taste, but simply and deeply disappointed, he said, by such predictability. He made me feel like I had peed my pants. Worst of all, I knew, even then, that this had been his intention.

I can understand this mania about gardening. Relationships of the human-to-human kind were frequently upsetting, so my grandfather chose to carry on with existence at a more basic level: plant life. Eva picked the human-to-animal plane, while HH kneeled right down on the earth. Dust to dust, and dawn to dusk, he tended to his garden. The only element that could disappoint him then was the weather: natural not human forces. For all intents and purposes my grandparents had found a place to retire that ran parallel to history, remote from the main current. Outside the institutional setting, he'd found an optimal healing environment—some peace and quiet, in which he and Suzanne could tend to their legumes with unconditional love. And yet, when I remember the humidity of those summers and I see him, shirtless, grey bearded and fit, grinding on a carrot or cucumber, I cannot help but think of the god Cronus munching on his children. He was someone, I now believe, who always had the ambition and the inner force of character to impose himself on his time—except not on those times. So instead he became a martyr in his own mind and imposed himself on his family. On my grandmother, Suzanne, on Roland and Jens and Ursula. They were on the front lines, and they bore the brunt, for he was no ordinary martyr. Maybe he did not understand that the good martyrs suffer alone. Martyrs are lonely figures. They do not share what is theirs.

In the weeks before his death, my grandfather had complained of pain in his lower right leg. It was bad enough that he drove into Winston to consult a specialist, a vascular surgeon. The doctor diagnosed him with a phlebitis. HH called it nonsense. Back at home my grandmother wanted to know why he had gone to see a doctor in the first place, if he was going to ignore the advice he was given? He took no notice of her and stomped back outside, grumbling about western science, spouting off something to the effect that this particular doctor was a buffoon, a clown, a know-nothing. *Taugenichts.*

He walked straight to the garage and pulled a metal detector from the wall. He used this gadget, habitually, to 'clean' his land. Now he set the detector beside his leg and the device went off directly at a spot where he'd injured himself some years before. Back into the kitchen. He made an incision. Pried back folds of skin. Just minor surgery. And found the piece of metal. A nail head, or the end of a screw. He rinsed the foreign body in the kitchen sink and placed it beside the faucet, next to the vegetables my grandmother had washed that morning.

But the pain in his leg continued. Go to a doctor. I am a doctor. Please go and consult him again. Nonsense. *Taugenichts. Dunkle Männer.*

He should have gone to the doctor. He had chest pain, shortness of breath. He knew the natural history of a pulmonary embolism. The simple story of a blood clot travelling through the vessels, circulating, upwards, until finally it lodges itself in the artery leading to the lungs. The last hours of his life he remained in bed, issuing commands, ordering my grandmother on a continual basis to inject him with morphine. He had stockpiled the sweet stuff for such an occasion. Yet, he must have misjudged just how long he would go on suffering because he did finally run out of morphine.

At this stage, I would like to bid him adieu, to suppose that HH sauntered off into a wild pain wonderland. To presume that, under the influence of narcotics and bodily insults, he went out of his mind. But my grandmother, she was not out of her mind. Pinguin, limping, was terribly alive. Her eyesight may have been failing, but she witnessed his end: the cruel reward for years of loyalty and obedience. When she'd taken his name in 1936 she'd taken on more than the Nuremberg Laws. Suzanne had agreed to support him in sickness and in health. Well, here was sickness. From the bed he shouted and abused her. In his declining state, between periods of semi-conscious drowsiness, he made use of each sober moment to bark out nasty and self-pitying insinuations. Effectively, he attempted to destroy her, she whom he was leaving behind. Where was all this coming from? I'd like to say that it did not come from deep inside, but from very close to the surface—but I don't believe this was the case. He would not admit outside help. No ambulance, no medics. No fuss, and, certainly, no heroics. None that would obscure his own. His messy final hours were the apotheosis of his long suffering—his curtain call: farewell to all that, amen.

Just before passing away, as his last request, he ordered my grandmother to retrieve his pistol—a token from their years in Colombia—from the bedroom closet. The last purge. For maybe the first time in her life she disobeyed him. There were no bullets anyway. It was symbolic, a gesture on his part. Put me out of my misery, or I will. If you can't do it, hand it here. I like to believe she played stupid then, and brought him a wet cloth instead. She placed it over his forehead. She gently rubbed his brow. For, last requests aside, there was no understanding him. Even an FBI security case file submitted by multiple agents, using phone taps and a mail cover, would shed no further light on Hermann Hans. HH was an experience—a total experience, like war—and you do not understand experiences as such. *They strike you.*

5

COOKING SOUP ON A
BURNING HOUSE

It has frequently been said of performances that the directing is more Marxist than the play and that on opening night in Berlin, 31 August 1928, the audience was treated to a demonstration confused with a drama, saved only by some brilliant show songs. Nonetheless, staging *The Threepenny Opera* established the Theater am Schiffbauerdamm as the left-wing theatre du jour.

Making note of the reactionary atmosphere inside Weimar Germany, the critic Kurt Tucholsky observed, in the spring of 1930, that the furor surrounding the play had little to do with its substance. About Brecht and *The Threepenny Opera*, Tucholsky remarked: "This writer can be compared to a man cooking his soup on a burning house. It isn't he who caused the fire." Tucholsky's image reaches into the visual lair of physical comedy. But what does it really mean? His turn of phrase predates the Reichstag fire. Even so, after the parliament was set ablaze by the mentally disturbed Marinus Van der Lubbe in February 1933, with the Nazi hierarchy pulling the strings, Brecht's name skyrocketed in the ratings and he was soon number five on the Nazi murder list. For his part, Van der Lubbe, an unemployed bricklayer with ties to organized labour, was found stark naked and trembling behind the Reichstag. This unstable character, clown or fool, played a pivotal role in the establishment of the Nazi state, and in justifying the banning of the German Communist Party, the KPD, on 1 March 1933.

In the days following the Reichstag fire, German storm troopers seized all Communist Party buildings. Eva and Karl did not delay leaving Germany. They fled to Vienna in 1933, then, after the Anschluss, to Zurich, where they separated in 1938, as I have said.

Simultaneously, in 1933, Brecht, with his third wife, Helene Weigel, son Stefan, and daughter Barbara, was off to Zurich and eventually Svendborg in Denmark, to begin a life of exile that eventually brought the family to the USA in 1941.

In September 1943, Karl performed in the premiere of Brecht's *Life of Galileo* at the Zurich Schauspielhaus.

In 1946, Eva and Michael left Zurich without Karl and returned to start life over in the Russian sector of Berlin.

In 1947, Brecht flew to Zurich from Washington the day after his appearance before the House Un-American Activities Committee (HUAC), at which he denied ever having been associated with the Communist Party. As part of his solo performance before HUAC, 30 October 1947, Brecht responded to a question regarding his study of socialism: 'Have many of your writings been based upon the philosophy of Lenin and Marx?' His response: 'No; I don't think that is quite correct but, of course, I studied, had to study as a playwright who wrote historical plays. I, of course, had to study Marx's ideas about history. I do not think intelligent plays today can be written without such study. Also, history written now is vitally influenced by the studies of Marx about history.'

In Zurich, while in transit, Brecht composed his concise treatise *Kleines Organon für das Theater*, Little Organon for the Theater, in which he opposed identification and catharsis, the lifeblood of the Aristotelian tragedy, with his dramatic theory based on detachment and the alienation effect. Modelling himself after Galileo, Einstein and Oppenheimer, Brecht praised the aesthetics of the exact sciences and endorsed a scientific attitude—which has its own kind of beauty, he said, one which suits mankind's position on earth.

By 1948—the year Eva and Michael and dog were airlifted from the embargoed city via the British airbase Gatow—Brecht and Weigel were back in Berlin, taking an apartment in the East.

The Berliner Ensemble, founded by Brecht and Weigel, moved into its permanent home at the Theater am Schiffbauerdamm in 1954, some twenty-six years after *The Threepenny Opera's* opening night.

By this time Eva was well installed in Canada. Her son Michael had a dream: he wanted to become an actor.

In 1955, Brecht accepted the Stalin Peace prize in Moscow.

Hannah Arendt comments that to become a communist in the 1920s and 30s was no sin, merely an error. But to persist, right through to the 1950s? In her portrait of Brecht in *Men in Dark Times*, Arendt correlates the passing of his poetic powers, after he took up residence in East Berlin, with an unconscious response to ideological failure.

While reading Arendt on Brecht, I remember that it was in 1956 that Eva's ex-husband, Comrade Paryla, went to East Berlin, performing at Deutsches Theater until 1961. The Deutsches Theater is where Paryla had gotten his start in the business, under Max Reinhardt, who had been director there from 1905 to 1930. Reinhardt—whose real name was Maximilian Goldmann—was long gone in exile by the time Paryla made his triumphant return in the 1950s.

After receiving the Stalin Peace Prize, Brecht carried on for one more year. He transferred his prize money into a Swiss bank account. Rehearsals started for a London tour of *Life of Galileo*. Then, on 17 August 1956, he died of heart failure.

The man is buried in the Dorotheenfriedhof cemetery in Berlin.

THREEPENNY BERLIN

Trümmerfrauen. Women of the rubble. Gangs of old women. Crows in headscarves pulling handcarts. Clearing stones from the street. Picking up torn newspapers. In every sector, the Russian, French, American, British. Bent over like birds pecking at specks. Hawking paper bags and newspaper. A bounty of scraps. I piled my bounty onto the wagon and pulled it around the grey streets of Berlin like Mother Courage, like Helene Weigel on stage against the backdrop of The Thirty Years War.

I used newspaper for bedding.

We slept in a paper nest, Michi and I. We dreamed in a bowl of newspaper and dust. At night I covered Michi in paper and rags—he kept warm covered in the old news of advancing armies. Allied Troops Land in Sicily. Allied Troops Land in Normandy. Paris Falls. Soviet Troops in Warsaw.

The *Kippensammler* collected butts from the gutter, half-smoked cigarettes, and sold them on the street corner instead of chestnuts.

The *Süßigkeitsgangster*. The sweet-stuff gangsters. They sold goodies, like chocolate, on the black market.

The *Schieber* operated nightclubs. *Kabarette* in Kurfürstendamm. Black market clubs stuffed with furniture and art pieces stolen from the embassies and from ruined state buildings. The famous clubs were The Femina, Rio Rita and The Tabasco. Inside you couldn't tell who was female and who was male, who a former Nazi and who from the military police. *Kabarette* were the only shelter we had, one of the few places you could go to reinvent yourself. Bunkers, inside piles of rubble, hollowed out by jazz. American music played loud. Your host opened the evening, standing on a low stage, taking a long shit on the Third Reich. The liberators showed up to relax with a girl on each arm. With one blonde for dinner and one blonde for after midnight. They went for the music, for all that jazz.

I left Zurich with Michi for Berlin full of enthusiasm. We will build a new Germany! They need us! Mother and child, we will help rebuild Germany! Blow the trumpet. New life, new order. Bread from sand, Jesus from Judas.

They need us. That's what I thought—what I believed: they need us.

Us: who had left Germany. Us: we were different, totally different from the ones who lived under the Nazi system.

And 'they'? They: our brothers and sisters. German like us? No longer.

What had 'they' been up to? Who had 'they' become? How did 'they' pass time—the last five, six, seven years? Twelve years. Twelve years of the Third German Zoo. Of course that was the question. Who is rotten? Who full of worms? Who did what and who watched and who did nothing? Who carried on day to day and fetched vegetables from the earth? Who milked the cows squatting on a stool and was bored by it all? Who applauded, and who closed their eyes? Who danced around the Christmas tree? Who drove the truck? Who closed the door? Who turned the switch?

We arrived in Berlin after a twelve-hour train ride. Michael and I, standing on the platform, two leather suitcases between us.

Twelve hours away but twelve years.

It was dawn when we arrived. It was November, and cold. Berlin had not only lost the war, it had lost its colour. It was grey. It was destroyed. It was something hard to describe, beyond nature. There was no turning around our Berlin. Grey Berlin with Trümmerfrauen. Süßigkeitsgangster. Kippensammler. History closed, and business was hard for the gangster, thief, beggar, prostitute. There was a void and we called it Berlin. We all were licensed beggars. Twenty years after opening night, *Threepenny* returned to the streets. And to Peachum's types of human misery, you could add another: winter in post-war Berlin.

Berlin of the black market, that was my Berlin. Berlin of dust and cold. Berlin of bricks and broken glass. Berlin of rats. Berlin of the uniforms—khaki army jackets for sale from the French, British, Germans, Americans, Russians. Prêt-à-porter. Every sector was in fashion. Every uniform was on sale on the black market.

The wool pants made by the British were prized. They were by far the warmest. Wool made the gentlemen feel at home.

Four sectors to choose from and we landed in with the Russians. We lived in an orphanage in the rubble. Several families together, more children than adults. More orphans than parents. In the morning I walked with Michi to the Grunewald and the Tiergarten to collect sticks for fuel. It was a strange life. Things happened one after the other without making even a small difference. To the Grunewald to collect sticks. To the Tiergarten. Cook soup from soup from soup. The next day soup out of the last soup.

We sucked hard on the wooden spoon.

At the table, one of the men bowed his head over his bowl: *Hurra, die Butter ist Alle*! Hurray, the butter is all gone!

He was remembering all the Goering & Goebbels' hits from the 1930s and 40s. *Iron Has Always Made the Empire Strong, Butter and Lard Make People Fat! German Speaking Republics as One!* He banged his fist on the table and frightened the children.

Quiet, we told him. Quiet. We collected sticks. We sucked on wood. We put words in our mouths. It was life.

Beware of Wolves. Winter 1947.

Beware of Nazis. Beware of Thieves. Beware of Mass Murderers. And now: Beware of Wolves.

Blessed Are the Dead, for Their Hands Do Not Freeze.

Survival revolved around ration cards. The meat card. The bread card. Each was marked with the number of calories. One card we called the Death Card. There was no food on the shelves. There were no shelves. There were no shops. We survived playing our game of cards. Our game of chance. Trading this card for that card.

But by the winter of 1947 it was useless to play pretend anymore. Ration cards were hopeless. The black market took over, and if you couldn't work the black market, you shrivelled up, you folded. Doing good did no good for you. In a big bad world, as Brecht said, the best thing you could be was a small bad person. To survive, I had to dirty my fingernails. I had to lie and cheat. I won't tell you.

That winter the wolves came into the city from the countryside and fought with the rest of us over the fat of the land. Then it got so bad even the wolves froze. They lay down in the streets, and slept. They also starved in the bitter dark winter.

An end with suffering or suffering without end.

Misery.

No mercy. I am in zoo. I have lice and I don't get washed. I sleep in my bowl of newspaper. Here I am licking the dirt from under my fingernails to stay alive.

This is special treatment.

So that is all there is to it. Act One, Scene Three. The world is poor and man's a shit. First Threepenny Finale Concerning the Insecurity of the Human Condition.

The young girl, she went to the cabaret at night to find some warmth, to forget Berlin. She followed the music off the street and went in. She was watched by a group of eyes through the smoke. She came from the street and she slipped on the wet floor and flew into the lap of Corporal Smith, her lonely liberator, who tossed peanuts into her mouth and placed a square of milk chocolate on her tongue.

When she raised her chin to swallow, Corporal Smith slid his tongue down the back of her neck.

Starvation. I had Michael. How long could I survive in Berlin before becoming Corporal Smith's girl?

Trümmer Trudy came to my rescue. Trümmer Trudy, from the worker's theatre of the Russian sector, wrapped in a head-scarf, dragging her handcart. Merchant and beggar, no teeth. Trudy, the picture of erosion. A crumbling woman, sliding through the hourglass.

One day in the winter of '47 Trudy followed me back from the Tiergarten. Michael and I were carrying sticks.

Come to my nest, she said. My man is sick. I have something for you. She pointed a finger at Michael. Something for you, she insisted.

He was not so sure.

And something for you! She opened her coat as we started walking. Here, she said to me, and squeezed a lump of coal from between her breasts. Take it for the child. Take as much as you need—so I reached in and pulled up a potato from further down.

Michael laughed. It was a miracle but he laughed. She was full of surprises.

Hurrah. *Mein Nest!* Trudy pointed to the entrance of her nest. There I saw a pile of stones. A hole. She tugged on my coat and led us inside the nest. Dresden Destroyed. First Atomic Bomb Dropped. Her old man was asleep in the whirlwind of history. Americans Land in Sicily. Paris Falls. Her man was coughing. There was no fire but the walls were black. And in that whole mess, she had puppies. A litter of German shepherds. Somehow. Sleeping and suckling from their mother.

Trudy wants to give us one. One for Michael. For protection against the wolves, for protection against Berlin.

Oh, I said, I can hardly refuse.

§ § §

Allegedly there was a street performance of *The Threepenny Opera* in July 1945, not long after the fall of the city to the Soviets. The fighting had stopped, Berlin was in shambles, and these theatre people were at it again? The play was staged in the open-air ruins of the Soviet zone. Kurt Weill's music struck a chord with an audience made up almost entirely of Soviet soldiers. The actors were haggard and tired. Many of them, purportedly, were only recently released from concentration camps. It was a workmanlike production *of course,* but nonetheless, nonetheless.

In all my reading, there were few things less credible, more difficult to accept as truth, than this: one Allied soldier's description of an impromptu performance of Brecht's play in the Soviet zone, some fifteen years after its premiere at the nearby Theater am Schiffbauerdamm. It smacks too much of after-the-fact sentimentality. Of fable, of urban myth. At first glance I felt it was about as unlikely as Eva's story about how she got her German shepherd, Romeo, a ticket for the Berlin airlift. The year was 1948. Berlin was under embargo. Eva and her son were desperate to escape to the West after only two years of zoo life in the old capital. The story goes something like this.

Act One. After months of grey misery finally Eva is offered a position, an engagement, at Radio Berlin. In the broadcast booth Eva reads transcripts from the ongoing Nuremberg War Crime Trials into a microphone, a grey puffball, "the size of a swollen skull."

She projects her voice into the microphone, fills it up with details about the sadistic Nazi monsters.

One day, she is summoned by the German Military Police. *Collect your papers and report tomorrow to the Polizeiprä-sidium.* She's not interested in their proposal. You must go, her colleagues insist. No, she resists: that is like asking the field mouse to carry a wire trap on its back when she goes to meet the farm cat!

The next day the German police return. *Come. We will escort you! Come with us, the sooner the better!* Thus they drag Eva across town to headquarters. They march up the steps, inside, then descend into the cellar, down a steep stairway and into the underground. Held by the elbow, Eva passes through a long corridor of cold cement. O, I have seen this in the movies, Eva mumbles: this leads then to the Russians.

Sure enough. When the German police come to fetch you, the Soviets want you.

There are a number of them. And the interrogation room is

small. They sit her down at the table. One official fires questions through a woman interpreter. The interpreter, wearing a brown sweater, sits at the table like a bored cabaret singer. Others watch the action, arms on chests. The official launches questions Eva's way and she sends her answers, his way, through the woman. *How did you get to Berlin? Via the Americans? Speak, tell us everything. Why did you leave Switzerland?*

The leader scratches his moustache with Eva's file. When the first official concentrates in one direction, Eva mumbles to herself, this other plans an attack in the opposite direction.

After hours of cross-examination the leader, the man with the moustache, says: *All right. You don't have anything to hide, good, and you have nothing against us, good, then you will spy for us, yes, from now on ... Such and such a telephone number ... Call once a week and report to us about Radio Berlin ... conversations between the workers ... who is saying what, why, when ... what you talk about, everything you overhear in the canteen ... Report to such and such a number at these times ...*

Well, Eva mumbles, this *is* the movies now, no longer theatre. This is a trap. The underground passage, the electric light hanging over the table, and the quiet woman interpreter. Soviets, where are your fur hats? I was made for movies after all, to be a spy for the Russians!

The man says: *If it works out ... well, you have no choice ... we will put glass in your windows ... You're hungry, you haven't much food ... you will have food and cigarettes ... you have a son ... chocolate ... You have a dog, too?*

Act Two. *Nacht und Nebel*. The war is over, but business continues. In the fog of the night, hundreds and hundreds disappear. Eva's nights are haunted by this disappearing act. She sits by the window and looks out: soldiers jump from the back of the military truck, call up at the building, civilians are led outdoors, put in the back of the truck, door closed and five more disappear.

The first week goes by. She phones the number. I am a stranger, she says, I am one of the newcomers and no one talks to me. I am not trusted. I have nothing to report. Before she can finish the voiceless comrade hangs up.

Meanwhile Eva is promoted to the position of chief newscaster. There is no position at Radio Berlin more dangerous than this. Before going on the air the news team meet in the canteen to smoke. They stare each other in the eye and duel with cigarettes. Spies are everywhere: spies for the Russians, spies for the Americans. One mistake on air and rumours fly:

This one is a French spy and dangerous.
This one works for the Americans.

Eva hears the footsteps below her window, and constantly the trucks.

Either we wait here for the end, she tells her sleeping Michael, or we disappear. *Verschwinden* is the word in Eva's head. *Verschwinden, Verschwinden, Verschwinden.*

Act Three. The Soviets impose an embargo. Circumstances are desperate. Survival revolves around ration cards and the black market. A game of luck. For Eva and Michael there is no exit by land—there is only one way out. Airlift over the top. Airlift to the West. But they need a ticket to ride. A pass, papers, a bribe. A ticket from the Americans, French or British. Airlift is the dream, Eva mumbles, the only dream we have left.

Via the French sector she makes contact with a journalist, an old friend, with connections. He sends her instructions: report to this address, take this letter to the military headquarters in the French sector and they will help you. Well fine. Off she goes to the French sector carrying her letter. It is not easy getting there but she arrives. Knock, knock. Here I am, she mumbles. A girl with a gift. I have a letter. Please let me inside.

The doorman treats her very well. *Come inside, come inside, you must be cold.* There is no password, no line of security. Eva soon grows suspicious. She hears music coming from further inside. She mumbles to herself, is this the wrong address? No, no, no. Not at all. Bienvenue. The doorman takes her by the hand. The place is a cut above a brothel—a private officer's club. The officers lounge on renaissance sofas with fat German *Mädchen*. The Whores of the French Sector. In a corner of the room, a black man plays the grand piano. Eva holds out her letter. Laughter. Nobody can understand why she would want to leave Berlin, now, when the war is over. Our Berlin is wonderful, they begin to sing. Our Berlin is wonderful, nowhere is better than this!

The piano player smiles. He shrugs his shoulders. Eva departs.

Next there is a Swiss friend, another journalist, who arranges to get the family tickets for the English airlift. Two tickets. Unfortunately, there is no way to get the dog out. Poor Romeo.

One week before takeoff, Michael breaks down. Eva grabs hold of him. She shakes him silly to sad strains of "No Exit for Romeo."

But Michael will have none of it. He's become a young man, at only ten years old. He insists that he won't leave Romeo behind, that it's not possible. He won't do it. Go yourself. But I cannot follow. What the war has made us do, and what this war takes from us … what this war wants … it will never stop.

Eva knows what she has to do. She arrives at Gatow, the British air base. She stands with Romeo before the iron gate.

There is no entry. I must speak with the highest official. Only he has the authority to write the end of my story. There comes a military truck and it stops at the gate. Eva knocks on the driver's window. He tells her he cannot possibly let her in the cab, but if she likes she can crawl in the back with her dog and then he'll take them in, no problem.

Inside Gatow Eva heads straight to the main building. Military police surround her. She requests an audience with the base commander. Romeo starts barking. *Watch out, young lady! We'll lock you up—or pack you off to Russia.* Eva sighs. It's no use. Eva understands that the truth is of no interest. She informs the men that she is a Russian spy. They listen more carefully, now. But what about … this dog? Eva kicks Romeo hard on the underside. Romeo starts to howl. Finally the base commander appears—Gloucester or Worchester or Manchester—a name which is gravy to Eva's ears. In the interrogation room again there is an interpreter. It is the same woman, except she has changed her brown sweater for a blue one. She offers Eva a cigarette. They both light up and it looks as if one of them might begin to sing, when the British decide Eva is harmless.

I have tickets for the airlift, Eva says, but unfortunately I have this dog and I cannot leave my dog behind. She breaks down and cries. She cries and she cries and the base commander at first looks helpless. One of the military police is about to take Romeo away. The base commander stops him. He turns, at last, to the audience. This is the base commander's turn to shine. Gloucester or Worcester or Manchester, he says: since this is real life and not art, reason will give way before humanity.

The MPs shout and helmets fly into the air. Hurrah! Humanity has authority. Eva remains seated beside the woman interpreter. The MPs gather around and Eva has the last word.

Thank the British, she declares. Nobody could believe that I got Romeo out. But all three—we all three flew together. It was my first airplane. My first ever flight was in a jumbo bomber if you can believe it. That's the way it was.

THE BELLS OF WESTMINSTER

The bells of Westminster are ringing. 'In her sleep. About an hour ago.' For close to a year I'd committed my days and nights to this form of attentive absenteeism, thinking only of Eva and her Karl Paryla, HH and Pinguin, Romy, Anneliese, Rudolf and the others—including my great-grandfather, Emil, the bald monstrosity in the photograph tacked above my writing desk: Emil with twenty workmen and the Cutting God. And yet, one phone call from Pavel, and Eva's father and all the rest no longer seem real to me, let alone like family. Dramatic personae, they were—puppets in the casting department of my imagination.

Eva died in the spring of 1994, ten months after her diagnosis of pancreatic cancer. She was eighty-two.

The service was held, at her request, at the Citadel, Salvation Army headquarters, in Sault Ste. Marie. I drove nine hours from Montreal with Roland and Stephen, and Pavel met us in the lobby of the Howard Johnson. What a place to come to. I remember pushing open the door to my room, nudging it with my knees as I picked up my suitcase, and then frowning at the insides. The carpet was manicured. It looked as though the heavy animal used for maintenance had stretched its massive claws and drawn them back across the surface. The shower, bathtub, toilet and sink were, as I knew they would be, scoured of the human. The chocolate-sized soaps and the drinking glasses nestled beside the sink were gift-wrapped. For whom? And the oval mirror ringed with light bulbs—pièce de résistance in this faux dressing room reserved for suicides, adulterers, and wan-white travellers—stared me squarely between the eyes. I broke down the first time inside that vault of illusions, amidst a heap of images, sitting on the closed toilet. I cried and cried and finally my brother came to get me. He looked worried.

From early on my brother Stephen had been confounded by my interest in genealogy, which is how he and others depicted my obsession with Eva's story. Genealogists are generous-minded, however, while from the outset I was single-minded in my pursuit of all things Eva-related. Stephen never could understand what the fuss was about. When I would relate my progress to him—new findings or historical references—he appeared to fall under the aura of an increasingly dull pain. I surmised that Stephen equated "genealogy" with widow's work: neither refreshing nor refined. It was like palliative care or weepy social work, or the good works of a church congregation.

I didn't say a word during the service the next day. The Salvation Army Captain described Eva as a woman of strong character and faith. She was, he said, a rare personality. He recounted to a group of her closest friends and relatives how, in her dying, Eva had turned to God. (*Who else is there,* to turn to at such a time? Pavel whispered in my ear.) This was a wonderful thing, the Captain continued. Eva was a beautiful person and her belief was whole and for eternity. Next Roland was asked to give the eulogy. It was a simply worded affair. He quoted from a number of poets: Tagore, an anonymous Chinese courtier, but not Brecht. I wanted to step forward and proclaim to the others: The World is Poor and Man's a Shit! But neither I nor Pavel went up front.

Sitting in the pew between Pavel and Roland I turned my thoughts to the only other funeral I'd attended, my mother's, some twenty years ago. I tried to summon that day but instead I remembered Eva's story from 1919 about her own mother's funeral. *The pastor seated the children on the wagon and they arrived at the funeral, pulled by horses, holding flowers.* I remembered how Romy, as Eva had it, watched stolidly as her mother's coffin was lowered into the grave. Romy was the youngest, only four years old. When her mother's coffin dropped out of sight, Romy emitted a gasp, a valve opening deep inside herself that she shut by twisting, turning her feet in the cold ground. So Romy was frozen at eye-level, as Eva said: she 'turned' mute.

But if Romy abandoned speech she did not desert language. The business of mime (Romy's specialty) is *our* deafness, Eva told me, *our* insensitivity, not hers. I understood. When Romy turns mute she must immediately come under pressure: the pressure of her own murky ideation, a sea of ideas and feelings and impressions in their larvae state; insensate things which then resound, rubbing sides, until there is that roar of static. That internal roar that prised her from the world.

I felt something of the same sitting in the pew inside the Citadel. Then I remembered something else. Another of Eva's stories. One time or other I had given it the title "Forget and Never Forgive."

Meanwhile my grandfather, Gustav, managed to die in a sensational story. As family history goes, his story wins top prize.

You know, my brother and father had a terrible time getting along. The same went for my father and his father, Gustav. Between them nothing was understood, and no one agreed to anything. One of them was wrong, and the other one had no right to defend himself.

Hermann Hans and my father fought on many fronts, for years they battled, and when he had enough, my fa-

ther sent Hermann Hans away, out of the house. Her-
mann Hans went to live with the pastor. Pastor Kohler.
In his final judgment, my father declared that the church
had taken from his house every donation and offering,
could it please take from him, straight away, his only son.

But watch him, my father warned Pastor Kohler. He is
not one of the sheep.

The boy was banished from his father's kingdom. Get
walking, he was told, take your walking-stick and get
wandering. From one day to the next, he disappeared.
That's how the family operated from an early time. For-
get him and never forgive him.

Forget and never forgive.

Another example of forget and never forgive came
from Gustav, my grandfather. Gustav was a saddler like
my father. He was also an amateur astronomer. About
the time Mutti was dying, Gustav had gone to Berlin to
buy his tremendous telescope. It was modern equipment.
He set it up behind the house on Briskestrasse. At night
he escorted the children outside into the garden. He
showed us the stars. He pointed out his favourites. He
brought his grandchildren a sky and filled it with names.
Antares. Sirius. We took turns looking through the tele-
scope. The bright one, Altar. His deity, Deneb.

Opalade. The children called Gustav 'Opalade' be-
cause he gave us chocolade all the time.

But unfortunately Gustav and my father had a long
complicated history. Gustav was annoyed when my
father chose to marry a girl from the lower class, the
daughter of a carriage driver.

Watch out, my son! Horror and shame! Look, every-
one: he deliberately wanders under the wheels of society!

Against Gustav's wishes, my father married below our
level. He tied a knot to this poor girl, who then became

our mother. Furious, Gustav cut contact. Forget and never forgive. We never saw Gustav for ages. He didn't come around, not until Mutti was ill. Then he came with his telescope.

Gustav first became sick the year after Mutti died. It was unexpected. Gustav was strong. One day he felt weak. So around came the doctor to his house. Gustav complained. He had lost his appetite, he felt dizzy. No pain, only a loss of strength. But he refused to rest. Against the doctor's orders Gustav kept busy, working in the shed until he was too weak to hammer a nail through rotten wood. He would not lie down! Never in the daytime—you know, the old are superstitious—he would not go to his bed, he dragged on right to the end.

Finally he arrived at that hopeless situation, when he got stuck drinking tea.

In the afternoon he was put outside to sit in the garden. Gustav sat with a blanket over his knee.

Drink tea, some more tea, his wife told him. She kept him in tea leaves. It's good for the stomach, she said. Strong tea is good for the stomach.

Gustav endured his ulcer by drinking tea. His stomach filled with blood. A flood of blood. Bloated, it weighed him down. It ballooned and slipped below his belt.

Poor thing. From his eyes, everyone who came to visit could see that he was struggling. He knew the sky, but he was not prepared for his journey into the sky. He wasn't well organized for the afterlife.

Visitors were kept away to shield him. He lived in fear, especially of the grandchildren. But we managed to sneak in to see him, once or twice more. We found him in the garden, in his chair. Fingers nibbling at the edge of his blanket, his stomach sliding further and further down.

Opalade! The children arrived, each one carrying a bouquet of flowers. Männe in his well-pressed sailor suit. Girls with pity on their faces. Quiet children with wondering faces carrying flowers.

The children have flowers for you!

Oh no. The parade of death! Here they come to say goodbye to the sick old man. There was no other interpretation. By then he knew he was finished. By the end it was popular knowledge.

It was very sudden.

Slow, then sudden. He was dying, then already he was dead.

And so, after a month or two, anyhow, not very long— when the mourning period was over—it was discovered that his wife and the doctor were guilty of something. They had been playing a game of cat and mouse. They had killed Gustav. This is the theory. This is the story everybody heard. Those two characters had poisoned him, day by day, slowly, until one morning he was found curled up in his bed, dead as the field mouse. The two of them had toyed with him, batted him up in the air with their paws. Then immediately after Gustav was buried, and the bells had stopped ringing, then those two, the old doctor and Gustav's wife—my grandmother, your great-great-grandmother—escaped into the countryside.

They found a village, out in the middle of nowhere, and they became lovers for the rest of their life.

Oh yes. She was sixty. She must have been an exceptional case.

But she's forgotten.

When the ceremony was over a number of us went to a Chinese restaurant to eat and exchange some last memories about Eva. Most people, including Roland and Pavel, discredited the Captain's account of Eva's deathbed conversion. I myself thought it was entirely in character. Yes, perhaps she had left it a little late, but Eva—who had improvised most of the last century—always made the most of her situation. You could never pin her down. She never settled into a role longer than was necessary, because for Eva the world was a steel cage, not a stage. Though, admittedly, the male world of Männe and his youth group, the world of her father and the patrons of his leather shop, the world of the doctor and pastor muttering to candlelight—to her, I bet, this substantial pageant was stageworthy.

Thinking back, I realized that what Eva gained from Ophüls' classes was not a metamorphosis but the art of metamorphosis: the ability to change and change again, never coming to a standstill. She was pure verb. And yet, again and again, she found herself enclosed—by fate? by circumstance? Or simply by life? The cage, I can see now, the cage was just the size and fit of her body.

Drinking tea, Pavel presented me with a jewel box. I opened it, and under the cotton wafer found the dog tag he'd discovered while triaging Eva's belongings. 1948 Berlin. 48506. Above the licence number there is the engraving of a dog, just the head of the animal. This is Romeo's ID. In return, I gave Pavel the portrait of Eva from 1927 that I kept in my wallet. *Verfremdungseffekt* go to hell. Eva demands attention straight across time. Identification is a poor euphemism for what happens when I look into those eyes.

Standing up to leave the restaurant, Roland gestured toward the bowl of fortune cookies. No one had taken theirs.

The bells of Westminster ring, and ring again. Deadlines have come and passed. Meanwhile in Montreal we have winter again. Winter and snow.

ACKNOWLEDGEMENTS

In tiefer Dankbarkeit!—Kate Kennedy, editor, and Gary Dunfield & Andrew Steeves, publishers, of Gaspereau Press. Tausend Dank!—Amanda Jernigan. Vielen Dank!—Stan Johannesen, Bruce Henry, Alen Mattich, Simon Dardick, Dan Birkholz, Carmine Starnino, Jaspreet Singh, Liam Durcan, Terry Taft, Eric Thorfinnson, Michael Harris, Fred Biggar, Robert Hutcheon, Peter and Michelle Kilburn. All my love— Nicolas and Birgitta Steinmetz, John and Nancy Tarasuk, Jill Tarasuk, Emil Dmitri Jan Steinmetz Tarasuk, Sonya Eva Steinmetz Tarasuk.

"Heimat" was partly inspired by a footnote in Norman Davies and Roger Moorhouse's historical study of Breslau, *Microcosm: Portrait of a Central European City*. "Happy End" was written in fond memory of Felix Mirbt. I am indebted to his personal essay, "My Story: Felix Mirbt Muses on his Career in Puppetry," in *Canadian Theatre Review*, Summer 1995.

"Acting is a process within the framework of becoming" comes from an interview with Manès Sperber in *Gestalt Theory*. Schafer K-H, Walter, H-J. P. (1984) Gesprache mit Manès Sperber am 5 und 6 August 1983 in Paris. Vol 6 5-41 (0).

"Monkey Life" was previously published in *The Fiddlehead*. "Briskestrasse, Good Night" appeared in *Queen's Quarterly*. I would like to thank the editors, Mark Anthony Jarman and Joan Harcourt, respectively.

Selections from *The Threepenny Opera* are quoted from the version translated and edited by Ralph Manheim and John Willett (London: Methuen, 1979). Selections from *The Oresteia*, Aeschylus' trilogy of plays, were taken from the version by Ted Hughes (London: Faber & Faber Ltd., 1999).

For information on Bertolt Brecht, Brechtian theatre and acting I have relied heavily on the following sources: *Bertolt Brecht—Poetry and Prose*, edited by Reinhold Grimm with the collaboration of Caroline Molina y Vedia (New York: The Continuum International Publishing Group, 2003); *Brecht—As They Knew Him* (New York: International Publishers, 1977); *Living for Brecht: The Memoirs of Ruth Berlau—Bertolt Brecht's collaborator and companion recalls her forty years of devotion to the man and his work*, by Ruth Berlau, edited by Hans Bunge (New York: Fromm International Publishing Corporation, 1987); *The Life and Lies of Bertolt Brecht*, by John Fuegi (London: Harper Collins, 1994); *Brecht, A Collection of Critical Essays*, edited by Peter Demetz (Englewood Cliffs, N.J.: Prentice Hall, 1962); *Bertolt Brecht's Berlin, A Scrapbook of the Twenties*, by Wolf Von Eckardt and Sander L. Gilman (Lincoln: University of Nebraska Press, 1974); *Commodities of Desire—The Prostitute in Modern German Literature*, edited by Christiane Schönfeld (Woodbridge, Suffolk: Camden House, 2000); *Men in Dark Times*, by Hannah Arendt (London: Cape, 1970); *True and False—Heresy and Common Sense for the Actor*, by David Mamet (New York: Vintage Books, 1999); *Playwrights on Playwriting*, edited by Toby Cole with an introduction by John Gassner (New York: Hill and Wang, 1960); *Stella Adler: The Art of Acting* (New York: Applause Books, 2000); *The Brecht Commentaries*, by Eric Bentley (New York: Grove Press, 1981).

For descriptions of post-war Berlin, I looked to *Berlin 45: The Grey City*, by Richard Brett-Smith (New York: St.

274

Martin's Press, 1967). For an update on Eva's view of Switzerland, I read *The Swiss, The Gold, and The Dead: How Swiss Bankers Helped Finance the Nazi War Machine*, by Jean Ziegler, translated from the German by John Brownjohn (New York: Harcourt Brace, 1998). For more information on the old family trade: *Artificial Parts, Practical Lives: Modern Histories of Prosthetics*, edited by Katherine Ott, David Serlin, and Stephen Mihm (New York: New York University Press, 2002). Other trophies taken on safari: *A Brief History of Cocaine*, by Steven B. Karch (New York: CRC Press, 1998); *Landscape and Memory*, by Simon Schama (New York: Vintage, 1995); *Library: An Unquiet History*, by Matthew Battles (New York: W. W. Norton & Company, 2004); *Photomontages of the Nazi Period*, by John Heartfield (New York: Universe Books, 1977); *Until My Eyes Are Closed with Shards*, by Manès Sperber, translated from the German by Harry Zohn (New York: Holmes & Meier, c.1988); *The Pity of It All—A History of Jews in Germany 1743-1933*, by Amos Elon (New York: Metropolitan Books, 2002).

For music day and night, I have survived on *Die Dreigroschenoper—Berlin 1930*, Lotte Lenya & Marlene Dietrich (Teldec, 1990); *Lotte Lenya—Kurt Weill: Berlin & American Theater Songs* (CBS Records Inc., 1988); *Teresa Stratas—The Unknown Kurt Weill* (Elektra/Asylum/Nonesuch Records, 1981); *September Songs: the Music of Kurt Weill* (Sony Music Entertainment Inc., 1997).

I gratefully acknowledge the financial support of the Canada Council for the Arts, le Conseil des Arts et des Lettres du Québec, and the Ontario Arts Council.

In 1960, a group of German master printers approached the major type manufacturers and asked for a single 'harmonized' text type that could be supplied in all the forms of composition then in use: hand setting from foundry type, mechanical composition on Monotype and Linotype systems, and film setting. Each system made compromises and subtle changes to the historical letter designs in order to compensate for the technical requirements of their system. Printers, however, simply wanted to be able to use type composed on these various systems interchangeably without problems. The type that resulted was Sabon, designed by Jan Tschichold and released by the Stempel foundry in 1964, with Monotype and Linotype versions following in 1967. Tschichold based his design on letters cut by Claude Garamond in the sixteenth century and named them for Garamond's student, Jacques Sabon. The type was a great success; however, within two decades the technical concerns that prompted its design disappeared and the four type composition systems Sabon harmonized were replaced by digital type composition. ¶ The digital fonts of Sabon used in this book have been retrofitted with a number of additional features at Gaspereau Press: some ligatures are new to the design; others (ff ffi ffl ft) are roughly based on those Tschichold originally drew but which are absent from most commercial releases of the type. Also, a long-eared f (in the spirit of Garamond) has been introduced to replace the short-eared f which Tschichold designed to meet the technological constraints of Linotype composition.

The display type is Neuland, a rough, powerful set of unserifed roman capitals designed and cut in metal by Rudolf Koch and issued by the Klingspor Foundry, Offenbach, Germany, in 1923.

The lettering on the jacket and title page was rendered by Jack McMaster of Wolfville, Nova Scotia.

This is a work of fiction.

Typeset in Sabon & printed offset under the direction of Gary Dunfield & Andrew Steeves at Gaspereau Press.

7   6   5   4   3   2   1

Library and Archives Canada Cataloguing in Publication

Steinmetz, Andrew
Eva's Threepenny Theatre / Andrew Steinmetz.

ISBN 978-1-55447-056-3

I. Title.

PS8637.T447E93 2008   C813'.6   C2008-903279-9

GASPEREAU PRESS LIMITED
GARY DUNFIELD & ANDREW STEEVES
PRINTERS & PUBLISHERS
47 CHURCH AVENUE, KENTVILLE, NOVA SCOTIA
CANADA B4N 2M7   WWW.GASPEREAU.COM